THE DOUBLE STANDARD SPORTING HOUSE

THE DOUBLE STANDARD SPORTING HOUSE

A Novel

NANCY BERNHARD

SWP

SHE WRITES PRESS

Published in 2026 by
She Writes Press, an imprint of The Stable Book Group

32 Court Street, Suite 2109
Brooklyn, NY 11201
https://shewritespress.com

Library of Congress Control Number: 2025918195
ISBN: 979-8-89636-052-0
eISBN: 979-8-89636-053-7

Interior Designer: Katherine Lloyd, The DESK

Printed in the United States

to Diana Gordon,
first and last reader

For a long time, there was no way
for a woman to be both free and good.
—Jia Tolentino, 2019

CHARACTERS

Nell "Doc" Hastings—owner of The Double Standard Sporting House, and a free clinic for women

Lavinia "Vivie" Curtis—kidnapped girl whose life Doc saves

Benjamin "Benno" O'Connor—Tammany Hall 16th Ward Boss

Elliott Vanderpoel—theatrical producer

Asa Vanderpoel—editor and publisher of *The Standard* newspaper

Historical Figures Rendered in the Novel

Peter Sweeny—city chamberlain and member of the "Ring" atop Tammany Hall

George Barnard—Supreme Court Justice of New York

Oakey Hall—District Attorney of New York, elected mayor in 1868

"Diamond Jim" Fisk—financier

Josie Mansfield—Fisk's mistress

Junius Henri Browne—writer, former newspaper correspondent and Confederate captive

Red Light Lizzie and Jane the Grabber—procurers of prostitutes

Lydia Thompson, Pauline Markham, and Lisa Webber—members of the Blonde Belles Burlesque Troupe

Rebecca Salome Foster—matron of the Tombs

Dr. Marie Zakrzewska—founder of the New England Hospital for Women and Children

At the Double Standard

Ciara and Meg—hostesses known as Mary and Magdalena

Perlie Bixby—housekeeper

Israel Bixby—butler

Bertram Hibberd—chef

Aunty Laure—pastry chef

Willy Schor and Bud Bean—porters

Clemence, Corabelle, Georgia, Marianne, Ruby, Susannah, Sophronia, Tatiana, and Willow—harlots

In New York

Nina, Betsy, Jodie, and Ellen—student nurses at the clinic

Minnie Templeton—nurse trained by Doc, working for Emily Wrigley

Emily Wrigley—owner of several downtown brothels

Vernon Trent—abductor of girls

Wallace Lacy—stage manager at Wood's Metropolitan Theater

Viola Brison Hill—anti-prostitution reformer

Reverend Albin Birchdale—anti-prostitution reformer

Catherine Farnsworth—Pennsylvania farm girl

Bim Farley—owner of the Wayward Academy

Honey—harlot at the Wayward Academy

Beatrice "Beadie" Korn—owner of The Silk Pillow

In Portland

Wren Hunt—laundress at Portland Hospital

Annalee Warren and Dara Bauer—nurse trainees at Portland Hospital

Christine Pell—nursing supervisor at Portland Hospital

Dr. Jordan—physician at Portland Hospital

Gwindolin Leger—brothel nurse at Rosalie's in Portland

Part 1

THE RIVALRY PLOT

ONE

September 1868

My day had seen a knotty birth, a giant prolapse, and rampant syphilis. I left the clinic well after dark and stepped into the back garden fretting over the prolapse. There were no good treatments for a wandering uterus, and after hours shaping a barrier from wax, wool, and resin, I was starving. What makes a womb so restless it leaves home like a hero setting off on a quest? What cuts its binds? Female bodies were criminally neglected by medicine, even as they inspired bountiful art, and a robust industry.

In a pragmatic adaptation to such paradoxes of womanhood, at the far end of the garden sat the establishment that funded the clinic. The Double Standard Sporting House served the richest, most discerning men in New York, and we lavished our girls with care. It was the only way for me to practice medicine as I wished, with no one above me and free to patients. Hardly anyone noticed, which was convenient.

The Double kitchen was winding down, and I asked a young maid for a plate. Before I could sit, Ciara appeared in peach silk looking apologetic, followed by a laughing Meg. My dearest friends who ran the house, they usually gave me time to pivot from patients to clients. It cheered me to see them smiling, but I hoped their news would not stand between me and my supper.

Ciara said, “One way or another we’ll look back on this day. Feeling lucky, Doc?”

“Tired, mostly.”

“Well, starch your petticoat. George Barnard is booked for Ruby tonight, and he sent a note. He’s bringing a rookie over now, and would take it as a huge favor if we could find him a girl.”

I liked George, and he was a favored client, but he knew we didn’t take walk-ins. Normally Meg and Ciara would so flood him with flattery he wouldn’t mind. But he was a state supreme court justice, fully owned by the Tammany Hall political machine and its boss Bill Tweed, and they were entertaining his request. They weren’t cowed; there would be an angle.

Tammany itself is difficult to explain, being a monster with many heads. It began a century before as a political club and now ran like a warring tribe. In the fall of 1868, they were poised to capture the mayor, governor, legislature, and supreme court of New York. We had several clients like George in its top echelon, amiable men who stole outlandishly from the city by padding contracts. They dispensed some fraction of the plunder to the needy in exchange for votes. This vast mob was seizing all the city’s levers of power.

“Do we have a girl for George’s mystery friend?” I asked, pouring a glass of cider.

Twinkling with mischief, Meg said, “For a price.”

“Who is he?”

Ciara said, “The note didn’t say, but the messenger came from Delmonico’s.” This was the city’s finest restaurant.

Meg looked me in the eye. “George is supping with Peter Sweeny.”

Well, well. The Double Standard just kept rising with the

city's reckless growth. The city chamberlain, second or likely first most powerful man in New York, the wizard of Tammany's epic theft, Peter Sweeny was famously odd and prickly, and a devout Catholic. I flashed them a look of wonder and worry. A high-ranking and volatile client put us at risk of ruinous public scrutiny, but—and here was the angle—would also bring access and influence.

"Little bugger'll need a world-class nickname," said Meg.

"They used to call him Spider at Harry Hill's. Maybe he's handsy," said Ciara.

I'd heard him called Brains and Bismarck. "What does Bismarck do for fun, I wonder."

A pious man either abandoned or punished himself in a brothel's pleasures. And how did one square churchy obedience with historic theft? I'd also heard Sweeny held renowned grudges. "Why the sudden interest in sport?"

A porter called from the stairs, "Miss Ciara?"

As we went up, I asked which girl they intended for him.

"It'll take some juggling, but we thought Sophronia," Meg said. This was our girl of the moment, an hourglass brunette with a guileless face, good with a novice.

George Barnard stood alone at the salon piano, noodling a sonata.

"Your Honor."

"Evening, Doc, ladies." He was tall with dark curly hair and a particularly squirrelly version of the requisite moustaches drooping down the sides of his chin. He took my hand in both of his, and said his guest preferred to come straight to a private room.

Naturally Sweeny feared being seen at the Double, though many men got a charge from darting up the stairs. "He can come directly to the library."

Ciara went to find Sophronia, and Meg and I crossed the hall to wait for George to fetch his friend. She whispered, "Saint Débauche," and then, "Pope Pius the Libertine."

I said, "I imagine he's not so much embracing sport as he is falling into temptation. The Reluctant Pervert."

"Mommy's Little Miscreant. Tinpot Degenerate."

We put on our most pleasing faces as he slunk into the room and waited until the door closed to doff his hat and cloak. For all his fearsome intelligence, Peter Sweeny looked shy. Nearly my height of 5 feet, 8 inches with sloped shoulders and thick black hair stabbing in all directions, he might have been handsome given another soul within, but the man was wooden and remote. I began to see how he squared God with fraud.

George introduced us, and I let Meg lead the conversation, as she was an auburn-haired goddess in a gorgeous evening gown, and I was a middle-aged medic in a dirty shirtwaist. Taking a bourbon, Sweeny answered each of her questions with a single syllable.

Ciara knocked and entered with Sophronia, who wore an azure gown with a sweetheart neckline. Sweeny missed that most stunning décolletage while his eyes flew between Meg and Ciara. We called them the twins, but clients knew them as Mary and Magdalena. Given that he showed not one speck of humor, let alone about his religion, I said, "You're not seeing double, sir. These are our house hostesses Meg and Ciara, to whom you can appeal if you need anything at all."

Ciara noted my use of their names and introduced Sophie, who curtsied to good advantage and sat next to him. He froze, but her soft words soon put him at ease.

And then I remembered something particular. Sweeny had been elected district attorney in the mid 1850s but resigned early, having broken down in front of his very first jury. The man did not like eyes on him. I led George away to the draped window.

He murmured, "I mentioned the advantages of a private house, and he stood up, ready to go. I hope you're amused."

"Does he often take sport?"

"Never, to my knowledge."

Sweeny's attention had at last landed on Sophronia's figure and the elegant finger tracing her collarbone. He coughed and recrossed his legs.

Ciara joined us at the window. "Ruby awaits you upstairs, George. I can take you to her, or bring her here, as you prefer."

"All right there, Sweeny?" he called.

Sweeny dismissed him with a flick of the hand, so George and I followed Ciara out. I left them all to business and returned gratefully to my supper, curious if Peter Sweeny would turn out to be a one-off, a friend, or a difficulty. He was well worth cultivating, but the closer we grew to the Ring atop Tammany, the more implicated we became in their corruption and thievery. I tolerated the trespasses to law in brothel work, as women had so few options and respectability was so rank with hypocrisy, but this was different. Tammany was careless, and to be its favorite risked making me its captive. I would guard my independence even as the girls beguiled Sweeny.

Halfway through my cold squash and beef, I heard Ciara on the stairs again. She said, "Benno's here, asking for you."

I closed my eyes and prayed for patience. Benjamin "Benno" O'Connor was our new ward boss, the local Tammany muscle several rungs below George and Sweeny. "What does he want?"

"He asked for Ruby. When I told him she was busy, he demanded you. We can't manage a second walk-in."

"Is he sober?" I rushed through a few more bites of food.

"I think so. Mostly."

I said, "Peter Sweeny is settled upstairs, yes? He really did not want to be seen." He and Benno likely knew one another. We had two staircases and an array of dodges.

Benno had come up on the docks and the Big Six engine of Tweed's fire company, the type to sit on a hydrant watching a house burn before he'd let a rival company put it out. Tweed had gifted him our 16th ward, which spanned the docks and our fashionable uptown vice district, Satan's Circus. Fifty houses crowded the blocks between Twenty-Third and Twenty-Seventh west of Broadway, most of them far out of his reach until lately.

My plan was to be gracious and useful. Our power, which Benno had yet to learn, rested partly in charm, but mostly in secrets.

Ciara had settled him in the library with a beer, a porter at the door.

"I like that girl Ruby," he said, like he expected me to produce her before entering the room. He didn't stand. His square bald head sat on a columnar neck, inclined to fight.

"She's a peach," I said, sitting. "But Benno, our girls are booked weeks in advance for the whole night. Forgive me if you expected to see her, but that's not possible."

"Sure it is. I had her before."

His face was straight malice, with dead eyes, a thrusting jaw, and psoriatic skin. I guessed his teeth hurt. Time to appease him as best I could. "During our monthly Saturday parties, we have more flexibility. I don't mean to be rude or disrespectful, and I am sorry, but a gentleman has long since paid for the pleasure of her company for the whole evening. It would not do you or me any good to interrupt their arrangement."

"They see only one guy a night?" He cherished his prerogatives but was enraptured by money. Local Tammany bosses in each of the city's twenty-one wards took hefty graft from every enterprise including brothels, and bought the police. I found myself in the strange new position of intimate to titans, but servant to this hoodlum.

"There's a steep entrance fee, if you will, and then over the course of the evening they eat a very fine meal, and drink a lot of very fine liquor."

He grunted. "You got faro or dice?"

"No, we don't have gambling at the Double Standard."

"Why not? That's easy money."

Perhaps he had come to renegotiate terms. We paid the last boss a steep, round $1500, or about 7 percent of our monthly income, which was half of our profit.

I said, "Gamblers fight. They throw chairs and slap girls around, and it ends up costing more than it brings in. Plus we're not that kind of house."

"Well," he said, threats being his first language, "maybe now you are."

I had long experience delivering unpleasant news. "Did you know that I come from the street, Benno? Same as you. The house is fancy, but I'm no snob."

"Yeah, but I heard you were never a whore."

He smeared me with the word anyway. Men often found it suspicious that I profited from prostitution as a man did, without participating. Some girls found it disloyal.

"That's true," I told him, "but I still started with nothing. Less than nothing."

"Why not?" He looked me over. He was near my age of thirty-six, double that of most harlots. Pretty and feminine enough when I was young, my thick brown hair and hazel eyes my best features, I was tall and had the habit of authority. I didn't mince my steps or drop my gaze, and had a scar just under my jaw suggesting a violent history.

"Be a harlot?" I smiled. "I stick to what I'm good at. Listen, our clients arrive with the kind of cash a winning gambler throws around. They might go downtown on a different night or play *vingt-et-un* somewhere else, but sometimes they want sophistication and refinement. In our part of the market, the absence of gambling is an asset."

He turtled his chin. "That's no fun."

"There are many kinds of fun, my friend. Our girls are incomparable."

"Manzoe's Academy and the Hotel de Wood have dice."

These were other fine houses in the neighborhood, but they were public, admitting anyone who could pay. We required appointments and referrals, most of which came through the Union League and University Clubs. I said, "We've been booked solid for seven years."

He looked around at the mahogany bookshelves and did a double-take at a marble bust of Eulalia, a teenaged martyr. I put a hand to my collar, which brought a porter into the room with another glass of beer.

Benno watched the boy, who never raised his eyes, and said, "How many people work here?"

"We have nine harlots at the moment, plus two hostesses, and about thirty staff. A brothel runs like a small hotel," I told him. "Dishes and laundry." I left out the nearby stable and various other ventures.

The pressure would be on him to deliver votes and to expand his own interests so he could dispense jobs and favors in the Sixteenth, something I knew well. I said, "It took a while to build all this up. Years, really. Imagine where you'll be in a decade."

His brow dropped. "How'd you get this property?"

It began as a weedy lot purchased on impulse during the

Panic of 1857 when for once it was useful to know a gambler: prices were low, and he was desperate. The lot spanned Twenty-Fourth and Twenty-Fifth Streets between Sixth and Seventh Avenues. On it now sat twelve tidy brownstones, six facing north and six south with a big garden between.

He said, "You have tenants," wondering how to charge me for them too.

I needed to move him along. "Why don't we go see Ciara, who keeps our calendar? She can book you in for Ruby on another night. Are you hungry?"

As we left the library, I gestured toward the dining room, and heard Sophronia and Peter Sweeny coming down the stairs already. Sophie said, "Do you ever get word of what happens to the orphans after the church takes charge of them?"

Sweeny said, "The church does what's best for them."

"It'd be so kind of you to visit and see how they get on."

He mumbled an equivocation.

I wanted to get Benno out of the hallway, but he had stopped dead and I nearly bumped into him. I whispered, "Are you acquainted with Mr. Sweeny?"

In a blind panic, he took two steps toward the back of the house, and then two steps back toward me, looking trapped and very dodgy.

I said, "This way," and led him down the back stairs and into the hallway outside the kitchen.

He snarled, "What are you playing at?"

"Pardon me?"

"You didn't tell me Peter Sweeny was here!"

"We never discuss clients, Benno."

"What the fuck is happening right now?"

"Nothing at all. It's a regular night." Was he that intimidated by Tammany higher-ups? I'd have thought Benno would welcome any contact with the Ring, but maybe he was unsure of his footing.

He stepped right in front of me, and my heartbeat spiked. "If I find out you're messing with me I'll fucking kill you."

I raised my hands in surrender. "We had no idea you were coming tonight!"

He panted, trying to calm himself.

"Belt of whiskey?" I offered.

He glared venom at me for seeing his fear.

Pointing at the back door, I said, "If you cross the yard, there's an alley out to Twenty-Fifth Street."

But then the door banged open and we both jumped. One of my newest student nurses stood facing a coiled Benno, his hands fisted.

"Yes, Betsy?"

She stuttered. "There's a girl. She's bleeding. Can you come?"

"I'll be there soon," I said, and lifted my chin to indicate she should go.

Benno paced for the minute it took to produce his hat, and he stomped out the door like a little boy who'd dropped his biscuit. That was not ideal, and I'd have to make it up to him, but I ran across the yard, more worried at that moment about what I'd find at the clinic.

My four students fluttered around an examination table, beside which stood Minnie Templeton, a nurse who had trained at the clinic a few years earlier, during the war. Minnie saw to thirty harlots in several rough-to-middling houses on Broome and Crosby Streets owned by Mrs. Emily Wrigley.

On the table lay an unconscious girl with a bruised and swollen eye and a banged up mouth. Lumps in the blanket meant bandages. There was too much movement in the room. "Everyone please stop what you're doing. Is there an emergency?"

Minnie said, "I don't think so. She has several vaginal tears made by something sharp. I had the bleeding under control before moving her, and I put every pillow and blanket I could find in that carriage."

I froze, then shuddered. The girl was very young and deathly pale beneath the bruises. "Which vaginal wall?" I asked, my voice small.

"Bladder."

"How much blood?"

"It's messy everywhere but the real problem is four or five punctures, maybe from the tip of a knife. I packed it but had no help and was going to send for you, but brought her here instead."

"Well done, Minnie, thank you." I knew I should diagnose and delegate, but could only siphon tiny bits of air into my lungs. I hadn't been so rattled in years, and had to clear the room. To the students I said, "Whose night is it?"

Betsy, who had started with us two weeks prior, raised her hand. I thanked the rest and sent them to bed, and then only three of us stood around the girl, who was very pale and very young. "Concussion?"

"Definitely. And they keep her on a lot of laudanum."

My vision began to cloud at the edges, but I couldn't let students see me fall apart. I leant my legs into the table and pressed my feet into the floor, swamped by memories of my own long-ago immobility, muscles wasting, shadows moving across colorless walls and ceiling. "Who is she?"

"They call her Vivie. She was kidnapped from a party she went to with her *parents*. The father is important somehow. They kept her chained and sold her virginity to some villain who had a nervous fit when the deed was done."

"Sweet Lord," I said, wavering in the past, a ghost of myself. There'd been newspaper stories about a fifteen-year-old girl's disappearance. The father was a Vermont legislator. I felt her head for fever. "About six months ago?"

"Sounds right. Mrs. Wrigley got her from a dealer type in Albany. They don't let her out at all. Making a bloody fortune on her, five a day or more. You all right, Doc?"

I reset my jaw, willing my proficiency forward. "Just sorrow for this poor girl." I listened to Vivie's heart and lungs, and palpated the bones of her face. My hands began to steady. She had a split lip but I decided not to stitch it. "You haven't checked the bandage since you arrived?"

Minnie shook her head no.

Hands on my belly, I stood straighter. "I'd rather wait until morning for surgery. We'll need a lot of light."

Betsy said, "That east room on the third floor is brightest."

I looked at her. "Indeed. Let's check the external bandage to be sure she's not hemorrhaging." Later the problem would be the leaking bladder but right now my concern was blood. I said to Minnie, "Do you know anything about her cycle?"

"No menses in all these months."

Small mercies. The carriage ride did not appear to have spurred new bleeding, but the girl's pelvis was covered in bruises and abrasions. I added one more plaster to the half dozen applied already. There was no sign of disease, for which I praised Minnie.

I said, "You both can sleep. I'll sit with her."

This met with shocked silence. Betsy stammered, "Doc, I promise to get you at any sign of trouble."

I tried to reassure her. "I know. I trust you, my dear. Give me two minutes upstairs and then find Minnie a bed, please." She still looked anxious, so I said, "It's fine."

Minnie said, "Doc, are you sure? I can stay with her. She knows me, and you need to rest before morning surgery."

"I won't sleep anyway." It worried them for me to do a

student's work, especially when I was acting strangely, but there was a certain kind of watch over a girl in this state, and I meant to do it. A patient like this was a good part of why I practiced brothel medicine. I wanted the next person she met to embody the possibility of recovery.

Betsey and Minnie shared a worried look, so I said, "When someone offers you the chance to rest, best to take it."

The fourth floor of the clinic building housed my own rooms. I changed my shoes, grabbed two shawls, two books, and some tea leaves. Minnie lingered, but when she left I brought a chair near the bed and watched Vivie breathe. Her inhales had begun shallow but were slowly deepening.

I sighed, remembering Benno's odd reaction to Peter Sweeny. And his intention to squeeze the house was worrisome. I would keep appeasing him, unpromising as it seemed. Smoothing Benno's way with the Ring might be the place to begin. I'd speak to Ruby about building on what he thought a woman was.

My eyes fell back to Vivie, to whom I had far more to give. "I'm so sorry," I told her. "They'll call you fallen, like you slipped on a mossy paving stone. Oh dear, so clumsy of you."

Traces of her childhood were still visible in the set of her mouth and the depth of her dreaming. She was all of us at that most precarious moment of reckoning.

"The road ahead of you is long, but we can help," I told her. "We'll try to restore some of what's been taken from you." Your health, your dignity, your self-respect. Family was trickier. "You'll be well hidden here as you heal and get your feet back under you."

Later when I had dozed off, Vivie cried out and twisted in the bed. I stroked her head to soothe her and to see if she'd spiked a fever. She was a little warm, and I took her hand. "It's all right, dear girl. You're safe here. No one's going to hurt you."

"No," she pleaded, squeezing my hand and pulling me closer. "No more." She wept in her sleep, and I hummed fragments of a hymn whose words I never knew.

At first light, Vivie flickered into consciousness. She saw me, her face sweet through the lumps and bruises: round blue eyes, bow mouth with strong white teeth, hair the color of maple candy.

"Hello Miss Vivie, I'm Nell Hastings. You can call me Doc."

"Minnie said you could help me." Her mouth was dry and stiff, and I watched her try to focus. "It's morning?" she asked, the night before shadowing her eyes.

"Almost dawn," I said.

"Please may I have some water?"

I shook my head. "I wish I could give you some. Later, but not now. I'm sorry."

She took it as one more cruelty.

I found some beeswax and dabbed it onto her lips. "You have an injury to your bladder. When the sun gets a little higher and we get better light, I'm going to sew it up. Until then we want it as empty as possible."

She blinked. "You'll sew inside me? With a needle and thread?"

I smiled at her. "You won't believe me when I tell you. For this we use thread of silver. I get it from a jeweler. And a curved needle."

"I'll have jewelry inside me?"

I laughed, but she could only cough, which gave her pain.

"Breathe slowly," I said and blew out a thread of air, rubbing her arm. "Let's put jokes on the list of things you can have later."

She watched me, and I almost asked if she remembered the night before. Silence and shame would compound her injuries, but so could forcing her to relive the worst. It was too soon to stand at the right distance.

I said, "If you would, please touch your head to find any lumps or bruising under your hair. Go gently." Again I demonstrated.

She said softly, "You want me to do it?"

"Please."

Phantoms of manhandling doctors stomped through the room. "So you don't hurt me?" She spoke like a New England patrician, as would a girl stolen from home in Vermont.

"Yes."

"How kind," she said, her voice breaking. I saw ballet training in the way she lifted her arms. She found a lump above one ear, and said, "I fell there."

I nodded. "You have a concussion."

"Like a headache?"

"It will give you a headache. Light and sound may trouble you. You'll be on bed rest for a few weeks."

Her hands fell to her abdomen.

"Yes," I said, "from those injuries as well. But after those few weeks, I have every hope you'll be fine." She almost scoffed at this, but swallowed it.

I nodded to show I understood that some things would never be fine. "In a little while, we'll bring you upstairs to an east-facing room. You'll be asleep for the procedure, so it won't hurt. Have you ever had chloroform, or ether?"

She shook her head, another worry overwhelming her. Inhaled anesthetics had been in use for about fifteen years, but a healthy child would never have seen them. I said, "Perhaps we should pause a moment. You didn't ask for treatment, and it has its risks."

She looked right at me. "But Minnie said I need an operation, that I must have it."

"Yes, your injuries are the greater danger in the long run."

Sounds of the nurses rising reached us. Vivie said, "Is there any reason to wait?"

I considered. "No." Her chances would diminish every day.

She nodded once.

"All right, then. Let's begin your recovery." I waited until she met my gaze. "You may surprise yourself."

Betsy appeared, and I left them to see to my own morning routines, and by the time I descended to the third floor, they had fixed reflectors on the gas lamps and carried Vivie, who wore a hat with a wide brim over her eyes. "Gracious," I said.

A table had been set with two bottles of chloroform, and a brass inhaler of my own design and manufacture. I picked up a duck-bill speculum, a two-sided hook we used to pull back the perineum, intending to disinfect it, but Vivie caught sight of it and recoiled, whimpering. I took a chance and handed it to her, explained its shape and lack of sharp edges. "Any metal coming toward your body is upsetting, of course. It's awkward but I promise it's not bad. It helps us see inside you. You'll lay on Minnie's lap and she'll hold you tight."

"Oh," she said with a jagged breath, feeling its heft and edges, still fearful but less agitated. "It looks dreadful."

She was right, of course, and went to the heart of medicine, which was often brutal. "Agreed. There's a lot of experimentation with new designs. Perhaps you'll invent one." But then I checked myself. She had not asked to be tutored in surgery. I took it back and sprayed it with a carbolic solution.

Nina had assisted me once before on a fistula repair, and Betsy had never seen a surgery, so I asked them to stay. When the sun cleared the Fifth Avenue Hotel two blocks away, we positioned Vivie on Minnie, who administered the chloroform. The four cuts from the vagina to the bladder, each under an inch, were indeed likely made by a pick or the tip of a dull knife. I closed them with nine silver sutures, and saw no evidence of pregnancy or disease, though extensive internal bruises mirrored the external ones.

I reminded the nurses that Vivie should have only liquids, and we began a log to manage her laudanum dosing and ultimate withdrawal. Minnie had to get back downtown and report to their employer, and I needed to check the patient with the prolapse. We all said a little prayer against infection for Vivie, and I felt a steeliness rise in me I meant to pass to this wavering girl.

Commotion rang from the main dining room as I drew near. We required attendance at harlots' breakfast at two p.m. each Tuesday and Friday. The girls were crowing over *cartes des visites* for Lydia Thompson and the girls of her Blonde Belles Burlesque Troupe, studying their clothes and hair, taking their poses. The Belles had crossed the Atlantic and the night before premiered their *Ixion* at the brand-new Metropolitan Theater. They deemed Pauline Markham the most beautiful, but Lydia herself the sauciest. Ruby and Susannah had attended the opening, and loved its spit-roast of sporting men. Burlesque, with its ribald, unruly humor and exposure of legs in flesh-colored stockings, was all the rage.

The table, draped in linen and lace at night, was laid with a checked cotton cloth and platters of cheese, eggs, and apple fritters. The girls' *dishabille* of wrappers and messy hair was pleasing within the room's grand proportions, its scarlet silk walls and fresh lilies.

Ciara, slumped in a chair reading a newspaper, squawked and sat up. "The respectable world has no idea what to make of the Belles. Listen to this: 'Though they were not like men, they were in most things as unlike women, and seemed creatures of an alien sex, parodying both. It was certainly shocking to look at them with their horrible prettiness, their archness in which was no charm, their grace put to shame.'"

Ruby said, "An alien sex! They're smashing the line between good girls and bad girls, between women and men."

"What's that critic's name?" I asked, thinking all his blood went to his pen.

Ciara checked. "William Dean Howells. Perhaps I'll write to him and offer to explain burlesque."

"Horrible prettiness!" I poured myself tea and marked the endless exuberance of twenty-year-olds.

"Will you go, Doc?" asked Susannah.

I rarely went to theater anymore, having suffered enough public insults for one lifetime. A physician once spat in my face at the Opera House, refusing to share a row with a "notorious abortionist." My friend Elliott had frog-marched this Dr. Murray to the aisle and sent him sprawling, and Murray brought his grievance to the *Herald*, which was most unfortunate, as our chief asset was discretion.

A low comedy leg show was not to my taste in any case, but I said, "I may sneak in next month to hear the famous Miss Thompson sing."

Meg caught my eye, and I nodded. She called them to order.

I said, "Ciara love, any out-of-towners this week?"

"Just the mid-week regulars on the calendar until Friday."

"Thank you. Does anyone else have news?"

"Gabriel Mayer gifted me this," said Corabelle, flourishing a ring with a fat sapphire circled by diamonds. Mayer was a middle-aged insurance broker she saw every Sunday.

Ciara said, "An engagement ring?"

"I'm not sure."

"Would you like it to be?"

Cora squirmed. "I'm not sure." She was the most approachable girl, a bouncy, elfin creature with a rolling walk that was halfway to dancing. She had arrived at the Double Standard heartbroken over a touring violinist. "He has good hands and keeps himself nice."

Marianne, opposed to marriage in general and for harlots in particular, said, "Pretty tepid for a lifetime."

"Piss off," said Cora cheerfully, extending her arm to let the jewel catch the light. "He's sweet."

She might stall, but a rare girl refused a rich and decent man. If she was uncertain about a suitor's character, we had ways to test his temper and his kindness. I said, "After you've enjoyed your bauble a bit, you might put it in the safe. Anything else? If not, let's discuss Benno's temperament. What do we know about him?" I was looking to shed light on his fear of Peter Sweeny without sparking gossip that might get back to him.

"Swankpot," said diminutive, black-haired Tatiana. "Needs everyone to know he's boss."

Ruby said, "Fucks like it's killing him, fast as possible."

"Thank heaven," drawled Tati.

Ciara said, "He's building a new clubhouse on Fourteenth Street near Eighth, so he may be pinched. Looking for new sources of revenue."

This was news he neglected to tell me, despite the obvious opening in our conversation about building the Double. I said, "He's edgy about fitting in here."

Susannah said, "Short man troubles."

Tati said, "Always on the verge of clocking you one."

That was a good reminder. I said, "Remember to be on your guard with him. He has a history of violence with women." A rumor had made the rounds that on the night Tweed made him ward boss, he threw a naked girl out the window of an assignation house. Maybe she didn't grovel enough.

Tatiana said, "He likes to be flattered."

"All men like to be flattered," said Ruby.

"He can smell insincerity."

"What kind of flattery doesn't smell of insincerity?" Ruby was a natural performer mugging to lighten the mood. Her jaunty beauty—blonde corkscrew curls, twinkling eyes, and big elastic mouth—reeked happy mischief, an interesting favorite for a grim man.

"The kind with something to it. Praise his best features, what you actually like about him."

"Aw Benno, I love you because your dick's so little and you come so fast!"

"Be his shoulder to cry on," said Willow, one of two newer girls.

"No!" I said sternly, shaking my head. "No. Men like Benno do not cry, and you are not to get maternal or soft with him. Softness makes him fearful, and fear makes him violent. Think: buddy, accomplice, one of the boys."

Meg said, "Okay, someone summarize what we know about handling Benno. Georgia?"

The other new girl looked up and sat straighter. "When sluggers like Benno feel out of control or vulnerable, they're dangerous. Be tough, be mean about his enemies, let him run the show."

The girls clapped, and Georgia took a reluctant bow. I wondered if Benno and I had common enemies and how much he meant to run my show.

During his usual monthly visit to collect Tammany's take from the Double Standard, Henry Philip Wotley, aka Hanky Pank, looked aggravated. Benno kept all the collectors from the old regime, and Hanky Pank and I had transacted this business for years. He owned two concert saloons, the Eureka and the Reveille, and dressed the part. A round, ruddy man, he brought a neighborhood policeman with him, which he'd never done before. The payment was in part to keep the police away from us. In other wards, houses paid them directly, but in the Sixteenth where sport was rampant, the ward boss made those arrangements. Martin Mitchell was a spry, friendly fellow who got along with everyone, and I noted the fix's new transparency.

I led them to the library. "Drink?"

"No thanks, Doc."

I sat at the desk, leaving them the comfortable chairs.

"What's eating you, Hank?" I asked. He sat there like the chair hurt him, his brow so low over his eyes it gave me neck pain.

He spat out, "What would be the big deal about letting a guy play a game of faro?"

I blinked.

He grew enthusiastic. "It'd up your take by half."

I said, "It'd up *your* take by half."

He ticked off elite houses on his fingers. "Seven Sisters, Millie Street's, they all have faro or *vingt-et-un* or the occasional dice game, but not you."

"Gamblers fight, Hank. As I told Benno, they lose, throw punches, smash expensive furniture, pull knives and guns, and then it's a whole other kind of night for me. That's not the kind of place I run."

He ran his thumb along his fingertips, a sign of money. Here was Benno putting the squeeze on me. "You don't like it because you have to patch up the damage done by losers."

"In part."

"See, that's a perfect arrangement. You get paid when they get messed up, you get paid when they get fixed up."

But Hank was sweating. He didn't want to tell me how to run my place.

"Is this shakedown happening everywhere, or is it special for me?"

Hank said, "Everywhere."

I sighed. "Well, it stands to reason he's going to make some changes. I know about the clubhouse. What else does he have in mind?"

Hank blanched, stumbled, and finally said, "He's still getting the lay of the land."

That was laughably awkward. Hank might be hiding Benno's mysterious problem with Peter Sweeny, or his dislike of me or the house. Or maybe Benno just felt invincible with Tweed's backing, and it left Hank in a strange position with his friends in the ward. The papers, the courts, and the police were all in Tammany's pockets, so no one stood up to them. Well, I would make a thankless stand right here on a faro table.

I turned to Martin Mitchell. "You drumming up business too?"

He winked. "No ma'am, just keeping Hank company on his rounds today."

Martin's ease calmed me, reminded me to stick to my strengths. I said to Hank, "Let me ask you this: does Benno appreciate what goes on here, on the whole block?"

"Sure, Doc. I told him how much you helped old Breen." The previous boss fancied Broadway dancers, who occasionally conceived. And I set his fingers now and then from boxing fractures.

"Well, remind him that I can take care of all those problems for him, and I keep my mouth shut." I paused to make sure he heard that. "I'm sorry to disappoint him, truly, I like to help him out when I can, but I won't have gambling at the Double Standard."

"That ain't gonna go down well, Doc."

I shrugged and slid an envelope full of bills onto the desk. "Next time Benno has an idea for my house, tell him to come by and he and I can talk it through over a drink."

"Funny about that," said Hank, watching me. "He told me he didn't have time to spend a whole night with one fancy girl." So Benno was that afraid of Peter Sweeny. I couldn't yet say if it was a tactical rift or a more personal beef, but I had my suspicions, given the peculiarities of both men. Meanwhile, I was pleased to let him rut elsewhere.

I shrugged. "Maybe he ought to try two, then."

Martin Mitchell shook my hand and gave me a crisp nod on his way out.

Vivie slept for three days, sometimes agitated. As the swelling of her face abated, she seemed to recede, hardly spoke. Worried she was giving up, I sat with her in the evenings, reading my letters and papers. One night she woke and bade me go to bed. I became a lion then, protective, but complied when she was settled. During my own convalescence many years prior, my healer Gwin had never fussed over me, and dark waking hours had been when the work of returning to myself got done. Gwin's ghost seemed often to be over my shoulder since Vivie's arrival. "As long as you know you're not alone," I said, and squeezed her hand.

Another night Nina, the lead student, waylaid me when I came in after dinner. Vivie had woken from a nightmare and cried so violently they worried for her sutures. Another girl said she would fetch me and Vivie pleaded against it, promised to calm herself. We didn't always get the laudanum dosing right. By the time I arrived she was asleep again, a tiny snore on each exhale. I smoothed her hair.

The next morning she and I disputed on her diet, as she was desperate for bread. I explained the danger to her sutures from pressure and strain, and she reddened.

I said, "Laudanum can be very constipating. Did you find that so?"

Her eyes widened in mortification.

"It's your body, Vivie. The more you know about how it works, the better you'll live in it."

She shook her head in disgust. Half a year of brutal prostitution and she was still squeamish about a bowel movement.

"One piece of bread," I said.

It appealed less. She said, "My mother used to give me castor oil." And with that chance mention of her mother, a cloud descended. She didn't want to talk about it.

The core staff of the Double Standard had been together for years, and we were family. Four days after Vivie arrived at the clinic, I asked for a few minutes with all of them, and we convened in the kitchen around midnight.

The twins were not actually twins, but first cousins born months apart to twin mothers who passed on their shiny red hair and enchanting cheekbones. In the winter of 1860 Meg burst into the brand-new clinic carrying a very pale Ciara on her back. She was hemorrhaging, having been about six weeks along and dosed herself with too much tansy and ergot. My standard hemostatic tincture (yarrow, shepherd's purse, and witch hazel, mostly) slowed the bleeding enough that I didn't have to go into her uterus. I might have sent them home the next day but kept them talking, so funny and seamless were they together.

Born in Galway, they grew up in Five Points and became waiter girls at a series of ever larger and lusher concert saloons, ending at Harry Hill's by the time they turned sixteen. They'd go upstairs separately or together with a good-looking high spender. Everyone told them to go on the stage. Then they met a pair of brothers, iron traders from the Alleghenies who took an apartment for them at Broadway and Grand. On any given night, some number of the brothers and their friends would drop by. Daytime the girls read plays to each other and practiced accents, worked up a twins act.

It was providential. The house was nearly finished so I offered them an as-yet to be determined part in it. I showed them the building out the window of Ciara's room in the clinic, and Meg looked at me like I had two heads.

"You own that?"

"I do. I'm calling it the Double Standard Sporting House."

They froze. Ciara's a bit more buttoned up, and Meg has a dirty mouth on her. In two blinks, Ciara smiled like an angel fresh from Sunday service, and Meg cocked her hip and looked me up and down like I was fresh pie. On top of gall, they brought a strategic grasp of New York's underworld.

As a compassionate and forgiving Mary, Ciara received confidences, and suffused the house with a benign, affectionate order. As party girl Magdalena, Meg helped everyone laugh and loosen up, and paired each man with the right harlot. Meg stoked extravagance, and Ciara noted each expenditure. They shared responsibility for the harlots' disposition, appearance, and performance.

Meg was also the longtime consort of my attorney and man of business, Lyman Beecher, the principal of a prominent law practice who managed my device concern and was its public face. It was an opportunity I spotted just as the house began producing enough money to invest in a brass foundry. As silent owner, I'd sold thousands of ether and chloroform inhalers to the Union Army, and hinged prostheses, for which there was sad demand. Lyman kept an office in one of the Twenty-Fifth Street buildings.

Israel and Perlie Bixby ran the house as butler and housekeeper. Israel worked the door and trained the porters who served food and drink, delivered messages, and directed traffic. Perlie and her fifteen maids and six laundresses kept the girls dressed and coiffed, and the house immaculate, with great tact. About half of the house staff, including Israel and Perlie, were Negro.

I first met Perlie on Fourteenth Street when I saw her helping a boy who had fallen into the gutter, fainting from hunger. She lifted him up though he was none too grateful, gave him an apple, and waited for him to eat it and stand. He scarpered with a curse, but I fell into step with her and said, “That was kind.”

“He did not agree,” she said in a voice brimming with humor and sense.

“Forgive my presumption, but do you mind if I walk with you a ways?”

“If you like.”

When I learned she had years behind her as a housekeeper of a Fifth Avenue mansion, I invited her to the Double. When I proposed to pay her three times her present wage, she exploded in great hoots of mirth and told me I was crazy.

Israel became my first coachman. A strong, fatherly man, every inch the Biblical patriarch, he had a facility for refusing guests without angering them. They had both grown up free in New York and had no babes of their own, a sadness that led them to bring in scores of street children as maids and porters and help them to become whatever they wanted to be. Perlie would sigh and say, “This is how the Lord made us, we do the best we can.”

With the five of us gathered, I described Vivie's plight and injuries, my suspicions about her identity, and how unhappy I would be to send her back to the miserable care of Emily Wrigley.

Israel said, "You like her."

Meg said, "Doc, what are you thinking?"

This was tricky, but I was honest with them. "I plan to buy her debt, and let her recover at the clinic."

"How much debt?"

"Wrigley claims a thousand."

"God forbid!" said Perlie, and then the table remained quiet.

I said, "I'll negotiate the amount, but I have a chance to save this girl's life and I'm going to take it."

Meg was doubtful. "Bringing her here won't solve anything, Doc. She won't want to see clients, so what then?"

"Then she'll have a choice and we'll help her."

Ciara rubbed her face. "She can't go home."

I said, "What's the best place for her?"

After a long silence, Perlie said softly, "With people who understand what she's been through, and won't shame her."

It seemed to them like a whim, answering no need in the house. Making an exception for one girl invited a hundred desperate pleas. I said, "It'll be two or three months at most."

Meg worked her mouth. She didn't like managing jealousy among the girls.

"Who was the last slaver girl we had?" asked Ciara.

With a sour face, Meg said, "Cordelia."

We all sighed. That girl came from a fancy house on Washington Square. She'd been snared at the dock by Jane the Grabber, who split the slave market with her great rival Red Light Lizzie. They each ran houses and sold girls, publishing regular stock lists. We had taken her on about four years prior, but Cordelia hid her troubles, stole liquor from the house and jewels from other girls, and never learned to ask for help. I gave her options and chances until the twins said to stop. The life was tough enough as a choice.

Ciara said, "Doc, to be clear, do you want to turn this girl Vivie into a Double harlot or move her along?"

"Let's come back to that later, when she's physically recovered."

No one agreed, but no one raised an objection. They didn't like it, but it was my choice. Israel was least likely among them to be troubled by Vivie's presence, but seemed the most irritated, and then I remembered that Ciara had called Cordelia a "slaver girl." He didn't like using that word in this context. I was about to say something when Ciara corrected herself with some distaste. "Sorry, Israel. *Stolen* girl, *abducted* girl."

Perlie faced her husband. "This girl was stolen from home and forced to brutal work. What else is it?"

He softened, looking at her. "The girl grew up free in a powerful family. She's no slave."

"Doc still has to buy her freedom," said Perlie, low and sharp.

Keeping calm, Israel said, "It's not the same. It's terrible bad luck, but she wasn't born to slavery, and thanks to Doc, she's escaped it now."

I said, "No, it's not the same. But that fancy father of hers was no protection." The differences between race and sex always reminded me of the differences between chronic disease and acute injury. Each could be endlessly debilitating or intermittently life-threatening in their distinct and intertwined ways. Perlie and I shared a look agreeing this was not worth arguing. The remedies for both were few and poor enough.

I said to Israel, "The word makes a point when you apply it to a girl like her for the exact reason you raise."

He shook his head. "Well, as you know, that's trading on the backs of real slaves in a way that doesn't sit right with me."

He was usually right when he took the trouble to correct me, but I was sick to death of minimizing and sidestepping around rape. “In the absence of a dedicated word for a girl being stolen from home into sexual captivity, what do we call it? Kidnapping, grabbing, snatching?”

“I don’t know Doc, but not slavery.”

I heaved a big sigh, thinking I’d reserve the word for certain people or situations. “Between us we can call it kidnapping or abduction.”

Israel nodded once, but Perlie looked vexed when we said goodnight. She might have been puzzling over the language, or she might have been unhappy that Israel challenged me. No matter how well we got on and how much I trusted and respected them, I still owned the house. I appeased myself by paying plenty and planning big settlements when I sold the house or we otherwise parted.

I stopped in to see Vivie on my way to bed. She was asleep, as were the student nurses. I went upstairs and scanned some letters and the evening papers. The quiet, usually welcome, felt hollow, and I imagined her living with the nurses. Had she seen herself as a slave? To be taken so abruptly from a safe, ordered world into forced prostitution was dismal, but I was overeager. Perturbed by the way I was imposing myself on this girl, I slept in a tangle.

As I checked Vivie’s eyes and temperature in the morning, she said, “Miss Hastings, may I ask, what is the meaning of the house’s name, the Double Standard?”

In pain and withdrawal, she asked a question I often asked prospective girls. I stopped what I was doing to watch her. “Call me Doc. What do you think it means?”

She swallowed. "Perhaps that women are supposed to be chaste, but men go to brothels whenever they please?"

A classic answer about sexual freedoms, expressed without rancor. "You put a nice point on it."

She showed no sign of infection. I asked how much blood and urine she was passing, and she shrank at the question. While I took her pulse, she said, "What do the girls talk about at their breakfasts?" She was artful in deflecting.

"Whatever's on their minds. Lydia Thompson and the Blonde Belles of Burlesque, lately. How to take care of ourselves. Crushes, of course, someone's always in love. And we talk about what they'll do when they leave. A harlot may work at the Double Standard for no more than two years, and we do all we can to launch them into some other line of work."

She blinked. "You must be the only employer trying to get rid of her workers."

I laughed, loving her already. "Vivie," I said, "how would you feel about staying here with us?"

She shook her head, downcast. "Mrs. Wrigley would never allow it."

"Putting that aside, would you like to?"

"Of course," she said in a tiny voice. "Anyone would."

"I'll work it out with Mrs. Wrigley, then. I know she claims you have debts, but that's not right. I don't believe girls should be kept against their will."

Still doubtful, she said, "I'd rather owe you of course. Is it true that Double girls see only one man a night?" She looked up.

"You'll owe me nothing, Vivie, except to be honest and do your best to shake the laudanum."

Now she grew suspicious, as well she should. "I don't understand."

I took my time deciding what to say next, and resisting the

urge to take her hand, sat down on the end of the bed. "Minnie told me you were kidnapped."

She swallowed, eyes wide and teary.

My eyes watered too. "I hate that above all things, Vivie, that some villain stole you from your life and your family. Do you know the man's name?"

She wept for half a minute, and I rubbed her back. "He called himself Vernon Trent. I haven't seen him since he left me at that first house in Albany."

"I'm so sorry. Did he drug you?"

She half shrugged, meaning she guessed so. "We were dancing, and I teased him because he wasn't any good. He's big and kind of lumbering. So many times I thought back to what I could have done to provoke him, and the only thing that might explain it were those few seconds of laughter." This came with a sob, and gutted me.

I did take her hand then. "Vivie, it was nothing you did, I promise. We search for reasons to give it some kind of sense, but there is none. All he had to do was see you. You mustn't blame yourself, you are not at fault in any way."

Despairing of her bad luck, she said, "I hate him!"

"He's contemptible. Listen now, my dear. I can't send you back to be that innocent girl who had such a terrible crime done against her. But neither do I have use for a fragile little chickadee addicted to laudanum. You can still be a strong young woman who once lived through something terrible, and take your revenge with a full and happy life, far better than that coward. I'd like to help you pick yourself up. Does that sound like the right way forward?"

"Yes, of course. Maybe I could find something else sooner than two years."

I was never as grateful for my wealth as I was in that moment, all my sacrifices seeming small. "You have months of recovery ahead of you but as I said, Double girls are never coerced. You must choose that line of work. After a few weeks' rest, you may decide you never want an old man in your bed until you're his old wife."

"What do you mean?"

"You don't have to decide now."

"I could give it up?"

"Truthfully, you're too young to be a Double Standard harlot. My girls are at least twenty when they start." Twenty was considered old for harlots, but younger girls could not, as a rule, do what I asked of them: read and respond to a sophisticated man's desires. If a man wanted a child, sadly he could find one in specialty houses near the Bowery and Chatham Square.

Vivie said, "Why would a girl ever choose it?"

Indeed. I could have spoken on that topic at length but considered what she needed at that moment. "For freedom. Money buys independence and there are precious few ways for girls to earn so quickly. You could do needlework or be a shopgirl your whole life and not earn what you can here in two years. You can launch yourself into a new life afterwards. It's a skill and an art, satisfying a man. But it helps to like men, and sex. And power."

"Ugh," she said.

"Well, from now on you get to choose whom you take to bed."

She sagged with bone-deep relief, tears streaming. Now she did seem like a waif, half child of another world. Her instability came from the shock of her abduction, and she had a better than average chance of not dying by Christmas if I could keep her with us. I could help twenty other girls with the money it would take to pry her from Wrigley, and it was a risk ten ways, not least that this Vernon Trent character might come looking for her.

Her sobs ran their course, and next she said, "I don't have any clothes."

I laughed. "Our dressmaker Philomena will fix that."

"Oh, I love you, Doc!"

She threw her arms around me and I laughed and choked up and held her close. "Aren't you sweet. I'm glad we met, Vivie." Was I so lonely I would buy myself a little daughter-friend to adore me? She was edging toward safety but not yet convinced, and I made her promise to rest.

When I went to see Emily Wrigley, she admitted that $1000 was steep for a top-earning girl abducted only months past, but was disinclined to part with her prize. I proposed to charge her $1000 for saving the girl's life. At last Wrigley confessed she'd promised the dealer not to sell the girl. He was probably still getting a cut.

"Tell him a client shredded her and you had no choice with her leaking urine on everything and everyone."

Her face knotted up.

I said, "A newspaperman spotting her would bring the whole Vermont State Legislature slashing their way through here."

"They can find their way uptown too," she said.

I sighed rather theatrically. "If they do, I'll tell them how she got from Bennington to Albany, your daily regimen, and what that client of yours did to her with a knife. I don't suppose you want to tell me the worm's name, or why he tried to kill her."

She narrowed her eyes and said, "Since when do they need a reason?"

"Seems personal. Or maybe contractual. Who does he work for?"

She feigned boredom, and when we settled on $650, she called me a dog-faced whore.

"Do yourself a favor," I told her. "Don't deal with slavers. A wretched harlot is never a good idea."

"What is a harlot but wretched?"

"On her way to someplace else."

I remember pine cones. Our lane was lined with Eastern white pines, giants raining these woody little carcasses in the fall, an endless supply of blocks and weapons. I kicked them at fence posts and skipped them off outcrops, built walled settlements. My father, always instructive, must have asked me to deduce their purpose. After cutting and gluing my hands with sap, I finally smashed one with a rock and found the seeds inside. My mother gave me lupines and bee balm and a lady slipper as introduction to the softer, more flamboyant side of reproduction, but I loved the pine cones' wooden petals, spiraling shields dug into strong resin, and the impossibly tall trees' knuckled roots threading beds of fallen needles.

We left Darmstadt when I was three, and I remember the sea. My parents took over a practice among the farmers and fishermen of Newbury, Massachusetts. He came from a city surgery with a hospital affiliation, she from midwifery at a lying-in hospital. In Newbury, she traveled constantly to births. After school I read or assisted my father, and I had one year attending her when I was twelve. My only distinct memory of that time is leaving a house at dawn with her weeping over a new mother lost to childbed fever, kicking the ground and pulling her face. But that was unusual.

She tended a thriving herb garden, and smelled of earth and leaves. I have her height, her eyes, and her industry.

TWO

In the third floor sitting room, I found Marianne laughing at a woodcut on a *National Police Gazette* cover. A girl was taking revenge on her faithless suitor with an axe. Sophronia, her bare legs entwined with Marianne's, couldn't decide if the cover girl was meant to be a villain or a heroine.

Marianne said, "And there you have the entirety of the woman question."

Sophie pulled her legs in and looked guilty, though I didn't mind if the girls pet or pleasured one another. This floor was their sanctum. The room was cluttered and homey and smelled of French perfume and fresh rolls with butter.

I said, "Who's first?"

Once a week I examined each girl for venereal disease. I also asked them to inspect themselves daily with a mirror, and taught them to identify various ulcers. We used a jelly bolus with boric acid as a preventative for syphilis, and in the rare case a girl did get infected, we treated her with calomel or other forms of mercury, though the benefits hardly outweighed the risks. I noticed girls infected in summer did better than those infected in winter, and had begun to experiment with steam and hot baths.

Exams took place in the third-floor bedrooms, where girls slept by twos when they weren't with a client. This arrangement minimized secret addictions and melancholias, and going into the rooms each week aided my assessments. Some girls like Tatiana stayed in the suites whenever possible, while Georgia and others bolted for their little beds.

During exams I collected their journal pages. I required daily notation on their sexual health: numbers and kinds of sexual acts, use of sponges, pessaries, douches, and suppositories, menses, level of sex drive, orgasm, infection. I wanted to know which days in the menstrual cycle were the most fertile, and which methods of contraception were most effective. Common knowledge said that a woman was fertile for two weeks after menstruation and the three days before. My teacher Sister Gwin called that malarkey, and maintained that it was around the midpoint of the menses. After eight years of excellent record-keeping, we knew that a pessary and a sponge together were over 95 percent effective at preventing conception, and that Gwin was as usual correct, conception generally occurred mid-cycle. If their menses were regular enough to predict fertility, Double girls took those days off or did only French. And we all began to notice that we could tell when we were fertile. Our juices changed, we craved sex more, and there was a certain pulling on either side of the abdomen, which I ascribed to bilateral ovaries. We hadn't had a pregnancy in a year.

I also kept records of my clinic patients, though not so thorough. There I studied broader questions pertaining to women in the larger population of shop girls, street girls, and occasional prostitutes, wives of laborers and clerks. We tallied pregnancies, births, disease, assault, and death. One in three or four had suffered sexual predation, and virtually all faced stalking and hectoring. Unmarried women were more likely to die of disease, married women by violence. Some days I thought my truest calling was to collect their stories, to let the lives of women and girls accrue somewhere and not, as usual, fade and vanish.

It was possible I was the only medical practitioner in the world with this depth of documentation on reproductive health, but there also might have been a hundred brothel nurses from Belfast to Hong Kong doing similar work. No medical journal anywhere would touch it. Predictably, the *Revolution*, a new women's rights newspaper published right down on Park Row by Susan B. Anthony and Elizabeth Cady Stanton, desperate to appear sexless and respectable, rejected two different articles, one on recognizing venereal diseases, and the other, just days earlier, summarizing what we'd learned about the menstrual cycle. I considered writing a pamphlet and publishing it at my own expense, but that would draw unwelcome attention to the procedures I did at the clinic. Any female surgeon was assumed to be a godless baby killer or a quack, but as yet there was no formal regulation of medicine or licensing. Midwives and healers were nonetheless pushed further underground each year. We depended on invisibility for certain clinic procedures and for client discretion at the house, but this same invisibility undermined the spread of vital information about fertility, and hid my expertise. Such was life. Only rarely did it get to me.

Clemence wanted to go first. She had come to the Double after a stint as a Mississippi riverboat dancer, and suffered from pelvic inflammation. A recent journal article made me think she had menstrual tissue growing outside her uterus, but offered no good suggestions for treatment. I had tried both stimulating and impeding bleeding and neither gave her any relief. After she told me her latest symptoms, we went down to the kitchen to speak to our beloved demon of a chef, Bertram Hibberd, to ask if he had ideas to decrease inflammation.

"Oh you peaky, lass? A vegetable broth and some fermented cabbages and cucumbers, I should think."

Bert was an unusual person who wore skirts and twirled in place when upset, which occurred when his efforts at the stove did not go according to plan. He was not chatty except with our baker Aunty Laure, a sinewy old bawd with a wealth of fables. Everyone loved their kitchen, a big room at ground level in the back with its round table and enchanting aromas. Here loitered idle porters and coachmen, maids and laundresses, drinking coffee and eating whatever Bert felt like giving them. Occasionally a deliveryman would bully Bert, and that person learned that Double Standard porters did not tolerate cruelty. Twice he was beaten on nearby streets. He rarely went out anymore and was happiest in the kitchen, where he practiced his art from early in the morning until late at night. He, like the twins and the Bixbys, lived in the building next door.

"That spirit need a sitdown," said Aunty Laure, having an animistic view of medicine and Clem's troubles. Laure was a light-skinned Creyol with West African, Haitian, and French lineages.

"Say more?" I asked her.

She looked at Clemence's belly. "The spirit in you is wandering, child. She needs to go back where she belong."

Clemence said, "How do we get her to do that?" I also perked up, remembering that wandering uterus.

Laure closed her eyes and nodded several times. "Strong song. A drum is good."

Clemence looked wary and I said, "When you feel like dancing."

The most persistent question I got the rest of that day was whether I would allow the girls to dye their hair blonde like the Belles. I told them no, as the chemicals burned hair and skin. "Get a wig."

Judge George Barnard burst into the main salon where I was having my first quiet moment of the day with *Harper's*. Though we were not strictly open, he had taken to dropping by on his way home. I didn't much mind the presumption, as he was good company. He lived nearby on Twenty-Third Street.

"I'll never play the piano again!" He clutched his right wrist like it was an injured animal. The judge was busy churning out new Tammany voters before Election Day on the third of November, three and a half weeks away. During the war, hardly any men became citizens because of the draft. But now in exchange for votes, Tammany dispensed plenty of no-show patronage jobs and wads of cash as they sought to install friendlies as mayor and governor. It required a lot of judicial signatures.

"How many new Americans did you mint today, George?"

"McCann does two thousand a day. I tried four at a time but at that rate I'll lose all feeling in my hand."

"Come over here," I said, waving him toward a small table.

"I can't hold cards, Doc."

I never played cards. "Take off your coat and roll up your sleeve."

"Why Doc, that'll keep my mind off the pain." I poured him a bourbon and sat to his right rubbing my hands together.

George came from a good family and went adventuring when he finished school. He tried the California gold fields but lost what little ore he found at poker, ran up a big debt that he worked off as a shill. Next he joined a minstrel troupe that toured the mining camps, having a fine tenor honed in the choirs of Yale.

After his western adventures, he read law with an uncle. Tweed, alert to a sporting toff with a price tag, plucked him from that drudgery and installed him in a vacant spot on the New York Supreme Court. In session George wore a white top hat, whittled sticks, and sipped brandy. He was hardworking and knew some law—how much was in dispute by those with occasion to know—but he was wholly owned by Tweed, and had recently helped him to steal the Erie Railroad. Tweed's new friends Diamond Jim Fisk and Mephistopheles Jay Gould used dubious bonds to float their Erie bid, and when it landed in the courts, George had issued the crucial injunction.

The exact price for his cooperation was not known, but Peter Sweeny (I had lately informed myself) got $150,000 and a seat on the Erie Board for going along. The rate for a friendly vote in the legislature, where the Erie fight landed after an appellate judge begged to differ with George, was about $4,000. Safe to say the judge was flush.

That fight had ended in July, and by October George's utility to Tammany—and to his own election to the bench he occupied—was in creating voters.

I dug my fingers into the tissue between the two bones of his forearm, and he moaned like I had performed some new French twist on his cock. I put gentle pressure on the tendons of his wrist and thumb before turning the hand palm up and addressing the flexors. His mouth hung open in stupefied relief.

"My God," he said, "are you sure you don't see clients? If you can do that to my hand, I'd love to find out—"

I cut him off. "Perhaps Clemence is available this evening. Someone should work on your upper arm and shoulder as well, and she's good at that. Strong hands."

He gave a penitent look. "Doc, I hope I didn't offend you."

"Not at all, George, but I'm no more equipped to be a harlot than you are."

"I don't know," he said, "I can be very entertaining when a man comes before me with his pants down."

I went to work on his elbow, and he closed his eyes and relaxed further. I wondered what else it did to him to write his own name over and over and over. Like many men, George came to the Double Standard to unfurl his full self. At work he pretended to serve the law, at home he pretended to worship his family, all the while violating countless oaths, statutes, and common sense. He dissipated the pressure of his many hypocrisies with drink and by riding himself to oblivion on luscious, unjudging girls, for whom he paid a fortune. It was a strange way to live.

I went fishing. "So we have a new ward boss, Benjamin O'Connor. I understand Benno was a childhood friend of the boss."

"Mmm, yes," he mused, speech slowing. "Sorting the docks. It's a jungle down there. Rival gangs, bloody mess."

"And Benno's the man for that?"

He sighed and opened his eyes, gave a wry smile. "He's a bulldog. Tweed said when Benno was about twelve, he fought off a much bigger kid by biting off his ear, which he then wore on a string around his neck."

I blinked, and while it dawned on George that his story did not commend Benno to me as a boss, Meg came into the room and greeted him brightly. While still out of his sight line, she mimed drinking. To his face, she said, "I'm awfully sorry, George. Willow's not feeling well. She sends her most profound regrets. Would you like me to arrange another girl for you?"

He sighed. "Oh that's all right Maggie my dear. Tell her I hope she feels better soon. I'm so tired I'd probably fall asleep on her anyway. I'll mosey on home."

I released his hand. "That should feel better tomorrow."

"It's reviving already," he said, shaking the wrist, "but tomorrow will be a respite. They've run out of naturalization forms. Can't print them fast enough."

We laughed. Tweed owned the printing company, and the prices were surely astronomical.

I made my way downstairs to Willow, who was sitting at the kitchen table with Aunty Laure. They had a nice rapport.

"Evening, friends," I sat on Willow's other side. "How goes?"

Laure kept quiet. Willow worked her mouth a bit before saying, "Sorry, Doc. I don't know what I was thinking."

"Where are you in your cycle?"

She blinked a few times. "It's coming up, I suppose."

"Bit of a black mood?"

"Pissy, Meg called me." She laughed a while, full of self-loathing. Oh dear.

We all made jokes about the week before bleeding, women turning into gorgons and medusas, carried off by ill-tempered goblins and what have you. Some Harvard physician had lately published a book about how women had to rest during those days or suffer dire consequences. I wondered if this genius gave his housemaids a week off each month.

Willow had been at the Double about two months and was landing. She had built some trust and might shed some of her protective layers. I asked her, "Pissy about what?"

"I just want to be left alone for five minutes."

"That's easy, ask Perlie for a key to 134." A brownstone on Twenty-Fourth Street had apartments set aside for a discrete encounter or a quiet night off. "Are you getting along with Georgia?" They shared a room.

"She's a sweetheart." She was still edgy.

"Out with it," I said gently.

She blurted, "I can't do this anymore."

"You mean be a harlot, live here?"

"I love living here, I—" She couldn't spit it out.

"You don't like the work."

"I don't mind the men. It's, it's . . ." She started unbuttoning her jacket but her fingers could not quite manage it.

I said, "May I help you?"

Laure's eyes grew round. Willow was named for her form.

She was a tall, slender girl with no curves whatsoever, long legs with the least fleshy thighs I had ever seen on a woman and just a whiff of breasts. She had grown up off the Bowery, and become a waiter girl and eventually a Broadway dancer. As we removed her overskirt, underskirt, and crinoline, I asked if there was a kind of costume she preferred to wear.

She was too busy tearing off the jacket and blouse.

I shooed a couple of staring maids. Bert didn't take his eyes from the stove.

Aunty Laure said, "Have you seen those bloomers?"

Willow stopped moving. "You mean like trousers?"

"They're looser, they go under skirts."

This made her angry. After another moment she stood in a lawn camisole and petticoat, red-faced and huffing. "I can't stand all that!" She kicked the pile of clothing. "It weighs a ton and it's suffocating!"

Calm, I said, "I'm always jealous of teamsters' dress. Trousers and a shirt, a jacket if it's cold."

She kept kicking at the pile of silks, and I stood and lifted a beautiful pale green overskirt off the floor. The kitchen was clean but it was still a kitchen. Laure took over and I took Willow's hand and bid her sit again.

"Why don't we get you some new clothes? Dressing like a driver might not work, but you could try dressing like a gentleman."

"How could I?"

"Why not? People dress as someone else all the time. Let's lighten your load. You don't need all those underclothes, and you certainly don't need a corset."

She mocked me. "I'm a Double harlot, Doc. There are certain standards."

I gave her the sharp look she wanted and then turned speculative. "The standards of behavior still apply, and the clothing must be high quality, but there's room to play with what it signifies. Your legs would look rather splendid in trousers. You'll still need day and evening dresses for some occasions, but why don't we bring in a men's tailor because Phila won't cotton to making you a suit."

"Hunh," she said.

"Hunh is right," Laure said to me. "I can't tell if the spirit is bum-boozling you or you're boozling the spirit."

Meg arrived with an empty wine bottle and took in the pile of clothes and Willow sitting nearly naked at the table.

I said to Willow, "To be clear, are you off harlotry, or the clothing?"

"I'm off flattery and talking in little baby voices. I want, I want . . ."

"What?" Meg said, a bit loud with impatience.

Willow said, "I want to tell people to piss off and not apologize. Not to be interrupted and spoken over and condescended to and told what to do all the time!"

We all laughed in agreement. "I'm not sure a change of wardrobe can provide that, but it's a start. It might not suit all your clients, but plenty will enjoy it."

"It'll suit me!"

"All right," I said, pushing the mess of corkscrew curls out of her face. "Do you want to cut this short?"

She grabbed at her hair with both hands. "No. I can pin it up, can't I?"

"You can wear it like a princess with a tiara with your trousers for all I care. In the house, anyway. Nothing too odd outside until we settle on it, all right?"

"Mmm," she said, still holding onto a hank of hair draped over her shoulder to protect it from me. The drink emboldened her, as did shedding her clothes, so Willow threw out the next thing that irked her. "Seems like I heard, Doc," she said, "that you bought out a girl's debt for a thousand dollars."

"Where'd you hear that?" I said, startled by the sneer in her tone.

She shrugged.

I took a breath to compose myself. Trusting in the house meant testing me. "It wasn't that costly. The girl was kidnapped from home and much abused, and finally attacked with a knife. She was brought to the clinic for treatment, and I bought her debt."

"Why her?" Willow asked.

"She's my patient," I said. "Why not her?"

"They say she's well-born. Educated."

"Yes, and barely sixteen."

This made her sink and stew, her face a deep pout.

It was a question of who deserved so much care. "Do you suppose I wouldn't have done the same for you in that state?"

Her mouth twisted up.

Meg said, "You do recall begging for a place here? Pleading for it."

I shook my head at Meg, who put up her hands. To Willow I said, "You think because she had rich parents, what? I think she's more deserving? That I don't treat poor girls as well?"

Meg said, "Doc, it's your money and you can do whatever you want with it. She'd congratulate you if you'd bought jewels and furs."

Willow said again, "Why this one girl?"

Meg inhaled to speak and I put up a hand. "It's all right," I said to Willow. "You should ask questions if something seems unfair to you. Vivie was in very grave condition when she arrived. I operated, and saved her from leaking urine for the rest of her life. I couldn't stand the thought of sending her back for more abuse. I would have done the same for any girl."

Still she glowered. This was about her own history, whether she knew it or not.

I said, "That seems like a plenty good enough reason to me. But actually, as it happens, there is a more particular answer to your question. Vivie reminds me of another girl from years ago with similar injuries. At that time, I was unequipped to help. That one was not born to rich parents, but when I saw Vivie, she returned to me." I put one hand over my heart, and then the other, expected to say more but found little to add and no voice to add it.

Meg scanned her memory for whom that other girl might have been.

Then I said, "I did it for that other girl, and for many others I wish I'd been able to help."

Willow's face slowly shifted from defiance to collapse. She began to cry and then to wail.

"Oh honey," I said, and embraced her. The only details of her background I recalled were her dancing and that her parents were both gone. My care for Vivie had conjured her own losses.

"Doc," she sobbed, trying to compose herself. "My father was a brute. He beat us all the time and nearly killed my mother more than once."

Meg crossed herself, and I held my breath.

"One night she reached her limit. She thought about slitting her own wrists with her sewing shears, but instead she slit his throat while he slept."

"He an angry spirit, she a vengeful one," said Aunty Laure.

"Oh my dear," I said. "What a burden. Were you there?"

She threw herself into my lap to heave out the first layer of sacking she'd built to carry the weight. She was indeed shedding. I rubbed her back and held her hair from her face.

"How old were you?"

"Sixteen, just like that girl. They put Mama in prison and she died within weeks."

Meg got up and began to pace the kitchen. On her path back toward the table her expression was still impatient but also sorry.

"What a body goes through," said Laure.

"Tell us about your mother," I said.

Willow settled across my legs. "All she ever did was work. She did piece work, you know, never enough light or hours in the day."

"What was she like?"

"She sang. I tried to learn new songs for her because she sang the same three or four over and over and it could drive you mad. She loved pralines. That was her favorite, she got some for her birthday. Any kind of candied nut. When I smell them I want to cry."

"Did you have a funeral for her?" I asked.

She sat up and looked at me. "No."

"Maybe you still could, a ceremony or some occasion she would have liked."

Her mother was buried on Hart Island, the potter's field off the Bronx, but Willow seemed scared to visit. She said she'd think about it.

Having spit this poison out, she was now crumpling before us. I glanced at Meg and Laure.

Meg said, "Let's get you up to bed."

When she was on her feet, I stood and kissed her. "I'm glad you told us. That was brave. We'll talk about it more soon." As I watched Willow stumble out, I pondered whether her change of clothing meant she was embracing her mother or letting her go. Hard to know with these peculiarities what's our own and what's forced upon us. Brothels turned out to be my best venue for the free practice of medicine, the stick in the eye to respectability sometimes a sadness and sometimes a bonus.

When they had gone, Laure said to me, "That girl Vivie got under your skin."

I sighed. "Yes."

"She can't fix the past."

My look said no kidding.

"You hardly ever get messy, is all. I don't mind, but watch out you don't boil over for waiting so long."

"She's still a child. Have you seen her?"

Laure shook her head no, like Vivie was contagious.

"Tell me," I asked, "Why is everyone so suspicious of this girl?" Laure was dubious. "I couldn't stand to see another innocent life end in a bloody ruin, and for that I'm made to feel like a bigot, or a predator, or a head case in my own house!"

The corners of Laure's mouth turned up. "How's the air up there?"

"I'm really not in the mood, Laure."

She hummed to herself a bit, and then said, "Maybe not. But when you paint yourself into a corner and then moan you're trapped, I just can't help myself."

I slammed a hand on the table as I stood up, startling Laure, and seethed a moment. Huffing a breath, I strode out. Finding myself in the garden, I pulled up short and detoured to the one bench out of sight from both house and clinic, under a grape arbor reeking with preposterous sweetness.

Wanting to scream or break something, I sat still. There was nothing wrong with helping Vivie: it was *me* everyone found unsound. The girl had unsettled me, and so what? I hadn't hurt anyone. I hadn't changed course. Here I sat in the same old rictus of restrictions as if my limbs were tied with rope, grinding my teeth together and casting about for what might help me calm myself. There was nothing. Unfit for company, unable to walk abroad alone, rejected for the work which could help thousands of women, and all of it my own fault, apparently. Laudanum appealed, but that betrayed Vivie. Even the late, rotting grapes with their whispers of an easier, quieter life within my means were infuriating.

I had few satisfactions and fewer prospects. Those *Revolution* hags hadn't even returned my article on fertility, probably kept it to consult for themselves. I meant to write and demand it back but never got around to it, because in the end I fled upstairs and guzzled several tumblers of Scotch whiskey, counting the obstacles to study and practice for a capable nurse, let alone a female surgeon, the physical and social insults of brothel life and the endless, insulting suspicion of my service to women, the need to hide my achievements, and now this mortifying self-pity, never mind the more pressing threats of Benno's mysterious plans and the specter of Vivie's kidnapper or her assailant showing up to finish her. I took another belt, retched, and passed out in a chair, waking to hours of vomit, failing even at dissipation.

As Vivie regained strength and could move around a bit, she grew bored. After I removed her sutures, I decided to move her to the fourth floor of the Double. In daylight the girls would be good company, and as they got to know her, resentments would fade.

The night before the move, I stopped in to see how she was feeling.

"A bit of a headache today, but all right."

We discussed her withdrawal and her discharge. She looked glum and had some chafing around her mouth. "Ask Nina for a salve."

"I get dry when the weather turns colder."

"Vivie," I said, "we haven't talked much about your family. Is it all right if I ask some questions?"

She flattened her lips as if to hold back words, and I saw why they were chapping.

"Would I be right to think your full name is Lavinia Curtis?"

Her eyes widened. "I heard there was quite a fuss in the papers."

"Your parents must be heartbroken."

She sighed. "I want to write to them, but I can't have the story in the papers again, what happened to me, all the questions. I can't do that to them, or to me."

That was a good instinct. "If it could be done quietly, do you have the kind of relationship with them where you could tell them the truth?"

She looked doubtful. "My mother might understand but I don't think my father would."

"Would he blame you?"

"I don't know, but I could never go back to Bennington." She began to agitate, breath fast and shallow, and I sat next to her on the bed. She said, "They'd have to keep it a secret. It might be better for them and for me if I stayed disappeared."

Would it be better to suspect your daughter was dead or know she'd been a sex slave? "Tell me about them."

She described a prosperous third generation dairy, and a father who took up politics because he wanted to form a dairy association and found there were no clear rules for it. Her mother was a devoted gardener and cook, who would now be canning applesauce. She played the piano. I could see my own mother at the work table in our kitchen, smiling at the slow autumn flies as she peeled the hundredth apple.

"Do you play?"

She wrinkled her nose. "I hate practicing."

"There are two pianos at the house. You'll like Erroll, our professor."

She couldn't imagine being interested in anything.

I said, "Would you like me to write to your folks? We might arrange a meeting at a hotel here in New York."

This alarmed her and she held her breath, finally letting out, "What would you say?"

"I would tell them the truth about what happened, and say you are now recovering in a safe place."

"Maybe," she paused. "But not yet, all right? I want to think about it."

I took her hand. "My dear, I have one more tough question for you." One emotion after another flickered in those blue eyes. "You don't have to answer, but I want you to think about it for your healing. It may take time before you're ready and that's fine. For tonight it's a question to consider and you can take time to sort it."

She sat frozen.

I reminded her to breathe, and said, "We need to sort how you got the injuries to your bladder. They were made by something sharp." Her eyes filled with fear and confusion and I held tighter to her hand. "We don't want the injury to be mysterious or unclear to you. It's your body and you'll have to manage it your whole life, so let's not dodge the facts of how you got it." For starters, I wanted to know if she had been conscious.

She nodded but was still in a panic.

"Take a breath."

"I don't know." She cried freely as she spoke but never broke down. "The laudanum made it all so strange and mixed up. Someone gave me a drink and that may have had more in it. I don't know what was real. There were so many men and I just wanted it to stop."

"Naturally. You were hallucinating. Do you remember pain, or metal, maybe a knife?"

"I heard a name, but I'm not sure it was that night. Danny, maybe? Sometimes I thought it was Daddy, but that can't be right. I don't know, it might have been a different time."

I said, "I wish we knew if he was connected to Vernon Trent." The hectic way she scanned her memories told me she wasn't ready. "That's all right, my sweet," I said, embracing her. "Pieces of it may come back to you with time. You survived it, which is plenty."

One Sunday afternoon when I was upstairs at home, Nina came to tell me that Martin Mitchell the policeman was waiting to see me. She had put him in an exam room, which I found funny.

"You're the picture of health, Officer Mitchell."

He blushed and said, "I wanted a word." We stood across the exam table, one of us imagining him taking his pants down. "I heard some stories this week and thought you'd be interested. Three different girls disappeared, two street tarts who worked Broadway and one inmate of the Seven Sisters."

"That's awful, but not very surprising."

"No," he agreed, "but what caught my attention was that the two people who told me, a maid on the Row and a friend of the Broadway girls, told the same story. The girls were real standouts, and in a particular way. They seemed high class. And they disappeared off the street in daytime without taking their stuff."

We shared a rueful look.

He said, "Abduction at the wharves and stations is one thing. I mean, it's not pretty but no one ever shows up to ask what happened to a girl from upstate or Ireland. They don't have friends in the ward to ask questions. This puts me in a tough position." He was more agitated over working harlots than innocents. It was oddly endearing.

"Yes," I said, "kind of like that conversation with Hanky Pank." We shared another look. It was why he'd come. Who else would have the nerve in Benno's ward? This would certainly explain Hank's nerves when I asked about Benno's plans.

I didn't tell him about Vivie, but did ask, "Have you heard the name Vernon Trent?"

"No, why?"

"A high-class girl he took six months ago."

"Does he know Benno?"

"No idea." All the elite houses in the ward were run by women, something Benno doubtless hated. "If he's short on cash, trapping girls in debt is lucrative."

"And who's going to stop him?" he said, telling me that his hands were tied and it angered him. This visit could be a test from Benno, but I didn't think so. Perhaps Martin was the rare cop not captive to Tammany.

"Do you know their names?" I asked. "The girls."

"I think the one who worked Broadway near Fifth was called Catherine."

"Catherine Farnsworth?"

He perked up. "You know her?"

I swore, and nodded. She was a fresh-faced and healthy girl, well-spoken and funny, who came to the clinic for white patches of skin on her hands and feet. I diagnosed vitiligo, a loss of pigment with no known cause or cure. She worked up her courage to ask me if we were hiring girls for the house. For her grit and sweetness, I conveyed her interest to the twins. They liked her but passed because of the vitiligo.

I decided to trust him a bit. "Do you think Benno's behind it, that he's kidnapping girls?"

Martin said, "I don't know," and then looked dismayed.

"What?"

"They had a little party at his new club. It's not finished, but a few nights ago Benno and a few of his boys brought some girls in there."

My voice got low. "And?"

He swallowed. "As I understand it, they made the girls strip against their will, and did as they pleased."

With every splendid harlot in the ward at his disposal, Benno preferred force. "Gunpoint or knifepoint, presumably? Or just fists?"

Martin shrugged, and we shared that look again. He said, "Tell your girls to be extra careful when they go out. I'll visit Jane and Lizzie and see if they've heard about competitors moving in."

I said, "How about I take one and you take the other?"

"I'll take Lizzie, we have history. Thanks, Doc. I wasn't here."

I asked Israel to augment the girls' security without alarming them, and lost hours regretting Catherine and agitating about all the stolen girls, where they might be, and if Vivie's injuries were an indicator of their captors' methods, what might be done to them. In the absence of evidence, I tried to hold open the possibility that this was just an unusually bad week of unrelated violence in the ward and things would settle back to normal, but I knew it heralded something dreadful. I might have asked the twins to investigate, but I wanted better confirmation, and also to settle my own response. Undercooked warnings of coming catastrophe would only deepen their worry about me.

The family surgery faced the street, joined to the house by a short hallway. A series of unhappy girls lit fires and made meals. Neither parent cared for décor, though my father dragged his favorite chair from fireside to window according to the season. When not sleeping at odd hours, my mother made poultices and ointments, rolled bandages and cleaned instruments.

Some of my school friends were forbidden to visit me. Their fathers preferred the old doctor, and their mothers fretted about all the German medical journals and poisons. But I was welcome at a few homes where one more child made no difference at the table. I was good with little ones.

My mother was blamed for the household irregularities. "Why must she traipse about in all weathers?" She had a trap but sometimes rode the horse. In a storm she'd go in snowshoes. I once heard a woman in the neighborhood say that no respectable man would ever want me, with a mother always on the loose. I laughed so loudly, she heard me.

THREE

Judge George Barnard and Oakey Hall, District Attorney and candidate for Mayor, arrived at the Double Standard fresh from a ceremony to christen the newest locomotive of the Erie Railroad as the George C. Barnard. Apparently she was a beaut. The night before, several Tammany stalwarts had been installed as Erie directors and collected heaps of stock, all made possible by George's summertime injunctions. Impudence and cheek were the new virtues.

A group of men in celebration was always the same. The essential trait of masculinity being dominance, they kept score. They rehearsed nuances of their victories: their abilities, advantages, strategies, and skills, and their opponents' deficits, errors, flaws, and failures. Unrelieved, such stories left me sad; the endless need to perform was a terrible burden. But a man who brought some self-awareness to his need for approval, some wit to the preposterous mix of sheer effrontery and dumb luck that enabled success, I understood.

Elegant Oakey's waistcoat was a lemon-yellow paisley silk, matched by a cravat and pocket-square of gold-edged *broderie anglaise.* He was highborn and well-educated, a prolific playwright and essayist, and man about town who'd been seen with half the actresses on Broadway, though he had a society wife. I wondered why he'd agreed to be mayor of Tammany, though it was a big stage, and one could hardly say no to Tweed. He put a satin coat and a silver tongue on their rampant thievery.

After some gossip about the ceremony, Oakey said, "Something must be done about Sweeny's manners."

George groaned but I was attentive to any word on Peter Sweeny. He said, "That is one rude pirate." He must have embarrassed Tammany among the other Erie tycoons.

George told us that Slippery Dick Connolly, the third member atop the Tammany ring with Tweed and Sweeny, claimed to have spent an entire evening trying to teach Sweeny to be a swell, literally to glad-hand, to grab a man's fist and smack his shoulder. After several hours, the best Sweeny could manage was a rictus smile and a flick of his gaze to the person's eyes.

Sophronia said that in their brief encounter, he never expressed a desire or acknowledged their relations, never put a hand on her. He simply opened his trousers and spent at her touch.

Oakey did a double-take and stared at me. "Doc, could you do something with him? Give him an inkling of how to be in company?"

Address the bad manners of a powerful and volatile man? It was a big risk, but then Benno showed signs of becoming a big problem that Sweeny could solve. "He'd have to be willing."

Oakey grew impish. "There are a few enticements on the premises. He's well into his forties and his mother is agitating for him to marry. We could lure him with the promise of how to woo a bride."

George said, "The woman who marries that will be hard up."

Oakey said, "They'll queue fifty deep."

A widow perhaps, someone with experience. I said, "Propose it when he's relaxed, if that's in his repertoire. Ease into the subject, see if you can get him to ask for help."

George raised his glass to Oakey. "I'll leave it to you, your honor. I'm subtle as a locomotive."

My dear friend Elliott Vanderpoel appeared in the doorway, and I warmed at the sight of his lanky grace and gray-green eyes. A sometime theatrical producer, he was a rich libertine who could seduce anyone breathing.

He took in the company and said, "Lo, accomplices! Shall we hatch a conspiracy to overthrow some hidebound institution? What can we make of this cabal?" Elliott fancied himself an artist and rebel among these obedient footsoldiers. He kissed my cheeks before sitting.

Oakey said, "Where's your brother, Vanderpoel? I haven't seen him in months. Does that paper run itself?"

Elliott's elder half-brother Asa was a well-regarded newspaperman, publisher of a paper he founded after the war called *The Standard*. I'd never met the man but had myself a good laugh when I heard the paper's name. He meant to signal a fidelity to facts amid the rampant partisanship of other papers, but it made a splendid foil for the Double Standard. I did admire his principles: he'd been fired as city editor of the *Tribune* for fiery anti-slavery editorials and in 1863 gone off to work for the secretary of war. Oakey, always tending his own public image, would cultivate him like a hothouse rose, but Elliott once mentioned that Asa loathed Oakey. Annoyed, Elliott said, "He's getting every last minute on his sloop."

Ruby came in after Elliott and surveyed the room for where to sit. Elliott brightened and gestured to his lap. She wiggled her bottom and eased it over him, settling with a sigh. George and Oakey were entranced. Elliott might have been spiting Oakey for using him as a conduit to his brother. Ruby played with Elliott's hair and avoided my eye as they all swilled their drinks. I preferred sex play to stay in the suites. She said, "So what's the latest, gentlemen?"

As if suddenly faced with the existence of prostitution, George said, "Some judge in Albany proposed a reform bill with stiffer penalties for brothel clients than for the inmates. Talk about a non-starter!"

Oakey said, "I can imagine how that went over at Delevan House." The informal seat of power in Albany was a posh hotel where Tweed, who was himself on the ballot for the state senate, had lately taken a seven-room suite he filled with caged canaries, and presumably girls. That reforming judge was likely prevailed upon by the ladies of the Female Moral Reform Society or their ilk, whose assessment of male behavior was more acute than their political calculus.

Hands roaming Ruby's bodice, Elliott asked her, "Ever been to boarding school, my darling?"

"Have you?" she came back quick. Of course she'd been arrested. We all had.

"As a matter of fact," Elliott said, "the officers of Princeton, New Jersey did not appreciate the altitudinous hijinks of a certain band of youngsters."

"You were a very bad boy," Ruby said, goosing him somewhere, because he jumped. He tried to retaliate but her bottom was well padded by skirts, so instead he nipped at her neckline. She slapped his arm but arranged her breasts closer to his face. Their physical rapport was so easy and familiar, one could well imagine how it would proceed when they were alone, as the rest of us were now doing.

As he watched them George said, "No one regulated the hordes of diseased tarts following the Union Army. Did any of you actually see Hooker's Brigade?" Joseph Hooker was a sporting Union general whose brigade of "soiled doves" followed his army from Virginia to a neighborhood of Washington called Murder Bay. Eventually the vice district so overflowed the bay that the girls were herded onto a steamship and deposited on a beach in New Jersey, where they promptly founded a town called Loveladies.

Oakey said, "It was not wholesome."

Elliott said, "What do you think, Doc? Will the faithful make way on regulation?"

Tammany Hall conduct anti-vice reform? I tried not to laugh. I said, "Some smaller cities may try, but can you imagine New York registering six hundred houses and twenty thousand girls?"

Oakey said, "The Superintendent of Police says it's three thousand girls."

"That's very low," I said. "Most girls taking money for sex are not full-time harlots. They're seamstresses or factory workers supplementing an inadequate wage. If they regulate, they'll force girls to choose between one and the other."

George said, "Reformers do agitate over it."

Elliott said, "Get rid of one form of slavery, on to the next. Though they might do better eradicating marriage."

I loved him for that, and said, "I'd rather they looked to expand women's rights to make a decent living and own property than curtail one of the few ways we have to make a buck." I said to Oakey, "Do you suppose regulators ever consider how hunger weighs in a girl's choice of the life?"

Oakey was a bit shocked, but that discussion was cut short by a squad of porters arriving with a fine-smelling pork roast, a bushel of potatoes roasted in herbs and garlic, various salads and sauces, and several fine vintages that would cost the Tammany machine a fraction of its treasure.

Ruby relocated her bottom to a chair and kept George's attention with the opening and placement of her napkin. The meal was excellent even by Bert's standards, and we spent a few minutes in gustatory rapture, but I dreaded the prospect of regulation. I took the chance to discuss it with Oakey before he was elected.

Keeping my voice deferential, I said, "Oakey, you think it unbecoming that a woman earn her living standing up?"

He said, "Single women have to eat, I suppose. Six-hundred-thousand dead boys will leave a whole generation without husbands. You prompted me to consider the life choices of several actresses of my acquaintance, and questioned if they chose the theater quite voluntarily."

"Girls with no family wealth or education, I take it."

"And no temperament for embroidery," he laughed.

I tried to make it a game. "If they had your latitude, what do you suppose they would have done?"

He thrust out his lower lip. "One is quite funny. I suppose she might make a playwright, but that's less a living wage than acting."

Elliott said, "She might have been an attorney."

Both Oakey and George laughed. With a wink and a smirk, Oakey said, "I would love to see that."

"I could stand up in court and make a right good argument," said Ruby.

"I'd be all ears," said George.

"Would you rule in my favor?"

"Would you be wearing pants?"

"I don't have any pants," she said.

"You can have mine," said Elliott.

Oakey drank and turned to me. "Doc, I'd have thought you would welcome regulation. If they were registered, girls would avoid arrest and see licensed physicians."

"Who would no doubt treat them with care and respect," I said drily. Elliott and George laughed, and Oakey shifted in his chair.

Matter-of-fact, I said, "Regulating prostitution will increase the stigma and shame around a difficult choice. It would bolster the industry, and draw in more pimps and exploiters of women, more procurers." I thought of Israel and said, "More slavers. It would bring more tourists to New York to sample the flesh, including young children."

Oakey said, "You show no high regard for your profession."

"Doc is not a harlot, Oakey," said Elliott with a bit of steel.

"No indeed, I meant the owners."

As plaintively as I could, I said, "It's the only way many girls survive. Please don't make it any harder for them."

George raised his glass. "To girls doing the best they can."

Raising his glass to Ruby, Elliott said, "And to the Double Standard, where you can do the best girls." After we drank to that, he said, "Doc, we're due for a blowout. Let's use that beautiful ballroom of yours."

My first impulse was to demur, but I stopped to think. Flourishing our popularity with Tammany's top echelon might aggravate Benno if he was worried about fitting in, but done well it could ease him into a whole new level of access. He could have a drink and a laugh with Peter Sweeny and be reminded of my manifold utility. Plus the higher-ups should know that Benno was snatching girls off the street, if the signs were correct. "All right, friend. What do you say to an election night soirée?" It fell three weeks hence, Grant ordained for the presidency and Tammany candidates poised to take New York from aldermen to governor, with Tweed in the senate. It would be their coronation, their absorption of the entire city and state government.

"Americana!" said Elliott with a sweep of his hand. "Acres of bunting."

I agreed, but wished for a pirate theme to skewer Tammany's swaggering nerve and brazen thievery.

George said, "By God there was a corker at Josie Mansfield's last night." That townhouse adjoined the Opera House on Twenty-Third Street, recently purchased by Diamond Jim Fisk, who moved his office in. He'd met Josie at the Hotel de Wood, and installed her in the place next door, where George played poker with Tweed and Fisk. He once told me that Josie's pet name for Fisk was "Sardines," and I amused myself imagining why. In a pitiful failure of imagination, he called her "Dolly."

I said, "You gents can celebrate your victories, and we can invite the local celebrities as well." Elliott had a question about that remark, but saved it.

"Who is your local chieftain?" asked Oakey.

"Benno O'Connor."

"Christ," he said. "There's a specimen."

I said, "He wants me to add a faro table."

"Sticking his nose in, is he?" asked George.

"Is that what you boys are calling it now?" said Ruby, bless her.

"It's settled, then," I said, looking at each in turn. "We'll toast the future of New York in style." If not a clear strategy to roust kidnappers, a brothel ball flourished our strengths, and was always diverting.

Elliott followed me into the hall for a word before I made my getaway.

"What weighs you down, friend?" I asked him.

"It's my brother. I had a letter this morning." Elliott had given Oakey the brush-off on this subject but something was amiss. The half-brothers had a complicated history, their father having married Elliott's dancer mother rather soon after the prolonged illness and death of Asa's patrician mother.

"Is he all right?"

"It's from the housekeeper at his wife's family's summer place in Connecticut. He was supposed to return to the city two weeks ago, but instead he's sitting up there drinking, not sleeping, not answering letters, not making plans to leave. It's very unlike him."

"What will you do?" I asked.

"I'll go in the morning. I wanted to ask you, Doc, would you please come with me? If anyone could sort him, I'm sure it's you."

It never occurred to him that respectable men and women did not travel in pairs unless they were close kin or husband and wife. "Oh Ell, that's not possible. I'm sorry."

He said, "I'm no healer."

"This behavior is sudden?" I asked.

"Yes and no. Relations have not been smooth at home since the war." That was three years or more. "His wife took the children to tour the continent, and now he's too much alone at home."

"I'm sorry to hear it. He seems a good citizen."

"He's been kind to me. I must do all I can."

I said, "Be a compassionate listener for him. Ask if certain days of the war have been on his mind, or if he's thinking of friends from the past."

"What's happening?"

"No idea, but you said the war changed him. Get him talking if you can—gently."

He looked doubtful.

I patted his arm. "From what I know, he's a man of strong character and will right himself."

"Thanks, Doc. And please think about coming with me. It's a beautiful place, a few hours' journey on the train."

"I'll see him in the city, if it comes to that."

I informed Meg and Ciara of my election night party scheme to sweeten relations between Benno and Sweeny, and went to look in on Vivie. She was asleep in the third floor sitting room, *Persuasion* open in her lap. I stood quiet in the doorway enjoying the artlessness of her face, weighing how much of my present irritation was my own fault. When I stepped into the room, Vivie opened her eyes and smiled.

"Doc," she said, an endearment.

"Hello," I said, falling onto a chaise. "How are you feeling?"

"I'm all right. I can read a little more, but I'm monstrous itchy." She patted her belly. We'd discussed that this was likely a sign of healing.

"Make sure to use both those rinses before you sleep. I'll check you tomorrow."

"What about you, Doc?" she asked. "Are you tired?" Her kindness touched me.

I sighed. "I am."

"Did something happen?"

I thought back over the day and said, "The usual indignities of being a woman."

She nodded. "A rock and a hard place?"

I mused, "I wonder if somewhere in the city at this moment two men are sitting around wishing they were women."

She said, "If they are, it's because they want breasts and pussies always at their disposal."

I burst out laughing, all my vexation vanished.

She flushed crimson. "I'm sorry, was that too frank?"

"Just unexpected." We enjoyed it awhile. I said, "Any more thoughts on your future?"

"Not really. I have the same dilemmas."

"Take your time, my dear."

She wrinkled her face. "What do you think I should do?"

I met her gaze, and gave a more honest answer than I usually did to such a question. "Much as I like having you here, for your healing you need to choose a kind of work. And it's important that you leave New York."

"Why?"

Because the man who kidnapped her, or the man who attacked her, if they were not the same person, might try again, and too many people knew her link to me. "Mrs. Wrigley is not discreet."

She nodded, saying, "Vernon Trent knows where I am, then." She could identify Trent, which in normal times was reason enough for him to want her dead. Vernon Trent may have felt invincible, but Vivie was still at risk.

"We should assume. As soon as you're able to travel, you should. I have friends outside New York who can help you get set up. You're not to worry about money, all right?"

Tears fell. "Thank you, Doc. You saved me from hell on earth."

"You've done your part."

"Everyone here is so kind. I hate to leave. It feels safe."

I nodded, remembering that relief. Seeing the book in her lap, I said, "Anne Elliot is such a paragon, we long for her happy ending."

Vivie said, "Her suffering is rather quaint, don't you think? Reduced circumstances in a splendid Bath townhouse, lost love, annoying relatives."

I murmured assent. "You have a bit more to overcome. But you also have far wider latitude."

"Yes," she said. "Anne Elliot should have run a school or a hospital."

"That's the spirit!" When choosing girls for the house, I looked for a desire to escape the strangleholds of femininity while wielding its chief weapons. Girls with clear vision about the options actually open to them. "You'd make a wonderful teacher."

"I do love children," she said. "I have a lot to learn myself, but I suppose schools out west aren't too picky."

I said, "We work in schools because loving children aligns with what a woman is supposed to be. Nursing does too."

Vivie reflected, and said, "I can't tell if you approve of that."

I told her why nursing as it was done in most hospitals would not satisfy me.

"It's true, some schools are awful." Then she squinted. "I don't know that my imagination has ever ranged beyond womanly choices."

"It can be difficult to tell the difference between what we love and what we're allowed. Fluff your feathers a bit, and consider."

She looked at the door to the hallway as if the world beyond were opening, and shook her head.

As I crossed the yard toward my apartment, I felt far too much in the dark. Martin Mitchell had learned nothing more about the missing girls, nor had the Double porters asking around for Catherine Farnsworth. At least we hadn't heard of any new abductions.

Just after dawn, I was awake and dressing in my rooms above the clinic when someone began laying on the bell. I hurried down.

Two Negro men and one girl were seated in the hallway. Nina knelt before one man with a busted hand, while Betsy hustled in with a clean cloth for a wound to the arm of a pretty girl I took to be a harlot.

I said, "Good morning."

Nina said, "Morning. Brothel riot on Bleeker Street."

Heaven's sake. That was more than twenty blocks away, and I realized. "Bim Farley's?"

The man not being treated stood and said, "You Doc? Bim said to bring Honey to you."

"I am. Are you injured yourself, sir?"

He blinked. "I can wait." He held himself like he was in pain.

"Nina, are you all right?" Her patient appeared to have at least two broken fingers, probably from throwing a punch.

She said, "We'll get this wrapped up."

"Bring him to west and let him lay down." Our exam rooms were east, north, and west.

"Betsy, let's take this lady to east. You're Honey?" The girl nodded. "I'm Doc." I looked to the third man.

He said, "John Herman, ma'am."

"You'll be all right here? Call out if anything goes sideways."

"Yes, ma'am."

"Call me Doc. You work for Bim?"

"I do, ma'am. Doc." Bim Farley was a flinty old saloon owner who let anyone of any race rent rooms. I met him soon after I came to New York.

While Betsy settled Honey for me to stitch her, I asked John Herman, "Riot?"

"Bunch of drunk boys from downtown, wearing the clothes." He meant the foppish Bowery outfits. Gangs. "Some traded out their fancy coats but they all had the shoes."

"A lot of damage?"

"They set a fire, and while we put it out, they barged in. These two got the worst of it."

In general brothel riots meant drunk working men looking for someone lower on the social ladder to terrorize, though sometimes they targeted upper class brothels they couldn't afford. We had a few at the Silk Pillow, where I worked when I first came to New York, and one at the Double after the Draft Riots in '63. Before the war, rioters often wore blackface and targeted Negroes, abolitionists, and reformers as well as bagnios. Farley's made a likely target. Bim was a legend but growing old, and Tammany was squeezing anyone they couldn't control.

"They got inside?"

"They barely got out, I can tell you that."

Bim's was in the Fifteenth ward, which bordered the Sixteenth only at one corner, Sixth Avenue and Fourteenth Street. If Benno was involved, it was one more sign of his ballooning ambitions.

John Herman was in more than a little pain. "You sure you're all right?"

He looked aggravated. "One held me and the other kicked me pretty hard."

"Ah." He meant his testicles. "Well, if you're not bleeding there's not much we can do until it announces itself in some symptom. Do you want something for pain?"

"No thank you. I'll keep my wits about me."

I pointed to the north exam room. "You can lay down in there, and that's a water closet. Feel free to use it and check for blood in your water."

He nodded his thanks.

Honey was a lovely girl with clear, smooth *café au lait* skin over beautiful bone structure. I wanted her family history, eventually.

"Miss Honey," I said, "I'm Doc. I'm going to give you medicine that will put you to sleep while I sew that arm up."

She whimpered and pointed to her shoulder. Hell, I'd missed a dislocated clavicle under a feather collar. She wore a black velvet ribbon around her neck with a dangling heart charm, which I untied and put into her pocket.

"I'm sorry my dear," I said. "We'll fix that collarbone too. After we give you chloroform, you may feel pain when I set the bone, but it won't last long. You will hate me with your whole being for one moment, and in the next it will feel much better and you'll sleep." I tried to estimate how much blood she'd lost.

Honey licked her lips to try to speak. I gave her a sip of water. "I don't want to die," she said. "I'm scared to die." Her wounds were not mortal; something else scared her.

I brought a chair to sit right next to her and held her hand. "Good," I said, "very sensible. I don't want you to die, either. Those men are gone, and you're safe here. Your injuries are serious but not grave. I expect you'll be fine."

She held my hand tight. "Tell me something. Anything."

I told her she reminded me of a harlot called Alma Johnson, a beautiful girl I wanted to hire for the Double Standard during the war. Israel put his foot down. He flat-out told me not to mix girls, that I was out of my depth, that it would be no good for Alma, the house, or anyone. I told Honey only that Alma ran her own boîte with another girl.

"What became of her?"

I didn't know. Given Honey's demure mouth and the shreds of a classic coiffure, I said, "I heard she married and settled in Philadelphia."

"That's nice," she said.

Betsy was back with the inhaler. She was worried and I inquired. "Someone had a go on the medicine closet lock with a knife or some other tool. I don't think anything's missing, but you should take a look." Criminy, what now?

Honey panicked when she saw my concern, and I told her it was nothing to do with her arm. The trick there would be staving off infection. I'd keep her at the clinic for a few days and experiment with hot towels and astringents. Early on at the Pillow I'd lost a maid who fell down the stairs. Her extensive wounds festered despite our best efforts. In the end I gave her a fatal dose of morphine, the first time I'd used a syringe. I pressed my teeth together as I thought of what I could do to make sure Miss Honey fared better, and how we'd guard our drug supply. When she was out, I set the bone. As I washed my hands again before stitching the wound, Betsy and I smiled over John Herman snoring in the next room.

My mother contracted a respiratory infection, probably strep that became diphtheria. Germs were not well understood, but my father sent me to stay with Mrs. Tisch, a widow outside of town.

I stopped home after school and stood in the garden to hear how my mother fared. One day my father came out and slumped on the doorframe, his head in his hands.

"May I see her?"

"She won't know you."

I charged past him but he grabbed my arm and flung me back. "Not you as well," he said, and locked the door behind him. I cried in the garden until Mrs. Tisch came looking. She took me by the shoulders and bundled me down the road, murmuring kind words. In the morning she came to my bedside with a posey and the worst news, and held me while I rocked and writhed against it.

My father was raised to believe that strength was found in silence, but that's a brittle strength. If you knocked him he would shatter. After my mother died, he steered around everyone.

I gave him room to grieve, and we slid into distance. It was easier to make meals or read alone, and learn by example.

FOUR

Elliott and I sat on a bench in the garden, our faces turned to the October sun, discussing the ball's scheme to sweeten Benno with access to a higher grade of crook. As the producer of the Double's occasional parlor theatricals, he had come to help the girls with their skits.

"Oakey and George can't protect you?"

"Those two? Not from a warm breeze."

He twisted his mouth to one side, a tic I found charming. We became fast friends when we met at the Silk Pillow. He was barely eighteen to my twenty-six, full of sly wit and uproarious plans for stage extravaganzas. He was raised among his mother's dancer friends. When we met he had just lost her and we bonded as orphans. As he matured the arrangement of his limbs or the way he turned to me sometimes prompted warmer feelings, which I tried to hide.

Once I had occasion to treat his back. He'd fallen from a scaffold at the Olympic and arrived at the clinic in terror of bleeding to death. The wound was messy but not deep, and I stitched it and cleaned him up. I left the room to get him some clothes and when I returned and saw the dip of his waist rising into the swell of his hip, desire hit me like a blow to the head and a heart attack. I told myself it was the near miss to his spine and kidney and the chance he could be lost to me. It was the only time I remember becoming confused by the intimacy of treatment. He was a classic sport, handsome and rich, plowing his way through showgirls and harlots. His love for me was singular, and that suited. His laughter was my tonic.

Exhausted by the barriers and stigmas around respectability, I asked him, "As you pass back and forth from, say, the Double to a society drawing room, do you find yourself changing the way you speak and act? I mean, of course you do, but does it ever bother you? Do you ever resent hiding parts of yourself, living across that divide?"

The side of his mouth kinked again. "I used to amuse myself by acting upright around society ladies, you know, playing the gentleman to the hilt. Even with my tainted bloodline, the Vanderpoel name and fortune were just too alluring for certain young ladies or their mothers. There was a girl, oh, maybe ten years ago. Victoria something. She was delectable, if I was inclined for that sort of thing. Exquisite breeding, the most spectacular cheekbones and golden almond eyes. But I wasn't interested in a cage, no matter how fetching. My only defense was to act the reprobate with her friend. Word spread and they all cleared off in a hurry. I probably play the bad boy more in society than I do here. Keeps the gnats down."

Well, that was a breathtaking answer, completely devoid of sympathy for a woman's entrapment. After adjusting my hopes for commiseration, I smiled. "Yes, such a bother."

When no smart remark followed, I looked closer at him, and the golden light revealed exhaustion. I reached behind us and tore two sprigs from a giant arching sage plant, handing him one. While I crushed mine to release its warming scent, Elliott said, "Well, I got him back to the city." Right, he'd gone to Connecticut to retrieve his brother Asa. "Please come have a look at him? He's never been a drinker, let alone gone on a binge like this."

I said, "He's not a sporting man. He wouldn't want me in his house."

"He'd be fine with a nurse in his house."

"Would his wife be fine with it?"

He shook his head. "She's on the continent with the *kinder.*"

Opening my mouth to refuse, I noticed his jacket was creased and dirty. Elliott was always spotless. I wanted to ease his mind and couldn't rightly ask Asa Vanderpoel to the clinic. A patrician publisher would make a change from Benno, at least. "I'll need a name."

"Florence?"

"Annalee Warren," I said, surprising myself.

"Who's that?"

"A nurse." My best friend in training, whose name I had not said aloud in fifteen years: tall, quick, and hilarious. I wondered how she'd view the proposed errand and alias.

He said he'd arrange a time. Before he left, I asked him whom we knew backstage at Wood's Metropolitan.

Peter Sweeny, doctor of ledgers and dispenser of payoffs, prince of disappearing percentages, arrived with George Barnard on a dreary afternoon. Ciara and I led them to the library where he took a bourbon. That unruly head of lush, graying hair topped a neglected body in beautifully fitted clothing. We edged onto today's tightrope.

I welcomed them, saying how glad I was to see Sweeny again. "I congratulate you sir, for your wisdom in seeking education in these delicate and confusing matters." He stared at his knees and did not appear to breathe. "We can help you sort how to speak to respectable ladies, and also in the greater latitude of a sporting house."

"It's a muddle and a waste," he said.

I said, "You understand negotiation as few men do, I imagine."

He was caught between pride and false modesty.

"I would venture to say, some people, no matter how much they read in the papers, would not see the angles on the Erie deal."

He scowled.

"Mr. Sweeny, have you heard of color blindness? Some people's eyes cannot differentiate blue and yellow, or red and green."

This surprised him. "So I've heard."

"Most," I continued, "could never finance a railroad or shepherd the passage of legislation. Others find the nuances of, say, a dinner party, quite opaque."

His head snapped up. "Are you saying that I'm party blind?"

I smiled warmly, but this alarmed him. He read it as seduction. "With instruction, people with color blindness can learn to differentiate colors just fine."

"I see."

Again a joke. I shook my head in wonder and he flinched. I said, "That was funny," but he looked ill. Could this punning wit be accidental? "What would be useful to convey, say, at the dinner table with the wife of a business associate?"

He looked blank and then confused.

"Or in any situation where you wanted someone to feel at ease with you, or even that you care for them?"

He turtled his head as he tried to answer, but his lower body remained still, even frozen. "All right, Doc Hastings."

"Pardon, sir?"

"I can't do that. Teach me three things."

"Three things?"

"I learn three things at a time. What three things should I learn about this now?"

Gracious, the adaptations. "That is a most useful detail to understand about your own mind, sir. We do have some guidance for you on this."

I turned to Ciara, who had prepared it. "First," she said, sitting up a bit straighter, "show interest in the life and opinions of your conversation partner by asking open-ended questions and responding gently and approvingly to their answers."

"Excellent," I said, "Let's try that out. You and I are not yet much acquainted. Why don't you ask a question to begin a friendly conversation to learn more about me."

He blinked, thought for a beat, and said, "So how's the brothel business treating you?"

George and Ciara laughed, and he flushed, eyes darting to gauge if the required response was anger or more laughter, and he decided the latter.

"That was perfect," I said. "You asked me an open-ended question about one of my businesses. Now I'll answer: Much the same as ever, thank you. The house runs on rails. Right now my medical clinic is taking more of my attention."

We all looked to Sweeny but he sat motionless. Ciara said, "Was there an element in Doc's answer that interested you?"

"No."

"Did you know she runs a medical clinic?"

He was pouting now, his ineptitude on display. "Why is your clinic demanding now?"

"Well in addition to the usual conditions I treat, there's a bit of ague going around."

That interested him. "What do you do for the ague?"

"We try to keep liquids up and fever down."

"My mother uses leeches."

Here was a chance to see him handle conflict. "Most modern medical practitioners have stopped using them."

"She has not lived to seventy by following fads," he said, no doubt parroting her.

I held my ground. "Only a rare person would adapt at that age."

He darkened. "Don't insult my mother."

"Forgive me, Mr. Sweeny, but I did no such thing. I only pointed out that her information is outdated. You could convey your loyalty to your mother without giving offense by saying, for instance, 'I yield to my mother on such matters.' That way, you avoid a conflict and give a favorable impression of your filial devotion."

He lowered his brow. "Gentle, approving answers. She said that."

"Let's try again. Would you like to ask Ciara something?"

He inspected the carpet and said, "Do you like being a whore?" It was still unclear if he was inept or lashing out when threatened.

More laughter. I intervened before it escalated. "Can you see why that question might be considered indelicate or insulting?"

"She might not like being a whore. I can't see why anyone would." Interesting that he could see prostitution from the girl's vantage.

"Well, we refer to them as girls or harlots, which is a bit more respectful than 'whore.' If you wanted to show respect with your question, how could you ask Ciara about her work in a way that's more open-ended?"

He screwed up his face at the idea of showing respect to a whore. "What do you like about your work here at the Double Standard Sporting House?"

Ciara said, "That's a great question, Mr. Sweeny. There are many elements I enjoy about working here, but the best part is helping gentlemen like yourself feel happy and satisfied, making sure they enjoy themselves and feel valued."

"And that happens through copulation?"

"Sometimes. Also through conversation, eating and drinking, and enjoying the company of other people taking a break from their demanding lives."

"Some people like to stop work and go on vacation, but I do not."

"I sympathize," I said, and winked at Ciara. "Forgive me, Mr. Sweeny, but I feel obliged to point out that such a direct question about copulation is fine here in the house and we're glad to discuss it, but you would never refer to it in a dinner party environment."

"All men seem eager to discuss it."

We laughed yet again and I saw how his odd wit had arisen. The more direct and challenging his remarks, the more he was rewarded as strong and funny.

He said, "Is that one or three?"

"Pardon?"

"We were going to start with three things. Ask open-ended questions, show interest, respond gently with approval. Is that one or three?"

I said, "Perhaps that's enough for today. You are very amenable, sir, and I thank you for your liberality. May I add one more observation?"

Sweeny nodded.

"Business negotiations and interactions among men in general tend to be combative and competitive. Men enter each encounter expecting it to end with a winner and a loser."

George was taken aback but Sweeny said, "Naturally."

I continued, "Friendly conversations are neither combative nor competitive. They have a spirit of mutuality and harmony. The goal is not to win, but to end the encounter with pleasant feelings of connection, if not trust. You might even work to boost your friend's self-worth."

Sweeny said, "And that can be attained through showing interest, open-ended questions, and approving answers?"

"Yes," I said, "and by suspending the urge to win."

Sweeny's face then did some remarkable things. He doubted, he rebelled, he caught a glimpse, and finally understood. "Live and let live," he said.

"Yes, exactly," I whispered, and nodded with enthusiasm. He glanced at me with a shred of respect.

Ciara asked, "Were you gentlemen interested in sport?"

George said, "Our intention is to be out before you open."

I said, "You're welcome anytime. I do hope we'll celebrate your victories together at our Election Night Ball."

Sweeny did not stand on ceremony; he got up and walked out. George flashed a smile of profound amusement, and followed.

Ciara puffed out her cheeks and said, "Did we budge his understanding of a harlot?"

"Once he establishes a relationship with one, he'll tell himself she's different from all the others."

Peter Sweeny made a tempting target for those who could manipulate his tribalism and his vanity. Ciara and I traded ideas on how we might brace his strengths and bolster his deficits. The trick would be never to let him feel weak.

As we left the library, she said, "We should advertise: The Double Standard Finishing School for Awkward Racketeers."

I had another visitor that week, an old friend who came to deliver a most surprising bit of intelligence about the Election Day Ball. Years earlier, on a Sunday morning when the overnight guests were coaxing their crusted selves from bed, a phalanx of moral reformers agitated over the "Social Evil" barged their way into the hall. This was their preferred tactic, to shame clients when they were most apt to repent. Ciara detoured departures out the back, and I invited five starchy females to tea in the main salon. At loose ends since the war's conclusion, they had chosen a new cause. They ogled the pleasant room with its portrait of Eve, its marble Mars and Minerva, and its bronze Eulalia, and surged in their righteous intent, with one exception. A black-haired young lady in a fine burgundy ensemble did not peel her eyes from my face. After a few moments, I returned the stare with patient curiosity, as if to say, "How may I help you?" She flushed, widened her eyes further, and swallowed.

Meanwhile, the leader, a Mrs. Washburn, informed me that they had reconstituted the Female Moral Reform Society of previous years, a woman-led philanthropy that sought to escort prostitutes into repentance and more respectable employment. What did I think of such an effort? This was an unusual group. Alone among reformers, they actually engaged with prostitutes, and placed more responsibility on predatory men than preyed-upon women. Their kind would have been behind the non-starter regulation proposal in Albany that George had mentioned.

"I also urge my girls to choose more respectable employment, Mrs. Washburn. Often they marry, but others have become shopkeepers or nurses. Many leave with a considerable nest-egg and do very well. My house is not a route to drink and a lonely death."

The silence in the room signaled disbelief.

"May I respectfully suggest," I continued, "that your efforts would be better directed to the poorest and most desperate streetwalkers. My girls have medical attention, good nutrition, and education. They drink little alcohol. We also perform a public service in channeling, shall we say, the most vicious impulses of our clientele. We do try to blunt the edges of implacable seducers."

Mrs. Washburn was clearly the type who prepared her speeches in advance, but did not adapt well in the face of the unexpected. She blurted, "But what of God?"

"Indeed, Madam," I said. "God has made men and women, yet we have such unequal power to control our own lives. At the Double Standard, we use what power we do have to better our condition and help others to live a more peaceable and satisfied life. We do not generally invoke the name, but we are God's servants in our way."

The staring girl said, as if we were the only two in the room, "You see men as natural predators? And you work to reform them?"

I looked at her. "Some men are indeed predators. More are simply in need of friendship and reassurance of their manhood."

"But you study the predators."

"By necessity, we do. May I ask your name, mademoiselle?"

"Forgive me Miss Hastings, I am Viola Brison."

"Well, Miss Brison, as you might imagine, many girls here have personal experience as victims of predators and seducers, so we have profound incentive to prevent such behavior."

The matron found her tongue. "Do you not believe that leading these men and women to repentance and to our Lord instead would be to their eternal advantage?"

"Madame, I suspect we are in agreement on many aspects of the plight of fallen women. Our chief difference may be in our assessments of the inevitability of licentiousness. I do not believe that sporting men can be diverted to church very often. You are of course welcome to try. I take a more practical and incremental approach to the betterment of men and their salvation, and help them to be kinder and more sympathetic while their appetites run their course."

She had turned beet red. "Are you mocking me?"

"I assure you, I am not. Ask anyone who knows me."

"Well, Miss Hastings, your education is certainly in evidence, if not becoming."

"Thank you, Mrs. Washburn."

Flustered to learn of practicalities that might manage men's appetites, they took their leave. I declined to provide girls to them for prayer, but two or three ladies lingered across Twenty-Fifth Street to identify any departing notables. Miss Brison came to shake my hand as they departed, saying, "What a fascinating discussion, Miss Hastings. I'm so pleased to meet you."

I thought no more about it until two years later, when the shiny Miss Brison came to see me again, coming three times before finding me in the building. Now she was Mrs. Geoffrey Hill, and asked to speak to me in private. While her voice was steady and her hands still, this time she did not meet my gaze. She was troubled at the root, displaced. I led her to the library.

"Would you like some water or perhaps a brandy, Mrs. Hill?"

"Please don't take the trouble."

We sat facing one another, and though her eyes flicked once to mine, she kept her hands in her lap as she said, "In three years of working to curb the predation of men upon women, you are the only person I met who spoke from sense and experience."

"Thank you, that's very kind."

She swallowed, her eyes on her hands. "My husband beats me."

My pressure dropped, like the atmosphere before a storm. "I'm sorry to hear that."

"He says I like it." She meant violent sex.

"Do you?"

Her composure wavered and she wrestled herself into control. "I don't know."

"May I share something with you that I have seen in others?"

"Please." Her voice was tiny, and it came in a sob.

"When someone first becomes acquainted with sexual experience through violence," and here she looked up and watched me, "it can be difficult to separate pleasure from pain. And though such a person's temperament may naturally be more tender, her body has learned something else."

"Can it be unlearned?" she whispered.

"Certainly, but not if one's partner is intent on that style of congress."

"It's a style?"

I swallowed a laugh. "In a manner of speaking. There are many varied tastes between lovers, and you might interest your husband in others. If you tell him you welcome mutual gratification but not violence, it may encourage him to approach you differently. Tell me, does he welcome your opinion on other matters? Is he cordial at other times? Can he be led?"

"Sometimes."

"Was he raised in a church?"

"His father was a Presbyterian church elder."

"Ah," I said. Often they were more stringent than Catholics. "I believe he may feel his desire for you is sinful or shameful and he cannot allow himself to enjoy it, much less you. Speak to him of God's blessing on the sacrament of tender married love, and see where that leads him."

Shortly before Election Day, I had a third visit from Viola Hill. She was expecting, and appeared content.

First, she brought me up to date on her marital relations. "I did as you said, Miss Hastings, and it proved most useful."

"Please call me Doc. All my friends do."

"And I'm Viola. Well Doc, at first Geoffrey collapsed in mortification. He had no words for the feelings within him. As soon as I spoke the simple and honest words I learned from you, we found ourselves in far better accord. Sometimes by agreement we indulge his particular taste, but more often we enjoy what you termed, 'tender married love,' especially now," she said, sweeping a thumb out from the hands crossed on her abdomen.

"That's a delightful outcome," I said. "We are brought up so overly reserved that these simple conversations can seem impossible. I commend you for your courage and your honesty, but that sweet news is perhaps not why you're here."

She sighed. "No. I came to warn you that the Society is planning to infiltrate several elite houses to identify their clientele, and the Double Standard is on their list of targets."

"Gracious. Whom will they send?"

"One man is a reformer, a friend of Mrs. Washburn called Arthur Beltron, and another is a reporter and sketch artist for the *Herald* called Victor Myers, though I expect they will use other names when they visit. Is it true that you're having a bit of a do on Election Day?"

"Yes, we are." Amused by this bit of intrigue, I said, "You're a kind friend to tell me."

"Well," she said, satisfied, "I don't like to say we are even, but I am glad to hear that we are friends. I have one more small question for you, if you don't mind."

"Of course."

"My husband intends that I should deliver at Women's Hospital. What is your opinion of that option?"

I told her they treated women like livestock and wrote a list of three midwives who delivered women of her distinction.

"I don't suppose you could attend me?"

"Thank you for your confidence, Viola, but let's not challenge Mr. Hill quite that strenuously—yet."

She laughed.

"You're brave to come here. Aren't you concerned someone will see you?"

"Everyone knows I work with the Society. One of my friends did tease me after I spoke well of you. She said I had a crush."

"Well that's respectable," I laughed, imagining how the *Police Gazette* would explain a pregnant society bride at an exclusive brothel. "When is the child expected?"

"In two months. I'd prefer to go to our house in Cortlandt."

"There's your answer then. Tell your husband you must have fresh air and quiet, and once there visit the local midwives and choose the one you trust. It may be self-serving, but I believe you're an uncommon judge of women."

As I said good-bye to Viola, I mused that the scrutiny of the Double Standard from the Female Moral Reform Society was my daily fare, and that perhaps Tammany was not very different, and might be managed with our same strengths in discrete care and entertainment.

At that hour the twins would be supervising hair and dress on the third floor. I found Ciara and asked her to locate a porter or other lad who could draw faces from life, and three clever street girls. Then I began to wonder if our Election Day soirée wouldn't be a triumph and a legend.

Vivie noticed the rather fusty portrait of Beadie Korn hanging above the kitchen table and asked who it was.

"Beatrice Eugenie Kornblatt, the woman who made all of this possible."

Aunty Laure, rolling pie crusts at the pastry table, said, "I met her once."

"Did you! You never said."

"Mean cow."

I laughed. "Tell."

"I tried for a job at one of her houses, oh a long time ago. Turned me down and insulted my ancestors too."

Beadie was a grumpy, paranoid wretch most of the time, but was also capable of stunning kindness. She had lost her entire family in Kohn, Germany, to a fever when she was fourteen. She stayed for a time with the family of a friend, but the friend's brother climbed onto her while she slept and his father threw her out. Pregnant and destitute, she landed in a cheap flop house where she contracted syphilis, lost the child, and nearly died birthing it. A brothel doctor saved her life and took pity, buying her passage to New York where her mother's brother was reputed to live.

The uncle proved elusive so Beadie went to work in a third-class house, doing needle work and taking every job she could. Better clothes brought her to a better house and so on until she sat near the top of the trade and retired at twenty to run other girls. She catered to the new class of clerks, young men off the farms who had come to the city for cash and action. As they rose, she rose.

I arrived in New York in the summer of 1854, her name at the top of a list in my pocket. From the train I went directly to the Silk Pillow.

"*Gott in himmel*," she said with a sour face, "no harlot dresses like that."

"How about a nurse?" I said in German. I explained my background as the child of a German immigrant doctor and midwife, my year of training as a nurse in Portland, and my year assisting Gwin at Rosalie's. "I suppose you have a doctor who sees to your girls?"

She spat. "That *goniff*! All he does is feel them up and smell his fingers."

I said, "What do you pay him?"

"Why? You'll take less?"

"I'll take room and board and twenty dollars a week, and your girls will thrive. Is your cook any good?"

All this time I was standing with my hands folded in front of me. She sat in a chair that echoed a throne, her feet perched on a velvet footstool.

"I tell you what. If you can say what ails me, I'll give you a week's trial."

A faint scent of nectarines made a picture with the tenderness of her legs. "It's your sugar," I said. "You're always thirsty and you urinate a lot. Perhaps your eyesight troubles you, and your feet get numb."

Her lower lip stuck out and trembled.

I took a step forward. "Does your *goniff* doctor tell you how to take care of yourself? You may not like what I tell you but you'll live longer."

She blinked away her tears and said, "All right, *mamzer*." She liked my German rigor, I suppose.

"No more candy or cake or wine."

"Bah," she said, "Some pleasures make life worth living."

"When was the last time you walked around the block?"

She growled.

"Two weeks," I said, "and no cheating. You eat and drink only what I tell you. The first few days you'll have a headache and feel miserable, and on day four or five you'll turn a corner, and after two weeks you'll walk around the block on my arm." I overestimated so that when she felt revived after two days and walked to Stewart's Department Store in seven, she felt she got the best of me.

Complicated did not begin to describe Beadie Korn's moods and whims. She loved me, she hated me. I was brilliant, I was a quack. I had come to save her, I had come to kill her. But in the end I was the person she trusted. She taught me how to run a house and invest the proceeds. And she was the one who called me Doc. I had to hide my name in Portland, and Gwin had dubbed me Rafaela, meaning "God has healed," but Beadie deemed that too baroque for New York.

Vivie and Laure watched me as I recollected Beadie, waiting for my reply. "I worked for her for most of three years and when she died, she left me most of her property." That was in 1857, perhaps the best moment in history to invest in New York. "Beadie gave me a chance, and I pay her back as best I can."

The visit to Asa Vanderpoel arranged, Elliott fetched me in his carriage and on the ride told me more about his brother. "When my mother died, Asa and Caroline invited me to live with them. They were kind but the house was full of babies, so I went away for my last year at school. The first time I visited, I thought I'd wandered into a madhouse. There was paper all over the furniture and floors. They were laying out articles from the Cyclopedia." Asa Vanderpoel co-edited a twenty-six volume compendium of knowledge patterned on the Encyclopedia Brittanica.

"A year or two later, we were at Canonical Bay, Caro's family's place where Asa was lately holed up. Beautiful property on the Connecticut coast. He sits me down for a talk. No introduction, he's a bit nervous and launches into this speech about how he hated our father for remarrying, but that the old man had actually been much happier with my mother than his, and he wanted to apologize for his youthful idiocy and anger at my mother and me." He blinked and shook his head at the memory.

Such precipitous honesty made me more curious to meet Asa Vanderpoel. I'd seen him rendered in the odd photograph or cartoon, fomenting war for Union or championing Grant. Thomas Nast of *Harper's* drew him schoolmarmy in a clergyman's coat and tall riding boots wagging a sanctimonious finger, but perhaps he could still learn something new.

For such good friends, Elliott and I knew little of each other's history. He once reported a conversation among the girls about my origins. "Sprang directly from the head of Zeus," was the consensus, though rumors of both assault and seduction circulated. I offered to tell him the outline and he said, "No need to stir it all up now and upset yourself." Part kindness and part avoidance, this was classic Elliott, and doubtless the heart of our alliance. I had to remind myself that this opacity was of my own manufacture, and for good reason. As usual I hid, and then resented my invisibility.

We alit at a brick townhouse with an ionic pediment. The sun lay at the treetops of Gramercy Park as Elliott delivered me into Asa Vanderpoel's bedroom. It was spacious and sumptuous with silk bed curtains and a sitting area by the fire, all thick with tobacco. The dark-haired man on a settee in elegant, disheveled clothing, his long legs crossed with a bottle and glass at his elbow, was a gorgeous wreck. I saw the kinship but nothing prepared me for the man's sheer splendor, the distinguished head and stalwart shoulders, the stewed acumen. He drew every speck of energy toward him, but did not get up and likely couldn't. It disrupted gravity, a being of so much power listing toward the floor. A bubble of laughter rose in my chest. Elliott, but with heft.

"Asa," said Elliott, "this is Miss Annalee Warren, a good friend of mine. Miss Warren, my brother, Mr. Asa Vanderpoel." He stumbled on my introduction.

The man stared at me. In a slurry baritone I felt in my ribs, he said, "That's not your name." A timid nurse would not get this job done.

"No, it's not," I agreed. "But I will ask that you use it."

Without taking his eyes from me, he said, "Why have you brought this prevaricator into my room?"

I said, "If I may, Mr. Vanderpoel, I'm a nurse with some particular experience. Your brother thought I might be able to assist you in your present distress."

"My distress." He found this amusing and displayed his composure by taking a drink. His dark hair, uncut for months, curled about his ears, but he was clean-shaven. He had a lazy eye, which amplified the general fearsomeness.

I said, "Yes, you've been sleepless and medicating with what I take to be whiskey."

"And what would you recommend to remedy my distress, Miss Warren? Sea bathing? Or is it vegetables and Graham crackers? Laudanum perhaps."

He fairly scorned charlatans but showed little faith in Elliott's judgment for having brought me. I said, "If you enjoy sea bathing or vegetables, I hope you will partake at will. I would not recommend laudanum unless you're in acute physical pain. Are you?"

He twisted in his seat, but could not say, which vexed him.

"To answer your question, sir, I prescribe frank discussion."

"A lady who won't tell me her name prescribes frankness!" There was a warmth to his voice, the belligerence playful. I liked him. Alert and secure in his position; in pain; unable to untangle his emotions. I almost provoked a full-blown reaction to see what manifested and how he managed it.

"I withhold my name to protect your reputation, sir. What I offer is simple: you can tell me your story. Part of your past has re-emerged, I might say erupted into the present, and it disturbed you greatly, both this difficult memory and its unforeseen and uncontrollable flare-up. I suppose the original events took place during the war, but you may correct me. I have helped many people through similar episodes."

Vanderpoel kept his squinting eyes on me. There were spectacles on the table. He ignored my diagnosis and focused on my experience. "Who?"

"I couldn't say."

"Give me one name. Someone who's dead."

"I will not, sir." This was a test.

"And what do you call this line of work, Miss Warren?"

"I don't refer to it as such."

"Then how do you think of it in your own mind?"

"As telling the truth about painful events, from which we are so often constrained."

He stared into the distance for a moment and then returned, more focused. "And you have qualifications?"

"I'm a highly experienced nurse, as qualified in medicine as most physicians, though most physicians are unequipped for this. I am uncommonly direct and read emotions well."

"So you think I'm overemotional." He was enjoying me now, but had no intention of addressing the state he was in.

I took a breath and said with as much compassion as I could, "No. I think you're in terrible pain and fighting every way you know how against it overwhelming you."

He laughed and stared at me, got those long legs under him and with some trouble levered himself to standing, wobbled toward his brother, approached a window without seeing the view, looked at me, though I studied the painting above the bed, a very good seascape in a driftwood frame, his wife's I presumed. All the while he rubbed his forehead, and it struck me that he was shielding his eyes from something.

He said in cold control, "What do you want from me?"

"Whom do you see?"

He rounded on Elliott. "Who is this woman? She's a menace." Not even he believed it.

"Talk to her, Asa. She's the wisest person I know, and that includes you." This flattery was meant to soften him and steel me. Elliott went to his brother and put his hand to his shoulder. "She'll help you sort it."

Vanderpoel shook his head, and began to sway on his feet. "I can't."

I stood to take his other arm and we led him back to the settee. "There's no rush."

While my hand was on him, I took his pulse, saw him cast around for some purchase. "Your body is struggling to contain your rage and sadness. It's time to stop fighting, Mr. Vanderpoel. Lay down your weapons, and invite your ghosts to sit in the shadows nearby." At this he flinched. "They're waiting for you to speak to them. There are words each of you have to say to the other, tomorrow or the next day when you've come clear of drink."

"What ghosts?" he whispered.

I said, "That was a figure of speech," though now I knew something or someone haunted him. "When the body or mind suffers a blow, we often have a hard time taking it in, folding it into memory in the usual way. It doesn't want to go, or the brain resists or tries to expel it. That memory may return in unbidden or surprising ways. The mind may transpose it, so that, for instance, a young girl I knew had nightmares of a giant lizard. That was the shape her memory gave to the human predator who terrified her." It took me a moment to put a name to the face of that girl who'd been brought to the clinic sleepless and manic. Simone Lavery, a desperately poor seamstress who later left New York with the fifty dollars I gave her.

He listened intently, studying his own knees. “If your brain cannot accept the facts, does that mean you’re mad?”

“No,” I said, gently. “No. It means you’re injured. Your brain is trying to protect itself.” A whole gallery of faces passed before me, girls who’d been raped repeatedly over years by bosses, brothers, and fathers, whose minds would never be mended. A distant memory of looking at my hands, idled.

His fear fell back a notch. “And how does one heal such an injury?”

“Each person differs. Telling the story to a friend can alleviate some pressure. The passage of time. Finding meaning in the sacrifice. It’s most difficult when the suffering feels worthless, but if it’s in the service of others or an ideal, we can often reconcile terrible experiences more easily.” Girls who baited their fathers to keep them away from their sisters, girls who’d have done anything to escape home, girls who paid a steep price for their independence. Vivie might yet find her reason.

“Yes,” he whispered, “yes.”

I asked, “Will you speak to them?”

“I can’t,” he said again, and covered his face with his hands, pressing back whatever was surfacing. I waved Elliott to sit next to him while I withdrew to a nearby chair.

A few choked sobs escaped him and he clung to Elliott.

He said, “The room is spinning.”

I shifted the table in front of him and bid him come to all fours. He appeared rather helpless so I reached for his hand and pulled him forward. Vanderpoel tumbled to his knees and vomited onto the carpet. Elliott fetched some towels and water, helped him to drink, and wiped up the mess. I said, “Rest your forehead on this,” placing a pillow in front of him. “The floor will ground you.” He pushed down with his hands. When his breathing slowed, he rose to his knees again and faced me, green eyes mournful and more deeply askew. He had paused his battle but his obvious sorrow pained me. Kneeling together conjured both play and prayer.

"Would you like to lie down?"

"Yes, please." I offered my hand a second time. He was graceful even in this mess, and when we stood together, a wave of heat enveloped us. His mouth drew me and as I studied its color and contour from that close distance, a swift and unequivocal quake of desire ransacked my groin and my composure. This was preposterous, not least due to vomit. Our eyes met for an instant in mutual interest and recognition, and just as quick came his recoil, a self-effacement, his abhorrence to be seen. It was shame he was attempting to drown with drink, a holy disavowal and a deep grief. I stood mute with longing as Elliott led him to bed. I yearned to help and comfort Asa Vanderpoel, and then rushed to get as far away from him as I could.

In the carriage Elliott said, "I knew you could get to him."

A merchant's son, a bit older than my own age of fifteen, consulted my father. I stepped out to the kitchen when he saw male patients. It aggravated me to miss so many cases. My mother saw only women and I expected the same, but wanted to practice bone-setting.

Apparently a boil my father lanced on the young man's leg erupted, and he shouted for me.

"Hold this firmly," he said, indicating his hands pressing on a naked thigh, the boy's sex tucked adjacent under a single layer of muslin. The patient lay scowling, and I blanched.

My father said, "I'll be one minute, I want that lime and chlorine mash."

"I'll get it."

"I said I'll do it! Come, it'll be quick." So in the moment, he insisted on the dreaded exposure.

I kept my eyes on my hands, listening for my father's tread. His steps went past the kitchen and up the main stairs, and I exhaled in exasperation. The shrouded sex began to move. I glanced up and saw the choice hanging on the boy's face. He took my look as license and began pawing me.

I shrieked, "Stop it!" and swatted him with one hand. This went on for some moments until the sound of footsteps returning made him lay down and fix his clothing. "Rotter," I spat as I fixed the cloth on his leg.

"Slut," he hissed.

I slapped the patient's face with considerable force.

"What is the meaning of this?" my father cried in anger.

At me. He was glaring at me. I gaped, handed him the pus-covered cloth, and walked out.

Much later I thought to wonder what my father had in his room that he was so desperate to stop me from seeing. Drugs, alcohol, French postcards, all three? He was scrupulous about appearances and odors, but his eyes were seldom fully focused.

FIVE

When rising violence and corruption returned to nag at me, I remembered that fear of chaos was constant and ordinary at every time in history. I had lived the slide toward war and that cataclysm, and had worked among criminals and reprobates as one of them. I faced escalating threats, impediments, and punishments as a woman in medicine. But still: Tammany was trampling stops and precedents, and neither the law nor the newspapers had caught up. Our life felt ever more fragile and precarious, our underpinnings drifting, even as the days proceeded much as ever.

My options were few as usual, if familiar. I had arranged to see an old acquaintance, Hester Jane Haskins, better known as Jane the Grabber. I wanted very much to know where some combination of Benno, Hanky Pank, and Vernon Trent were holding Catherine Farnsworth and the other disappeared girls.

It took us weeks of notes back and forth to fix a date. Her redoubt moved every year or so; she never bought buildings because neighbors and police hounded her. Constant migration was more usual in the less favored forms of prostitution than my own rootedness. I had gambled that a high-class house would last five years and insulated it by owning the adjacent property. We had no lines of randy clients drinking in the street, but a brothel was always on borrowed time. We were at eight years; the longest I'd ever heard a house lasting was ten.

Jane's latest encampment stank of opium, tobacco, and men. Stupefied girls lounged and wandered in various states of undress, and someone was crying. The sounds of coitus erupted now and again, with the tread of men's steps upstairs. It was busy for mid-afternoon.

I had to reckon with why I'd given Jane a pass for all these years, but now found kidnapping girls insufferable in Vernon Trent and maybe Benno. My hypocrisies grew harder to carry.

Martin came with me, his meeting with Jane's rival Red Light Lizzie having yielded little. Jane eyed Martin like he was lunch and said, "Who's this now?" She might have been comely when young but her expression was vile, her condition chronic. A yellowish cast in her eyes and skin said drink, but her main symptom was a malevolence that could keep her alive for years.

Martin, in street clothes, shook her hand and introduced himself. "Don't be alarmed, we're here for your help. I'm a copper in Sixteen."

Her head whipped to me, and I said, "We're here for common cause, Jane, I swear. It's not a raid, as you can see."

We sat in a small dining room, and she offered drinks. "There's some wine kicking around."

We accepted out of courtesy when a girl brought some smudged glasses.

I said, "Have you noticed any new competitors in the last few months?"

She stilled and squinted, suspicious. "And if I have?"

Martin said, "Have you heard the name Vernon Trent?"

She cackled. "That's one he uses upstate. I chased him out of New York months ago."

Martin and I looked at one another. "He may be back. What other names does he use?"

"The scum!"

"Who is he?"

"Why should I tell you?"

Martin said, "I have a couple of problems with him. He's sloppy. He takes girls from my ward right off the street and makes a mess of them. You, Jane, have the wit to nab girls without local friends, and you do it cleanly."

She puffed up. "He worked for me for about a minute before I saw he was trying to squeeze me out."

"What did he do for you?"

She looked at me. "So now he's nosing into the posh side of town, is he? He wants quality girls for his friends."

I said, "What friends?"

"Why would I tell you that?"

"What do you want for it?"

"One of your girls."

I laughed. "I see your skin has a yellow cast to it. Why don't you come see me at the clinic and we can investigate."

"Not on your life."

I shrugged. "So it doesn't bother you that you itch and have red spider veins and are losing weight?"

"Witch!" she cried.

That was rich. I said, "Give me a name and I'll send you a tincture you can take twice a day. In a week you'll feel much better."

I could feel Martin tighten beside me.

"I'll tell you when I'm all brand new."

"No you won't," I said. "It's too bad about your liver. You've been helpful, though. I'd have thought you wanted help getting rid of Trent, but you protect your business as you see fit." I stood. "Thank you for your time today."

"Hold on," she said, and sighed. "He used to pal around with the boys at the Reveille." One of Hanky Pank's saloons, on Ninth Avenue between Fifteenth and Sixteenth, the Reveille was less than two blocks from Benno's new headquarters on Fourteenth.

I nodded, nauseous to have this confirmation that Hank, someone I had long known and liked, was working with Vernon Trent, who took Vivie, and suggested that Benno, more clearly than ever, was the boss behind it. "Twice a day, two drops and no more, in water, hot or cold. Stop drinking alcohol if you possibly can, or at least drink less. When it's almost gone, send me a line about how you're doing, or better yet come to the clinic and I'll give you more."

On the street, Martin said, "Damn, Doc."

"You object to my medical ethics?"

"She's touchy about her appearance. Into the lion's mouth!"

I didn't care. "Hank has an endless supply of willing girls at his clubs. I don't get this."

Neither of us could scout the Reveille. Martin said he'd send someone. I suggested he try to get a look at Benno's new clubhouse as well.

George brought Peter Sweeny for his second lesson in how to be in company with women, and we settled again in the library. I was pleased he liked and trusted us enough to return, and wondered if he knew about Benno's schemes. Today we would try to shake loose their troubled history.

Ciara said, "Were you able to use your new skills since we saw you last?"

His brows dropped and I gathered he had tried with mixed results.

She pressed on, "Today we might work on how to speak to eligible women."

"That sounds fun," said George, taking not his first belt of the day.

Still Sweeny did not speak. I said, "Mr. Sweeny, how do you know when you're attracted to a woman?"

"When I want to know what's under her clothes." He was staring at Ciara's skirts. She extended her spine and took a big inhale.

I said, "You feel curiosity, and lust. How could you tell her what you feel?"

"You're a very pretty whore, uh, harlot, and I want to get you alone."

"Now we're flirting," she said, lowering her lashes and twisting her shoulders a bit so he could see the curve of her breast. Ciara rarely saw clients anymore, but Sweeny would be an exception. "What are you thinking?"

"If your hair is that color everywhere."

They adjourned for a private tutorial. Ciara took him to the Blue Suite where he called her Mother and after exploring under her skirt and, removing it, fucked her from behind while chanting, "Bad boy, bad boy, bad boy," and at the moment of his climax, "God Yes!" No chance to discuss Benno arose.

The next day Sweeny sent a private note to Ciara inquiring if a nun's habit might be available at the Double Standard. At the subsequent visit, quickly scheduled, he was enthusiastic to find two identical nuns waiting for him. There was scolding, flagellation, and stern instruction on how to deliver a woman's pleasure, of which Sweeny was shocked to learn. He had some aptitude for oral, apparently, and spent while delivering it, always a plus.

"All women have spasms?" he asked. "That has not been my experience."

"That is all too common."

He was appalled. "Even Mother?"

"Well," Meg informed him, "it is not necessary for conception, but only a very selfish oaf will give no care to his partner's enjoyment. Partners who engage in mutual gratification are much more likely to be happy together and to have many children."

"Show me again," he said, taking out his pocket diary to make notes, but stopped. "Doesn't it interfere with business? If a lady waits at home, won't a man rush and leave tasks undone?"

Ciara covered her laugh with an exuberant, "Yes! It is exactly so for the happily married couple, but an able man will soon learn to manage it all efficiently."

Peter Sweeny made one more request. For his next visit he asked to add more girls and also men to the festivities. Such group encounters were common enough, as many men enjoyed sharing sexual conquests with their friends. This often involved humiliation or abuse of a girl, and sometimes covered sport between the men. The twins did not probe as to which of these aspects interested him.

The Double Standard limited multiples to two girls with one man. In the early years we made an exception for sexual initiations, but ended that after one dramatic misfire on the occasion of a mining scion turning eighteen.

On that evening, while the preliminaries were underway in the salon and liquor flowed a bit too quickly, the boy and his four friends asked for a demonstration of how to perform oral on a girl. A delightful harlot then at the Double, Brianna Dudden, provided a creative solution: to act it out. She donned a rose velvet jacket, and when she interlaced her fingers over her head, her strawberry blonde coiffure made a serviceable clitoris. Another girl, Penelope Baxter, used her hands wrapped in a woven shawl to enacted the giver's tongue. She demonstrated sinuous linear and circular motions and where pressure might be applied nearby while Brianna illustrated changes in the texture of the clit by messing up her hair.

The boys hooted and cheered and made the expected vulgar commentary, but when Brianna simulated climax with an operatic tremolo while spraying the boys with frothing champagne, they swarmed the makeshift stage and tore at the girls' clothing. Brianna went along, having come up in a rougher house, but Penelope was a more protected sort who'd been kept by only two men before coming to us. She shrieked in mortal terror, bringing Israel and a squad of porters running.

Each youngster was escorted to a suite for an individual tutorial and everyone left happy except Penelope, who declared herself finished as a harlot. I felt terrible for not having foreseen the melee.

In any case, Peter Sweeny likely did not understand what he was asking, and we'd have to find a delicate way to explain. But the Double Standard had captured his imagination, and he became a jaw-clenched and grouchy regular.

A girl arrived at the clinic with myriad injuries: a broken finger and deep slices to that hand, many old and new bruises, missing her front teeth.

Nina received her and did the first round of treatments, persuading her to stay overnight. She had spoken only her name, Reenie Byrne. When I heard the inventory of injuries I imagined she'd escaped some violent captor by breaking a window, and hoped it was the slaver's crib.

"Miss Byrne, I'm Doc. Do you mind if I examine you too?" I wanted to check if the blow to her mouth had damaged the joints or bones of her face. I sat beside the examination table where she rested, and when she looked at me, I said, "Husband? Boyfriend?"

Her face clouded, so I slowed my questions. A delicate creature with fine brown hair now matted and filthy, she smelled ripe and would have a bath when she went upstairs. The girls had given her a robe and sent her clothes for laundering.

At my touch she began to weep. Perhaps I was the age of her mother or some comforting figure, but the last threads of her composure gave way. I sat with her and waited to finish the palpation of her mandible and maxilla. She'd bitten her tongue.

"Did they give you laudanum?" I asked, now smelling it.

That surprised and frightened her, the allusion to captivity. The dosing would not have been regular, and the poor girl had probably alternated between opium fugue and withdrawal. She tried toughness and managed a raspy, "What do you know about it?"

"Well, I know it's tough to shake and we can help you. Ideally you could stay here for a few days."

This repelled her. "Why should I listen to you, anyway? Weird old bird."

"You came to us, Reenie. I'm very sorry but we'll do all we can for you."

She lashed out. "They say you're really a man. Bloody drab cow if you ask me."

That painted a picture. "Does the man who did this to you say things like that?"

I was sitting on a stool next to the examining table, and the little chit reached out and clamped down on my breast with grimy fingers. It startled me and hurt too, and I gave her a good elbow as I grabbed her wrists and pinned my full weight against her. She didn't resist, so I let go and stepped away. "If you stay for treatment, you'll need to apologize for that, Reenie. But if you don't, get someone else to help you off the laudanum. It'll kill you eventually."

I left her sobbing and apprised Betsy that Reenie was ready for her bath.

Betsy said, "You all right, Doc?"

Usually I soothed the spiky ones but could not abide physical attack. "She's angry. Watch her hands." I pushed out the back door and took a brisk turn around the garden, stopping at that massive sage, tearing and crushing a sprig in my hands. Not many girls made me spiteful, but I had to squash it to find out the location of that crib. I wanted to watch her face as I asked if she knew Catherine Farnsworth.

After her bath Reenie seemed worse, so I asked Betsy to give her a minimum dose of laudanum. We would calibrate and ease her off.

By the morning Reenie Byrne had absconded. That was ordinary, but somehow she had filched Betsy's keys. The medicine closet was open with all the laudanum gone, and also two full bottles of chloroform, confirming she'd been sent by slavers. I hoped to heaven Reenie would be freed for her successful infiltration, but she'd neglected to nick an inhaler. Anyone using chloroform for street abductions would soon learn it took several minutes to render someone unconscious, but that was small consolation. And now we had to watch for further intrusions. I sent word to Martin.

That week girls worked up vignettes all over the house. Susannah's beautiful alto rang in the stairwell, and Ruby could be found with a pen crumpling up paper and throwing wads into corners. They all worked on a voting sketch. Corabelle took over one end of the ballroom to practice an acrobatic dance routine with Georgia and Clemence. At the other end, Marianne and Sophronia worked up a martial routine with fake wooden rifles they swung like batons. Sitting with Tatiana, Vivie fine-tuned their choreography from a push chair.

"Where'd that come from?" I asked.

Vivie smiled and flushed, relating that the porter Willy Schor had found it for her at a shop over by Bellevue that made them for veterans. A strapping but shy and gentle young man, Willy had briefly been a soldier in the last months of the war. He had carried her from the clinic.

"Did he carry you downstairs today?"

She nodded. I was glad.

Surprised to find her with the most hard-hearted girls, I motioned for Tati to follow me into the hall and asked how that came about.

"I'm teaching her how to use a knife."

"Are you now. Thanks."

"I'll be sorry to see her go." Always a dark horse, Tatiana. Her mother, a legendary harlot herself, had sent her away to school but the girl had a gift for soothing angry men. Just in case, she kept slender blades in her clothes and bed.

"Me too." I'd sent out some letters but those arrangements had yet to be made.

I was wearing a fashionable green dress and deeply veiled hat. Tati said, "Where are you off to?"

I winked, which brought an admiring sidelong look, and went out the front. It was a bright cool day and it irritated me to ask for a carriage for one block east and five blocks up Broadway to Wood's Museum and Metropolitan Theater. The boys had real work to do, and though I'd have to be careful, I walked alone.

Most buildings along the way were five to six stories, the number of flights an able person could reasonably climb. At street level, I passed grocers, haberdashers, jewelers, bakers, butchers, leather workers, locksmiths, taverns, banks, hosiers, and a pretty new confectionary, the scent of which reminded me of Willow's mother. The sidewalk was crowded with clerks and messengers and groups of girls, the street thick with carriages, carts, and white horse–drawn omnibuses. Billboards touted the virtues of Pears' Soap, Fletcher's Castoria, Grandreth's Pills, and ten kinds of tobacco, and bills advertising the charms of the Blonde Bells were affixed to every flat surface.

The first approach was stealthy, as I never noticed a young man keeping pace with me. I flattened him with a look, but could take no credit as he took me for younger from behind. He melted away by standing still. Next a rougher type tried to catch my eye as I walked toward him. He opened his arms and became jovial, but was too slow formulating words and I stepped around him. I smelled the drink as I passed and he called out, "There's a stuck-up strumpet!"

The museum entry was mirrored, and I had to concur. My face was a stone mask. Young actresses and dancers huddled in packs around the entrance, their purpose much the same as mine, to importune Lydia Thompson and her ladies of burlesque. I paid the entrance fee and passed a note for the stage manager of the attached theater, Wallace Lacy, whom I'd met years before accompanying Elliott to Pfaff's Saloon. Writers sat at long tables below the sidewalk and took a name for their rebellion from the stage play *La vie de Bohème*, trying to conjure café culture in the city of the Forty Thieves (a.k.a. the board of aldermen).

While I waited for Wallace, I spent some minutes inspecting the museum curiosities. Seated on comfortable chairs were to be found a man close to seven feet tall with shoes as long as my forearm from elbow to fingertip, and a dwarf no taller than the man's coat pocket. They showed little interest in one another, the dwarf reading a book and the giant perusing the crowd, professionally bored. It saddened me that those born with such anomalies should have to display themselves for wages, but supposed they were making the best of it. The famed Siamese twins had the day off, and at least Wood's had no hermaphrodites displaying their incongruities. It was a master class in shame and defiance.

There were waxwork likenesses of President Lincoln and Queen Victoria, all the apostles and the son of God himself seeming rather abashed at the Last Supper. I could just hear the humorist Artemus Ward and all the bohemians holding forth on these attractions, on Americans always making a sideshow of everything right up to salvation. A stuffed whale hung from the ceiling. It was a perfect match for my present mission, to save my life's work and the livelihoods of dozens of people from a poisonous street thug using shapely legs and innuendo.

The shaggy mass of Wallace Lacy came striding in. "Sakes alive, Doc Hastings, you are a sight for sore eyes!" He enfolded me in a cloud of old sweat, tobacco, and paint.

"How delightful to see you, Wallace. You must visit the Double Standard."

"I'm not sure they pay me enough for that, Doc," he said, taking my arm and leading me toward the theater.

"You'll come as my guest. Come tonight for a good dinner after the show."

"That's awfully nice. It'll be great to catch up on all the news of the old crowd. But meanwhile, your note mentioned a favor?"

When he turned up that evening we fed him and I gave an idle Susannah a wad of cash to take him upstairs. A happier man never floated out the door.

When all the clients had gone up to the suites, I sat in the library with Meg and Ciara bathed in candlelight reflected off warm cherrywood, and knew myself to be losing heart.

Ciara said, "We circle back to this every year or two Doc, and we always conclude there's nothing better. We're not going to make dresses, and you can't run a hospital because anything bigger than the clinic would invite scrutiny."

I went to speak again and she said, "And a hotel would turn into an assignation house, and in that case we might as well be running the Double."

Meg said, "You're just tired."

I said, "Sport is getting uglier."

"Not in here."

We had launched dozens of women into independent businesses and decent marriages, each of whom promised to do the same for other girls. "We've gotten too conspicuous."

Ciara said, "The Double Standard is perfect as it is, and you know it."

I squared myself to take them step-by-step through the fragments of evidence: Benno's drive for more revenue, the disappearing girls, brothel rioting, Jane the Grabber's history with Vernon Trent and his patronage of the Reveille. Benno's avoidance of the Double and his weirdness with Sweeny were still mysterious, but perhaps related. They agreed something was out of joint.

"So what do we do?" Ciara asked.

"Well," I said, "my main hope is that the ball will convince Benno to leave us alone."

That baffled them.

I said, "He won't disturb the pleasures of Peter Sweeny and Oakey Hall."

Meg threw up her hands and Ciara threw me her sharpest glare. "He won't give two shites! A party?"

I closed my eyes and when I opened them, got up to pour myself a brandy. "What might be revealed. Balls shake things up."

"What else is cooking?" said Meg.

"Martin has people watching The Reveille. One girl who I think escaped from their crib came to the clinic, but she was in no position to help us."

Ciara said, "What do we think of Martin Mitchell? Did he buy his commission?"

Meg said, "Doesn't everyone on the Metropolitans?" Any cop who hadn't bought his position was called an "accidental."

I said I liked him and was on my way to trusting him.

Ciara said, "Benno's a cockroach, but would any ward boss be better when Tammany's taking over the world?"

I frowned. "Let's endear ourselves to Peter Sweeny, throw a legendary ball, and trip up the slavers where we can. I'm open to all suggestions."

"Impale Benno," said Meg.

I said, "That's what he would do."

The twins often preferred a forceful approach, to settle all questions at once as Benno and most men would. My instinct was usually to move more slowly, letting deeper currents reveal themselves. But in those depths, my strategy was changing. If Benno really was setting up a slaving operation, rather than trying to soothe and placate him, I was now wondering what I would sacrifice to stop him. I hoped someone else might have reason to trip him up, but could not imagine who. If stopping him cost me the Double, I would have to find a way to close the house while preserving the safety of everyone in it.

These lonely thoughts reminded me of an idea long floated between us as an insurance policy: to inscribe a list of our clients with their sexual history and unusual preferences in a document that could be stashed somewhere and used as leverage in a negotiation. Powerful men would move heaven and earth to prevent its publication. "Maybe it's time to write our affidavit."

"Boom!" said Meg. "Good, let's do it."

It could be used only when the house was at grave risk or one of us was facing death, as it torched our discretion and any future in New York. Ideally the threat alone would suffice. Disclosure meant closure, and wouldn't solve the problem of what to do instead. First: allure, and failing that: a self-destructive exposure. It'd be surprising, anyway.

I said, "What would you do if I closed the house?"

They looked at each other. "Are you serious?"

"Don't you think about it?"

Ciara looked stricken but Meg said, "I'd go to Paris."

"Well, we're not there yet." I counted the bookshelves. "It'd be a load of work to dismantle this place.

All three of us sat in our stews, pretty sure that what came next would pale in comparison to the last eight years. I took a swallow of brandy and wondered again where I could send Vivie before it all unraveled.

When I kissed Ciara good night, I said, "Don't worry."

She laughed. "You've given me a few things to think about."

As I trod the gravel path back through the garden to the clinic, I remembered the weeks after Beadie died, walking the streets in search of respectable employment. I took myself to hospitals and dispensaries, explained my background and years of experience, the surgeries I performed and treatments I had mastered. Not one would have me, and many threw me out the moment I mentioned a brothel, as if I were a carrier for sexual license. The most memorable interview was with the famous Doctor Elizabeth Blackwell herself at her Women's Clinic. She was the first woman to graduate from an American medical college. Her clinic was a paltry, underused affair. I challenged her to reach out to the vast population of girls who made their main or supplemental wage from prostitution. She turned up her nose and I got a bit heated.

"Don't they need care? Wouldn't it be better from women?"

She said, "Our enterprise is different. We're trying to bring women practitioners respect and respectability. That would hardly help."

I said, "It depends on whose respect you're after."

Pausing to look up at the night sky for my own north star, I said aloud, "Oh, Gwin. I meant to keep faith with you always." What would she make of the Double Standard in its present form, favorite and target of this grasping syndicate?

Her answers always surprised me, and I rarely liked them. "At root," she once told me, "everyone is pretty much the same." When I recoiled, seeing only predators and prey, she said, "We're born and we die, Rafaela. It's a short life, so don't waste it laying blame." I was still hoping to find something in Benno to admire, or for him to find something in me, but he was determined to live his story of vicious domination and vanquished rivals.

Just as Elizabeth Blackwell graduated from medical school in 1848, an alternative sprouted near Newbury. The Boston Female Medical College opened to train women as nurses and midwives. I wanted to attend as soon as I heard of it, and for years my father seemed to approve of this plan.

But as I grew near the age to begin inquiries, he resisted. We knew no one in Boston. We couldn't pay for it. He needed my help in the surgery. By sixteen, I was at war with him over my education.

I wrote to the Boston Female Medical College to ascertain their requirements, and after a long delay they responded that their finances did not currently support scholarships.

I was restless. My friends had begun to marry and move off, and I had no interest in the boys I knew. Thankfully my father had not picked anyone.

Arguments in favor of my improvement failed, tender solicitude failed, sulking neglect failed. I suggested a housekeeper if he preferred not to live alone. I appealed to the memory of my mother and all her skill and hopes for me.

One day he announced that his friend Dr. Gottlieb had a place for me at Portland Hospital, twice as far from Newbury as Boston, but to the north. They neither charged tuition nor paid wages. Room and board were provided in a dormitory attached to the hospital. I asked about the curriculum, and was told it was standard. Was there midwifery instruction? He mumbled.

"Do you really mean to dispose of me this way?"

"You wanted training."

"Why have you taught me since I was a toddler if you didn't want me to be like you?" He said nothing so I shouted the question again.

He scoffed, "All your mother's training did not protect her."

This made no sense. Her education had nothing to do with her death. And then I saw it. I said softly, "All your *training did nothing to protect her."*

His mouth grew ugly.

I finally saw what was before me, his pallor and low energy. Just when he might finally have drawn me closer, he arranged to send me away. I was so angry, I went.

He died within weeks, in part by choice, I think.

SIX

The question of what to wear to the ball stomped around my gut until I told Philomena to make me something lovely but to leave me out of it. She frowned over how to make a splashy gown I could put on without help. I always dressed myself and did my own hair, meaning the bodice had to fasten on the side or in front. The gown I found hanging in my room that evening was splendid, a dark cerise with unusual sleeves that were not sleeves but braided silk straps like bracelets around the upper arm. The neckline was high enough but the bust tightly fitted, and I felt every inch of my bare arms. One or two faint scars were visible on the underside of one but the light would be low. The bodice, skirts, and long black gloves were edged in the same trim. She'd given me a small cage crinoline so I could move in the crowd, but I wasn't used to wearing one at all and it irked me. I did my hair in a loose braid over one shoulder, and when I faced the mirror felt nauseous and turned away. When I agreed to the party I somehow forgot I'd have to attend it.

The Double kitchen was as busy as I'd ever seen it. Bert wore a checked suit with a black and white apron, and with a ladle orchestrated a parade of servers up the stairs. I climbed to the third floor looking for any girls not yet busy with clients.

"Woah, Doc!" was the first reaction to my appearance, from Ruby. She wore a wrapper over a skimpy costume for the revue. "Dazzling!" But as she said it, her face grew pinched.

"What?"

She tilted her head. "That hair won't do. Will you suffer an interference?"

"If I must."

"Did Phila make that? It's splendid on you." She was examining the bodice and I fisted my hands to stop from crossing them over my chest.

Cora and Clemence emerged from the girls' dressing room fully done up in hair and makeup with their tights and corsets. "Wow, Doc," Cora said. "So pretty!"

Clemence grew coy and said, "Do you have a date?"

I said, "If you count Benno."

A young maid named Verity was clearing some debris and froze when she saw me.

Ruby said, "V, can you put Doc's hair up?"

"Y-yes ma'am," she said.

"I don't bite," I said and smiled at her. "Please improve on this, but not too elaborate or fancy. It's a long night for me and it needs to stay put. Simple and elegant?"

She nodded, apparently nervous beyond the power of speech. I hadn't hired her or yet spoken to her, but she'd been at the house for several weeks. I put my hand out. "I'm Doc. You're Verity, I take it."

She shook my hand and also curtsied. "Yes ma'am. Please sit here." She showed me to a chair in front of a mirror, and covered me from chin to shoes with a silk smock.

Tatiana was in the next chair, her head in the hands of a longtime maid called Edith. They both watched me in the mirror. "Evening, ladies."

"Is this a first?" said Tati.

I'd had my hair done in that room before but could not remember when. "No, but I take your meaning."

Verity's hands shook as she undid my braid, so I asked her to stop for a moment and turned in the chair. "I'm making you nervous, but you needn't be."

She studied the floor and I put a finger under her chin and lifted her eyes to mine.

"I'm nervous myself. I don't usually dress like this or make myself fancy at all. You probably know that." She blinked. "It feels strange and wrong to me, if I'm being honest. So you could help me out. I'm going to speak to a lot of people I don't much admire tonight, and I'm thinking of the clothes as armor that will protect me and help me get it done." Let Benno and Peter Sweeny end soused and embracing, swearing to do better by womankind, and raising a toast to the perfection of the Double Standard, making me promise never to change it. "I want to look like someone who belongs at this fancy ball, but not like someone who's pretending. I still want to feel like myself. Does that make sense?"

"Yes ma'am," she said, starting to breathe. "A French roll is what you're after but you have a good head of hair. It's going to take a lot of hardware."

"Oh!" I said, glad it was my hair that daunted her. "You mean hairpins?"

"And clips."

"Do we have what you need?"

"Yes ma'am."

I closed my eyes and let the little yanks and pats to my head be calming. It took roughly forever, long enough that when Edith finished with Tati they discussed which lipstick would work on me, and Tati left to search out a particular hue.

Then Verity was done and Tati was back and Edith was dabbing color to my lips and they all moved to one side while I stood up. Edith said "Do this," and pressed her lips together.

I still hadn't looked in the mirror, but swept the smock off and said, "Good?"

Tati said, "Stunning." She took me by the shoulders and turned me to the mirror. I slammed my eyes shut but slowly opened them, searching past the stylings for my expression, which looked, well, ferocious. This surprised me so much I laughed, and took that moment to thank Verity for swallowing her fear. She must have thought I was pleased with her work but I could not have told you a single thing about my hair.

Walking down the hall, I told myself to stay away from mirrors and spirits. On the stairs I met Elliott resplendent in white tie. He whistled, kissed my hand, and took my arm as we descended and toured the first-floor rooms. The salon was bedecked with fir boughs and flowers, and the ballroom, seldom fully opened, was done up as a theater.

Not strictly part of the Double building, the ballroom filled the entire parlor floor of the adjacent brownstone, two big columns breaking the expanse. A stage at the back was garlanded with hothouse roses and lilies in the shape of a proscenium. Some few rows of chairs sat at the front for distinguished guests and the rest was open, overhung with crystal chandeliers. At the street end a bar groaned with champagne and bourbon.

Guests arrived in continuous waves, and soon the rooms were awash in excited conversation floating in clouds of whiskey and tobacco and the toe-tapping rhythm of a trio. George arrived with Peter Sweeny, and the presumptive Mayor-elect Oakey Hall trailed an entourage of actresses.

The financier Jim Fisk wore a double-breasted mulberry coat with dollar-sized gold buttons embossed with his initials.

As expected, a plump diamond took its place on his black four-in-hand over an elaborately ruffled shirtfront. His consort Miss Josie Mansfield was indeed lovely, with masses of crow-dark hair and a demure face over a lush figure, clad in navy with a shawl of valenciennes lace. We bowed to one another.

I came upon a favorite client, Junius Henri Browne. A war correspondent for the *Tribune*, he was captured at Vicksburg and spent two years in Confederate prisoner of war camps. Short and scrawny with a pince-nez in his pocket and *bon mot* on his lips, he gave himself a crash course in medicine in the filthy camps and saved many lives. Prison was his true university, and when he and the *Tribune*'s Albert Richardson escaped and walked overland for months to reach Union lines, he noted with gratitude, it was uniformly dirt-poor people and slaves who helped them along.

Junius retained his expensive taste however, and loved beautiful women. He spent a good chunk of the windfall from his captivity bestseller at the Double. He once told me that women had a frightening ability to beguile a man's mind, and I reminded him that the fright was his alone. We enjoyed one another.

He said, "If it's not impertinent to ask, who was that young man I saw you with earlier?"

I told him a bit about Elliott, and he asked if he was any relation to Asa Vanderpoel, who'd been his editor years back when he was a city reporter. "I always respected him. He's an excellent newspaperman."

Now he had my full attention. "What do you know about his war?"

"What you know. He worked for Stanton." This was Lincoln's Secretary of War, but I knew little of Asa Vanderpoel's actual wartime occupation. Junius said, "Not many men of his class or ability would ride a horse for twenty hours a day or sleep on the ground without a commission. He was Lincoln and Stanton's eyes on the battlefields, sending daily cables to Washington. At first the generals thought he was their spy but he gained their trust, especially Grant. They were close, and Vanderpoel became Grant's champion."

I said, "So he saw a lot of bloodshed."

"In the field a year or more—Vicksburg, Chattanooga, Petersburg—with trips to Washington and New York in between."

Why was he troubled now, I mused. "I'll read the memoir."

Junius said, "He's not the type to look back. Has his hands full building the *Standard*. When are you going to write your war memoir, Doc?"

I jumped a bit at that because of my plan to write an affidavit with all of the house's secrets, our last-chance weapon we could threaten to publish, but said, "My war?"

"The front line of debauchery and disease, of course."

"We never court attention," I said.

He closed his eyes as he nodded. "Understood."

Willy Schor whispered in my ear that Benno and his entourage had arrived, and that the twins were greeting them. It was past 11:30, so they were well-timed for the midnight show. I saw Hanky Pank, Benno, and two bodyguards traverse the hall toward the dining room and waited until they filled plates before following. I paused a moment to settle my look and tone. It was my first time seeing them since knowing their capacity for evil.

"Welcome, gentlemen," I said, and chatted blandly about the election and when results might be expected.

Benno, poisonous as ever in a new suit, said, "So who's here?"

"About sixty men so far, mostly tycoons of one sort or another. Jim Fisk is in the salon. Oakey Hall is here but occupied at the moment. Judge Barnard, Mr. Sweeny."

That last brought him to a scowling knife-edge. I waited, having already breeched decorum by mentioning names but trying to tempt him into confiding in me. Benno, I was now sure, feared Sweeny not in the way one feared a mercurial boss, but with the residue of a nasty personal history, some sort of bad blood or antipathy. Was the whole evening then completely misbegotten? Perhaps the difficulty could not be smoothed over.

"Would you like to say hello? I can find out where he is."

"No," he said, rigid.

"A man is often suggestible when he's most relaxed. Let us know if we can plant any seeds for you." Subtlety wasn't in his repertoire but he might imagine its uses in softer hands.

To his whole group, I previewed the imminent revue, and promised them seats at the front. "The girls have outdone themselves, and we have some surprises in store."

"I never mind a naked whore," Benno said, the equivalent of pissing on my shoe. He looked me up and down.

"How charming," I said, "I'm sure they love you too." Hanky Pank swallowed a laugh. The twins were probably right that there was no appeasing him, but I would keep trying.

At show time the girls gathered in the kitchen. I told them, "It's a good crowd. You're all gorgeous and I'm ridiculously proud of you. Please remember to keep your heads no matter what unexpected things happen." I winked as I said this last part, and their energy spiked. "You are professionals."

Marianne said, "Damn right, Doc." Willow twirled and Ruby said, "New York is ours tonight!"

Elliott strode onto the stage flourishing his wings. "Good evening sports and libertines of New York, courtesans and demimondaines! On this most sacred day of democracy, we welcome you to the Merry Hypocrites' Ball!" Cheers and laughter shook the floor. I was proud of the name, and hoped it would circulate.

"And now for your edification, emancipation, and titillation, the ladies of the Double Standard Sporting House present a celebration of our United States of America!"

They opened with "Yankee Doodle Dandy," the girls strutting and teasing in a luscious parade while saving plenty for the finale reprise. I squeezed myself into the ballroom in time to see Clemence and Susannah sashay downstage on two pairs of endless legs. They jockeyed for the best position, and their skirmish turned into an I-go-you-go dance. Erroll had brought in a five-piece band with exquisite timing. Susannah appeared to win, allowing Clemence to storm off shaking her shapely ass. Suze relaxed and removed a bottle from her décolletage, taking a swig before launching into "Little Brown Jug," a new song that was all the rage, with a mime of major boozing.

With the audience laughing and upending their own drinks, Union soldiers Marianne and Sophronia trooped in to a classic Army march, drilling with wooden rifles. They were straight out of burlesque: blue tights, fitted uniforms from the waist up, and fetching caps, a perfect mash of sexes with their feminine shapes taking precision positions with martial aggression. Horrible prettiness indeed. They twirled, they tossed, they planted and pivoted with all cockiness as the assembly whistled and hooted. In the end they aimed their weapons at the crowd, targeting one sport after another and pulling their triggers. Some got in the fun and fell over dead.

Tatiana came on next for our rendition of a minstrel show Tambo and Bones. She wore a lurid orange cutaway and flaming red boots, a floppy paisley tie and oversized *pince-nez*. The whole place erupted, Oakey himself down front beaming and delighted, pivoting in his seat and thumping his chest. She recited his qualifications for mayor, "I can sing like a bird, write acres of poetry, and mix a delectable lobster salad!"

Ruby fattened up as Tweed waddled out and tried to interrupt him. "We owe everything to the working man!" That got a big laugh.

Tati-Oakey effused with verbosity, promises of cultural uplift and street beautification: "We must have avenues and libraries to rival London and Paris!" Ruby-Tweed slung Tammany dogma: "The immigrant is the city's backbone!" In the end they agreed that, "When business is good, everyone loves it!" linked arms, and waltzed off arm in arm.

The voting skit that the whole house worked on came next. All the girls were bundled up in great coats and hats, dancing between ballot boxes to vote over and over in smashing, chaotic, intertwining choreography. When Elliott as a stern judge appeared, they switched hats on each round and danced faster. The girls wore men's wigs, but when Clemence's strawberry blonde locks tumbled out, they all froze in indignant shock and cold fury that a woman would dare to vote! The place broke up. Point delivered, daintily.

As the girls dazzled, I circled the room in the dark near the wall, though the damned hoop impeded me at every step. A sallow man I took to be *The World's* Victor Myers leant disheveled in one corner, his hand in the bodice of a curvy street girl. Later I heard that the upright reformer Arthur Beltron spirited two new friends into the Emerald Suite in search of a quiet place to testify on the gospel. Turned out he had never imagined the revelation of one girl on his cock and another on his face. He asked them to trade places and flip so he could minister to them from above, but changed his mind and gave himself up fully prostrate. They skipped out with his clothes. Thank you, Viola.

I stayed near the back for the next sketch, written by me with help from Meg and Elliott. It began with all the girls milling about at a party. One young man, Willow in a blazing red hunt coat, stood in front with his father played by Elliott, the two inspecting all the women. "All right Sonny my boy, happy hunting!"

"Thank you, Papa!"

First Sonny approached a very prim and proper little miss, Corabelle dressed for church, but his purposeful stride frightened her off. Next, he sidled up to a sexy tart, Marianne with a low neckline and a wink, who relieved him of his shirt (slit up the back) while lifting his wallet from his coat pocket.

The boy returned to his father, vexed.

"Sonny, you must target the right sort of woman for the right sort of activity."

"Activity?"

"You know, marriage, or . . . not marriage."

"How do I do that?"

The Papa said, "First you have to be able to tell which side of the line they fall on."

"Line? What line?"

The whole company turned to stare in shock and horror. "You don't know about the line?"

"I see no line."

"Well it's not an actual line, son, no more than the southern border of Pennsylvania is marked by a bright red ribbon to the far edge of Iowa."

"So I look for a line that's not a line."

Papa Elliott stepped back and spread his arms, cleared his throat and took a big inhale as the trio began a loping rhythm. "Look at her clothes, look at her face. Is she bold or coy, walk with flounce or grace? Does she look like a mother, or something other? Is she quiet and pliant, or spicy and a riot? High-necked or low, upright or prone?"

Sonny said, "Can't a woman be a bit of both, fear God and take a joke?"

The whole stage froze in shocked silence and stared at Sonny like he was completely barmy.

Sonny asked, "What am I missing? What's this mystery dividing women?"

Papa said, "Well, son, you must learn and now's the time, it's called the MATRON-VIXEN Line!"

The audience roared as all the girls lined up at the front of the stage shouting, "Matron! Vixen! Matron! Vixen!" As they called "Matron," the respectably dressed girls leaned forward to shake their fingers or cover their eyes, ears, or mouths. As they called "Vixen," the provocatively dressed girls winked, shimmied, licked their lips, crooked a finger. Back and forth they toggled, more and more extreme in their renditions. Susannah did a freakishly stern busybody while Ruby lifted her skirts to show red stockings.

Sonny stared in confusion and fascination, saying, "It's all too much, I can't sort it out. Don't all women smile and pout, stay in the house and also go out? I know, I'll go ask my sister!"

The whole company shouted, "NOOOOOOOOO!" as they lined up to protect Tati, dressed as a child, from his question.

He stumbled back aghast and asked, "So why must women be one or the other? What's the reason for all this trouble?" The audience was silent, watching.

Everybody onstage looked around, baffled and shifty-eyed, stroking their chins and scratching their heads. "That's just how it is!"

The boy asked, "Are they born that way? Hardly seems right, can't a girl of virtue be forced into vice by any man in just one night?"

All the players covered their ears in mortification, cried with pain and shock to hear that spoken. The crowd roared.

"I ask again, why the divide? What's gained from this insistence on floozy versus bride? Like everything funny, does it boil down to a question of money?"

The company was still shocked and mortified, but looked around at one another in confusion.

Sonny said, "Does a highborn girl always end a matron and a poor one always end a vixen?"

Everyone relaxed further, lower lips jutting as if to agree that was plausible, not a bad way to explain it, and began to affirm.

The girls dashed back to formation, this time with respectable women to one side and tarts to the other. "MATRON! VIXEN! MATRON! VIXEN!" Order re-established, Papa now proud of his son, they shook hands.

The boy said, "So rich people never fornicate?"

Everybody cracked up, howling with knowing laughter, while Papa Elliott buffed and inspected his fingernails. "Now remember son, we're talking only about women!" The audience erupted but quickly fell quiet again.

The boy nodded. "I see. So a poor woman cannot be virtuous. Definitely money, then. But wasn't Grandmother born to a collier?"

The kickline became rather desperate. "MATRON! VIXEN! MATRON! VIXEN!"

Finally Papa said, "Look son, it boils down to this. You must marry a virgin for wealth, but meanwhile take every chance to enjoy yourself!" He beckoned the vixens and they swarmed the boy, removing his outer clothes and grabbing his bottom while he reached for breasts and crotches.

Papa said, "You'll understand how it all works soon enough!" The vixens looked over their shoulders at the audience and winked as they led both Sonny and Papa away in different directions, the respectable ladies covering their eyes and dispersing into the audience.

At least this one sketch was meant to tickle women. Willow

had been splendid and the audience fully held by spectacle if not by implication.

Meanwhile, Elliott flew out again, straightening his clothes. I stood where I could see both Benno and Sweeny, who still had not spoken to one another. "Ladies and gentlemen, the Double Standard Sporting House thanks you for your delightful enthusiasm! Before our final number and parade, which we invite you to join as it makes its way around the room, we have a bit of a surprise for you." He really was a devastating flirt. "The city of New York has often in its history been set afire, but never so much as by these guests of ours. Merry Hypocrites, are you ready?" They cheered. "ARE YOU READY?" They thundered. "Then please welcome Miss Pauline Markham and Miss Lydia Thompson of the Blonde Belles Burlesque Troupe!"

The two stars strutted out as officers of the British Imperial Navy draped in gold braid, brass buttons, bicorn hats, and dark tights. I couldn't hear myself laughing over the ruckus. They waved and smiled and pointed at people in the crowd, who roared back. Benno was surprised. I saw the recoil in his neck and eyes, but he squinted in a quick recalculation. Sweeny's eyes were open but he covered his ears with his hands. Ciara was watching him from about six feet away. Meanwhile, the Double girls had come into the crowd and were jumping up and down with joy and adulation.

Having met the Belles backstage at Wood's, I respected anew the effects of costume, paint, and talent. At rest they were no more lovely than my girls, but on stage looked twice as striking and held the crowd with unforced command.

Lydia raised her voice to call everyone to order. "Well if this is the Sixteenth ward, I'd like to see the other Fifteen!" More cheers. "New York does throw a great party. Pauline, we ought to get out of the theater more often."

"I'll say, Lydia. I never saw a party like this in London."

"Except for that one time at the palace."

Pauline excavated a memory and her eyes widened. "Oh yes, the palace." She sighed. I wondered why she was playing dumb, but supposed it was a standard setup. "They don't have royalty here in America, do they?"

"No Pauline, this is a democracy. They fought a war over it."

"I thought that was North versus South."

"A different war. A hundred years ago they kicked out the king."

Pauline beamed. "And now we have a queen, our little Vicky."

"No, no queen. Not yet." Lydia winked.

"So who's in charge?"

Lydia surveyed the crowd and said with some awe, "I hear they call him the ward boss." That got a great laugh, and Benno looked around, alarmed.

"And what does he have that Vicky don't?"

"A pair of—"

"Crowns?"

"No, a long—"

"Royal lineage?"

"No, an enormous—"

"Treasury?"

"Yes! That's it. He has a huge wwwwww . . . wealth!"

Lydia began patting her body as if checking her own pockets.

Pauline said, "Some of you may have had a chance to see our show here in New York. Maybe you've heard of it, it's called *Ixion*?" Now I covered my ears. "Well, if we haven't had the pleasure of hosting you over at Wood's Metropolitan, we do an *adjusted* version of this song in the show. We thought tonight it might be nice for you Merry Hypocrites if we sang the original, written by your supremely talented countryman, Mr. Stephen Foster. Boys?" They launched into "Beautiful Dreamer," which was all wistful moonlight and soothing vapor, their voices immense and stunning, but showing the strain of eight shows a week. And then the song caught me up, cares of the rude world soothed, clouds of sorrow fading, a pang of longing for someone to croon to me of the bright coming morn. That flash of my heart revealed an empty weariness, and I felt quite alone in the crowded stinking room with my various tasks and burdens, but the Belles were that good: they moved me right along and out of myself with everyone on a wave of sweet adoration.

When the applause waned, Lydia arched an eyebrow, which promised more naughtiness. Dropping her voice a register, she said, "Might I meet the famous Mr. Benjamin O'Connor? Where are you, my darling?"

A pointing, a turning in the crowd conspired to throw Benno toward the stage. His first steps were halting, but he thrust back his shoulders and strode forward. The Belles each kissed a cheek and shook a hand, looked him up and down, winking at the crowd. Before he could decide how he felt about that, they pressed themselves against him, one under each arm, and stroked and tickled and wiggled. Benno was so busy trying to prevent or hide an erection he didn't dare speak, and in any case the girls gave him no openings. I would have paid a fortune for his thoughts at that moment, and realized I'd never seen him smile, even in spite.

"I hear you're a BIG boss," said Pauline, eying the front of his pants.

"I hear you're the BEST boss," said Lydia, looking him over front and back.

"We have another song, just for you this time."

"It's another number we play with in our show over at Wood's, specially adapted, Mr. O'Connor. It's a joy of burlesque, adapting the lyrics of our songs to the present moment. The words can change every night!" He had gone purple and I dared hope for a coronary.

The band struck up a familiar tune, the nursery rhyme "Taffy was a Welshman" with its bouncy beat. The real words, which everyone knew, loomed up as a catastrophic misstep by the Belles, a mortal danger. Taffy was a thief, a cheat, and a liar. The room held its breath but the re-written words showered Benno with exactly the kind of empty praise he required. It was snide genius. "Benno is a ward boss, Benno is a star, Benno came to my house and smoked a fat cigar." The Belles strutted around him in circles, using his body as a foil and prop. The words mattered less in the end than the sight of Broadway's biggest stars fawning over this curdled little man.

While the crowd cheered, Sophronia in her hourglass glory was wheeled down front on a cart, gave her hand to Benno, and pulled him right into an embrace. He put his hands on her in a way he had not dared with the Belles, who followed them onto the cart. The three beauties teased him as the band began the reprise of "Yankee Doodle Dandy," shouting on the line, "Yankee Doodle, keep it up!" The procession tried to circle the ballroom, everyone singing the chorus and trying to get in line or climb on. It was so packed most of the crowd was stuck in place so they danced where they were, feeling up their friends and neighbors. Hanky Pank, I noted with some irritation, had his hands all over Georgia.

When the song ended, Elliott bade the guests drink and sup in the main dining room. Half the crowd rampaged toward it while others rummaged in each other's clothing. Lydia and Pauline fled up the back stairs to change. I couldn't see Benno and could only hope he was gratified by the fuss.

Two other Belles, Lisa Weber and Ada Hartland, were chatting up Diamond Jim Fisk, now shed of Josie Mansfield.

Both plump and sharp, Fisk's eyes darted like little fishes. When introduced to me he said, "The famous Doc Hastings." He kissed my hand. "I'd heard of your skill but not your beauty, Madame. I believe I may forego my Fifth Avenue quack."

"How kind, Mr. Fisk, but I treat only girls and women. You are however, most welcome at the Double Standard." He squinted and moved on.

How many people kissed my cheeks that night? I preferred a simple nod, but a kiss might bring a sweet fragrance or frisson of affection. Drunks lunged in. Elliott made a remark about my sleeves being useful for bondage games, George kissed both cheeks and lingered, wanting to tell me about the eerie quiet of his chambers echoing doom all day, and Peter Sweeny nodded and went back to his cigar. Each of my girls, while resplendent and alluring, made me proud with their courtesy: Willow leading a frightened man toward the dining room, Clemence offering drinks, Marianne making jokes and overtures.

Lydia entered the salon in a lovely blue gown and was beset by admirers. She caught my eye, and while I was sure she could manage, I pretended to need her. We fled to the library. Israel saw and would bar the door. When we met backstage at Wood's, Wallace had kindly introduced me as a medical practitioner, and I told her about the Double. Lydia was undeterred, had agreed straight off to attend the ball as her Belles were dying to meet wealthy Americans.

"And you?" I'd asked. She'd put a finger to her lips. I'd heard a rumor that she was married to her producer John Henderson, but if that got out, it would shrink her audience.

I gestured to a club chair and she sank in with a sigh. I poured us each a brandy. "How do the Belles find the stock?"

She laughed. "Birth doesn't matter at all. Half these men started poor."

"A self-made man carries an advantage in masculinity. He's excluded from certain clubs, but walks taller for his pluck."

"I understand that," she said, "and I enjoy my advantage in masculinity."

Now I laughed. "Do you think men second-guess themselves when you poke fun?"

"All they see is leg. Some prig will think himself under attack and walk out, but I consider that a job well done. Where do you come from?"

"Me?" I told her, "Germany. My parents came here with nothing when I was three."

"It makes a difference, coming from nothing."

"It does," I said, noting the difference between having nothing and being nothing. "At the moment I'm focused on the limitations. Forgive me, you're the greatest sensation to hit New York in my lifetime, but you're still a showgirl. I'll always be a madam. You could fill Niblo's for a year and I could cure cancer, but it wouldn't matter." Niblo's Garden, where it was rumored the Belles would soon move, was the largest theater in New York.

"It's true they only let you get so far. The backlash has begun."

"How so?"

She scratched the back of her head. "Oh, the show is a disgraceful spectacle, and my hair isn't even blonde. I have no talent and they forget they ever heard of parody. Half of it is envy. Men proposition me and call me a whore when I refuse. Showgirls assail my character or beg me for a job."

The city's ardor for burlesque had spurred feeble revolution indeed.

She said, "We need a new show and *Ixion* is a tough act to follow. The vultures are circling. Broadway resents us, when they're not stealing our act."

That sounded like Benno and I mused, "I know what you mean. Sometimes I think I should have called the house the Double Bind. I get both praise and blame for serving fallen women, when it's my only chance to practice medicine, so save your praise, and I came to it quite unwillingly, so save your blame!"

Lydia smiled at me with great warmth and understanding. "Yeah, you're making a lot of noise but here we sit, quite comfortable in your gilt palace with the city at our feet."

I laughed and raised my glass to her. "To attracting everyone, yet changing nothing." She loved that.

The library was a bubble of quiet within the hubbub of the house, but then the door opened and a hundred voices flooded in. "Doc," Israel said.

"What a pleasure, Lydia," I said, coming to take her hand. "Thank you ever so much. Please stay and finish your drink."

She stood. "Back to the show. Let's do this again. The drink, I mean."

Israel directed me to the second-floor hallway to retrieve Vivie, which was odd because she was not supposed to be in the house lest someone spot her. I'd sent her to the clinic. She stood at the top of the stairs dressed as a fairy or nymph, with tulle ballet skirts to her ankles and satin slippers, a slender bodice with wings outlined in wire and covered in sequins. She wore a ball mask and carried a wand with a bell, her hair crowned and threaded with emerald silk ribbons. She was a vision, actually, except her posture and expression were those of a different sort of creature altogether, a hissing, spiteful sort of sprite, teeth and nails out. Ciara had her by the arm and was trying to drag her toward the back stairs but she wouldn't budge.

I came near and said, "Vivie, what is it?"

She looked at me, her eyes focusing. "Where is he?"

"Who?" I said gently.

"He came from there." She pointed to the Gold Suite. "With you." She looked daggers at Ciara.

"You saw a man from Mrs. Wrigley's?" Given her expression I might have guessed the man who cut her.

"Not there," she said, and had some difficulty speaking. She stammered, "The toad who took my virginity!" I pulled her close but she stayed stiff.

"Jesus, Mary, and Joseph," said a shocked Ciara, and I gathered it was Peter Sweeny.

Fragments aligned, and finally I grasped his history with Benno. Seeking to ingratiate himself with the Ring, Benno proposed to give Sweeny a gift so exquisite and memorable it would vault Benno into the top circles of power. He contracted with Vernon Trent for a special virgin, and Trent abducted Vivie for this purpose. But Sweeny was shattered by guilt and blamed Benno, who was now terrified of Sweeny's wrath. Holy mother indeed.

Ciara and I looked at one another over Vivie's shoulder, and she said, "What are the odds?"

Before I could answer, Vivie pulled back and snarled with perfect fury, "Who the fuck is he?"

The dormitory was threadbare and the meals repulsive. We were not trainees but janitorial staff in peaked caps and aprons. We were taught laundry and mopping and the serving of meals, and to say nothing. I became a joke on the wards with my endless questions.

My cohort offered consolations. Annalee Warren came from Ogunquit, a strong, smart girl with a sharp laugh. She was my roommate and the friend I always needed. She bolstered me after my father's death. The hospital spared two days' leave for his burial. I managed to store two boxes with Mrs. Tisch, mostly seeds, and left the disposal of the house and practice to a local attorney.

The nursing supervisor, Miss Pell, took Annalee and me aside some months into our residence and told us we were too kind to the patients. "They take too much of your time, and you'll get too attached." We must have looked shocked, so she continued, "We are not their family. Our job is to see to their prescribed treatment, and keep them fed, warm, and dry."

"Yes ma'am," said Annalee, always practical.

"You are professionals and representatives of this hospital."

"Yes ma'am."

"There is no need to smile so much."

I held in my huff. "Miss Pell, may I ask a question?"

She rolled her eyes. "One," she said.

"My mother always said that a kind word or a smile was the best medicine. Do you not agree?"

She looked disgusted, then sighed. "In the hinterland, that may apply. The patients in a city hospital ward are not your friends or neighbors. Half of them are reprobates who do not deserve such consideration. You must not offer warmth or the suggestion of any kind of personal connection."

The men's ward at that moment held an elderly man who'd had his leg amputated, and a child with a blood cancer.

She might have been trying to warn us off the patients we called "Lew," short for lewd, for their foul talk or gestures. A real jerk was a Lew-lew, like the teamster with cirrhosis who wagged his tongue at us and made slurping noises. Or perhaps her heart had been broken by losing patients. When we knew her, she was ice cold and power mad. Annalee called her "the smiting hand."

We spent our days serving meals and cleaning wards, patients, and bed pans, not too kind and not too educated.

Part 2

THE CAREGIVER'S PLOT

SEVEN

It took ten minutes to pull all the pins, leaving me a frayed Medusa. Desperate for bed, I oiled and brushed and braided my hair, covered it with a silk sleeping cap, and vowed never again.

Late in the morning I woke Vivie with lavender tea and honey. Her own hair fell in ten directions and she combed it with her fingers, sitting up to make room for me and cradling the hot cup in her hands. I watched the previous night come back to her. Her breath was steady and her eyes stared far within.

I said, "Tell me about the costume. It was pretty."

She flashed a smile that crinkled her eyes. "Aunty Laure called me a little bunny, but said bunnies could be awfully tricky."

"Did she!" Laure told occasional tales of Brer Rabbit and Brer Fox, the clever hare besting his betters. She improvised freely.

Vivie's mischievous face was new. "She said beware cute little cottontails."

The rabbit begins at a disadvantage but tricks his way out of it. Laure knew her business. "That wasn't a bunny costume," I said.

"Right. Well, all I could think was hasenpfeffer." We giggled. She chose not to dress as prey! She said, "Fairies carry magic and men fear them."

What would lure a bunny fairy onto the bedroom floor of a busy brothel where she must not go? "I do recall discussing with you the need to stay at the clinic last night."

"Sorry Doc. I am sorry. I stayed in the third-floor stairwell, mostly. I wanted to see the house in all its glory."

Ah. She wanted to interact with men but in passing. She was trying out the world with a role to play, a character who was not the victim or the fallen woman, and in her very first outing caught a glimpse of the last person she wanted to see.

I saw pawprints disappearing into briar patches. "Well congratulations, my dear. You took a risk for those bunny reasons of yours and yielded us quite the bounty of information."

"Peter Sweeny," she said, shaking her head in disgust. His identity was less shocking than what he'd done to her, but she held accountability in her hands now. "I suppose he's used to getting what he wants."

I had wrestled with this the night before and was still unsure what to do. "Do you mind saying what happened between you? You told Minnie he had some sort of fit."

Vivie said, "He recoiled as soon as he spent. I was bleeding and crying in pain and mortification, and he started tearing at his face. He was reaching into his pants which were around his ankles and he fell over. He was trying to get to his rosary, and then he was praying and shaking and crying as much as I was. I could only cover myself with a sheet since one hand was still tied to the bed. I lost track after that."

I kissed her hand and said I was sorry to make her recall it.

"The audacity," she said.

Sweeny probably thought Benno was testing his virility, and now feared men would call him cowardly about the rape of virgins. I'd been trying to heal the rift between them, when I should have been exploiting it. The two men had not, so far as

I knew, spoken to one another at the ball. I said, "To my mind, the nerve resides more with Vernon Trent, and with Benno. Not to minimize Sweeny's guilt, but it's an exception for him and an everyday profession for those two."

She squinted. "It was pretty exceptional for me."

"Yes, and of course you're angry."

"Is there a way to punish him? Can't he be arrested?"

I sighed. "Tammany pretty much controls the police, but there are other ways to punish him if that's what you want."

"Don't you want that?" she said, with a suspicious look I'd seen before.

I wanted to reassure her, but she was growing impulsive. "He may be the most powerful man in New York, and he's very peculiar. It would be a delicate feat to ruin him without ruining you and me too. We have to take our time and think it all through."

She found her own hesitation. "Would I have to confront him?"

"Not if you don't want to. Here's the rub, my dear. You now have a card to play, a powerful one. You may have a chance to use it to help other girls. It'll keep, so take your time."

Extortion never ended well, but if they realized where Vivie was staying and what we knew, they might volunteer reparation. They might also prefer violence. I was pretty sure Emily Wrigley had told no one about selling Vivie's debt to me, but that could change at any moment. Everyone in the house knew where she was.

Vivie assessed me more seriously than she ever had, and I wasn't sure if that possibility inspired or repelled her. Her voice was lower when she spoke. "Peculiar how?"

I paused by habit, but his personality was well established. "He has this criminal genius for hiding embezzlement, but doesn't know how to have a conversation. He fears God but is utterly corrupt, which must create terrible pressure inside of him.

I suspect the inner circle of Tammany tolerates him because his failures of understanding resemble toughness or humor. Benno or Trent must have talked him into a special virgin, because I don't think it would have occurred to him. He may himself have been a virgin. Certainly inexperienced. They were trying to do him a favor so he'd open up new worlds of graft to them."

One laugh escaped her. "Of course. And then he regretted it. I don't have a word for how horrible that is."

"No, that word has not yet been invented."

She laughed again but fell back to grimness, began to retch. I grabbed the wash basin and she slid down in the bed, laid her head on the pillow. Did it matter if the blame rested between several men? Or if no one got what they wanted?

I sat on the floor and stroked her hair.

"He told me I was lucky and should play my cards right."

"Who did?"

She come up to one elbow. "Vernon Trent. My God, he thought he was doing me a favor."

Her face was vital as she absorbed this pain, near adult. I'd seen many girls wrestle with Eve and the apple: ignorance and innocence, or knowledge? This was the first time Vivie savored the rewards of knowing. Her weighing of Peter Sweeny's character and Vernon Trent's calculus foretold that she might someday conclude her gains outran her losses. When she next met her parents, it would be this part of her more than the shattered girl that distanced them, the part of her that valued seeing through all the veils. There was no going home with such wisdom. You were cast out, and that was the worst part. But you gained a much larger world.

Hanky Pank came by for Benno's monthly payment looking oily and stiff.

"You feeling all right?"

"Never better," he said, grimacing.

We had several difficulties between us and I waited to hear where he'd begin.

He said, "Since when you been chumming around with Peter Sweeny?"

"I don't discuss clients, Hank." I was trying to be friendly but he was having none of it.

"What's your beef?" he said. "I mean, you've got it pretty good here. Most women in your position would show a little gratitude."

I almost laughed to hear him parrot Benno. "What position is that, exactly? Forking over my profits to you? Sure, I love that. Thanks so much for taking my money."

"Crazy bitch," he said with a shred of affection. Where he grew up you took whatever you could.

I said, "Look Hank, why don't you be straight with me instead of giving yourself an ulcer? Say what's on your mind."

Here was a man under orders he found ridiculous.

"What, Benno wants half the house, all my girls, to shut me down? Spit it out!"

He swallowed. "Let's say girls interest him."

"What does he want?"

Now he found ground level. "Well he sure the fuck doesn't want to look bad in front of Peter Sweeny."

I said, "Sweeny had a great time at the ball. I put Benno on stage with the most famous women in New York, if not the world. Did he not notice?" As I said it, I began to wonder if Sweeny, himself an embarrassment at certain clubs, wasn't embarrassed by Benno and his ilk. The papers had started calling them Tweed's "Shiny Hat Brigade" for their new silk toppers, which they didn't have the posture or bearing to wear.

Pinning on a diamond was at least more straightforward. Perhaps Sweeny saw the mess with Vivie as one more discrepancy between High Tammany and Low.

"Did he look happy? Benno's not the type for all that."

I said, "Who's Vernon Trent?"

He gave me a filthy look. Confirmation that Trent was working for Benno.

"What are you telling me, Hank?"

"If you want some advice, keep your snoot down. Go out of town for a couple of days."

Conversationally I said, "Is that a threat, or more of a warning?"

"Don't let Benno hear your name for a couple of weeks is all I'm saying."

I slid the envelope. "Watch your own back, eh?"

I hemmed and hawed, but wanted to consult sister owners. We gathered periodically to talk shop and keep the trade cordial. I invited seven women from the neighborhood, including two from the Seven Sisters with whom I was acquainted. These were seven contiguous houses on Twenty-Fifth Street near Seventh Avenue, reputedly the most expensive houses in New York and extremely formal, which I could never square with lines in the street. Who would queue to spend that money? People loved to imagine seven actual sisters, but the name came from an early burlesque.

Of the seven invitees, only two responded, to say they were awfully busy but hoped I was well. They were being careful, just as I had hesitated, since wealthy females banding together was more than enough to infuriate Benno. And now they'd be wary of me too, portending the end of a woman's right to her own bordello.

Via Elliott, Asa Vanderpoel invited me back to Gramercy Park. In the weeks since my consultation he had rallied tolerably and gone back to work, but now he wanted further guidance on his ghosts.

I'd make a mooning fool of myself. Asa Vanderpoel had crowded me at night after our brief acquaintance. "Can't you put him off? I hate to lie to anyone."

"Please," said Elliott. "I'm so rarely useful to him."

I began to doubt that Elliott saw me at all. "It's better for him that I don't."

"But I can't tell him that. Just one more time, Doc. You made such a difference."

Damnation. I was sorely tempted and told myself that seeing him would allow me to stop dreaming about him. "Promise to stay in the room with us?"

"Of course."

Vanderpoel was immaculate as he opened the door himself and led us to the parlor. His capacious sensibility and grace in motion were better governed in sobriety. He offered me a velvet settee, a glass of Madeira, and a plate of biscuits, as one would a spinster nurse. He sipped a whiskey with rather less purpose than before. The room was paneled in some exotic wood, the décor a mix of luxurious fabrics and eclectic paintings from old masters to newer folk art. Not a single servant was in evidence.

As soon as I was settled, Elliott said, "I'll leave you to it." I shot him daggers but he never looked at me, the traitor. I might have spoken up but found myself silent.

And there we were. The man was so familiar. Perhaps it was my long friendship with Elliott or some common element of our makeup. We sat at angles to one another, both of us shielding our power.

He saw me looking at the facing painting, a foggy coastline, the land and water more of a suggestion with the barest hints of color. It was lovely.

"My wife's work," he said.

"And the one in your room, I think."

He nodded, a bit abashed by my having been there.

I said, "She has a gift."

"She stopped painting years ago." That disappointed him.

"That's a shame. How old was she when she made that?"

His eyes shifted up as he thought back. "Maybe twenty."

She stopped when she started bearing his children. "Perhaps she'll return to it someday. You had an interest in poetry I believe."

He said, "Our youthful passions do get swept aside. Did you have one?"

Mine had been wandering rivers and shorelines, observing plants and creatures. "It was more attached to a place." Before he could ask where I grew up, I said, "You had a difficult war."

"Not in the scheme of things." He smiled, rueful. "Speaking with you is like I imagine bullfighting to be."

I did not apologize. "I see dozens of patients a day and don't have time to waste. I don't suppose generals and cabinet secretaries are any different."

"I suppose not."

"But you're unaccustomed to directness in a woman."

He made no answer.

"And I'm no general or secretary." He had thoughts on that but before he could voice them I said, "My questions are not meant to be impertinent. Some treatments are painful."

He found this interesting. "The surgeon wields a knife."

"Yes! Many medicines are poison. I don't enjoy making you uncomfortable."

"Oh, you do a little."

That made me laugh. We had definitely dispensed with propriety. I recomposed myself and said, "I might poke fun at your resistance. There's a difference between what troubles you and what you use to avoid facing it. When the patient is intelligent," I nodded to him, "I might use sarcasm to illuminate resistant behaviors like excessive drinking, but I would never make fun of your pain." This all felt unnecessarily revealing, and I was talking far too much.

"You think drink a form of resistance?"

"It's an anesthetic. You make the pain insensible but then instead of facing your difficulty, you're absorbed by the effects of alcohol poisoning."

He pursed his lips, ever disappointed with himself. Whatever had surfaced lately had put its thumb on a pattern that had long troubled him. It dovetailed with his deepest doubts. "Indeed," he said. "What are other avoidant behaviors?"

I was holding my breath and took a moment to recompose. "Bullying, hysteria, gluttony or starvation, any provocation that takes attention away from the underlying problem. An intellectual tangent, say, but those are shorter-lived."

"Fair enough." He contemplated that old habit. "Can I say that I see the value in telling the story of my war but don't feel ready?"

"Certainly." God, I sounded smug. Then what was I doing there?

"But?"

"Of course I respect such a clear and reasonable statement, but will also tell you that stalling to fortify your defenses might just make it harder. You can say it quickly. It need not run to twenty-six volumes."

He laughed deeply, which electrified me. "Even so, now that you're here, I need time to catch up to the proposed enterprise."

"Of course." It was possible the facts had become tangled, or he wanted to sort for himself the proper lines of contention. Perhaps the memory was knotty and confusing. Or maybe he was still taking my measure.

The only trouble with quiet was that it left me in the seismic disruption I felt in his presence. I caught an occasional whisper of his scent, lemony and also burnt. That might have been tobacco, but I wondered if it wasn't also the shame I had seen the last time we met. I wished he would speak, to distract me from the urge to lay myself against him end to end.

He spoke without looking up. "Do you ever think that the central issue of our age is hypocrisy?"

I choked. "Every day of my life!"

He crimped his mouth. "We're awash in pieties but starved for honesty."

"Gamblers, cheats, and demagogues," I said.

"Yes," he whispered, watching me so intently I thought I might faint. My face flamed as I held his gaze, the right eye raging, the left soft and wandering. The color was a marvel, green in blue water, in which I began to float.

He said, "And what do you do when you discover it in yourself?"

I did feel faint now, and resisted the urge to put hands to my face. My voice was shaky as I said, "I remind myself that although I have to live in this world, I did not make it."

This surprised him and he broke our gaze. He sat back trying to relinquish some grave responsibility. I rested for a few breaths, then told a story.

My teacher Gwindolin Leger had been a nun for many decades. Ninety pounds of nerve and backbone, she was born way out in New Brunswick to French Canadians, took vows very young and lived in a cloister in the Laurentians, studied herb lore and became a healer. Seduced by a priest, she conceived a child, a girl who was taken from her. They punished Gwin but not the priest, and in her rage and mortification she took a vow of silence she kept for longer than she'd ever spoken. And then she had the change. She loved to tell this part. When her courses were over, she saw through it. Her whole life in service to a church that abused and reviled her for fertility. Her first words denounced the lies that trapped her, condemned the abbesses for kidnapping, pimping, and complicity. She packed her herbs and walked out, proclaiming Jesus came with her.

Asa's listening was so intent he appeared to be praying, but he said lightly, "So you're not pious, then?"

I laughed, realizing he hadn't flinched at the mention of adultery or menstruation, and perhaps I had chosen this story as a test. I said, "I'm painfully proper and circumspect, and I might say faithful, but cannot stomach hypocrisy."

Elliott had told him so, he said with one corner of his mouth curling. Could that gesture be inherited? He grew serious again. "She knew it was wrong, though, didn't she? The priest?"

Gwin wouldn't mind me telling him. "He wore the uniform of authority and she'd been taught obedience. She wasn't asked to reason for herself through right and wrong, she was told at every moment to obey."

"Indeed." He shivered. "Why did you tell me that story?"

I discovered my reasons as I answered him. "Because one good can impede another. Obedience to a worthy cause can eclipse your own self, or your humanity." I fumbled around for a moment, and then added, "Because some of us carry the costs of epidemic injustice, and sometimes we decide we've carried them long enough."

He stared at me in shock, beautiful mouth opening, but then dropped his head in regret. "I can't find the beginning."

Softly as I could I said, "Then begin at the end. What happened lately?"

He forced out aching words, "I failed a friend."

I waited a few breaths and said, "What friend?"

The name he pronounced with love and regret, James Harrison Bigelow, was familiar to me. A Union general, an engineer, and a cavalryman in Grant's command, a few weeks dead. Did Elliott not know or neglect to tell me the man was grieving?

Vanderpoel closed his eyes and I watched a wave of pain flow from his gut to his heart, felt him hold his breath. With dry lips he said, "He wrote but before his letter reached me, he put a gun to his head."

Sweet Jesus. He glanced at me and I hoped he saw compassion. Both he and Elliott failed to speak of it for shame. That sickened me for all of them.

"I cannot bear that I abandoned him."

They had unfinished business. "What would you tell him, if you could?"

He resisted it as play-acting and shook his head no.

"It's an artifice, but indulge me. Picture him. Perhaps you have a question."

At some point he changed his address from me to his friend. "He couldn't sleep, couldn't reconcile, couldn't suffer the memories. We said we'd visit Vicksburg and Chancellorsville and Chattanooga in ten years. We could have climbed Lookout Mountain, could have ridden stellar horses from Chattanooga to Birmingham and slept in feather beds. We could have said our prayers for the dead together."

I nodded along. "What memories followed him?"

"Chickamauga, mainly, and the siege of Chattanooga. The horses starving, the men too." He began to feel the pain of it, but I couldn't tell if it belonged to him or to Bigelow. It was all I could do to keep my seat and not put my arms around him. Blast Elliott, who could have done it, for leaving.

At my prompting he told the story of their friendship, the moments of connection and tenderness, the ways they suited one another. He spoke of a splendid horse Bigelow commandeered for him from a Confederate officer taken prisoner, a rainy campfire, a hotel room shared in crowded Washington, a rare empty train compartment where they could have slept but talked all night instead. "We spoke best in motion, both facing forward."

I said, "What was difficult between you?"

"During the war, nothing. Nothing at all. He was my best friend. I trusted him completely."

"And after?"

He hung his head. "It was harder. He came to New York and I dragged him around to parties and theater, introductions to this one and that, a victory round if you will. And the night before he left he said, 'I'd have preferred to sit by the fire and talk with you.' I missed it, his pain. I was dense as stone to it."

I wondered about the nature of Bigelow's regard. "He wanted to mourn, you wanted to celebrate. Both legitimate."

He wiped his face. "I failed him. My one true friend."

I shook my head and said, "That letter?"

He looked at me.

"He didn't come to you because he wanted to die and he knew you could talk him out of it."

His shoulders, jaw, and eyelids dropped. One sob sounded. When he spoke, his voice was gentler. Bigelow reminded him of his father, who had a related view of manhood. At a certain point

I stopped listening very well. I heard the contour and direction, but it was a lengthy conversation after a lengthy day of them. I knew what ailed Asa Vanderpoel: he was sad and lonely. His parents never taught him connection but he stumbled on some forms of it. My task was to lead him back to himself with great care not to lead him to me.

My mind wandered to more amiable subjects. His hands were lovely, half again as large as mine with long square-tipped fingers. He gestured rarely as he spoke, but when he did I was riveted. Strong, alive, and agile, they spoke of horsemanship, and sailing, and typesetting. His touch had been galvanic.

His body became more legible, the crossing and uncrossing of his legs a measure of various kinds of comfort. He had an immense capacity for learning, yet beneath this strength was a hesitation, a boyish aversion, a fear of errors.

As he spoke of his father and Jim Bigelow and their high-mindedness, I focused on his heart, and could sense the blocks around it, a dark encirclement, maybe his dead mother and her fragility. He had been a teen and grief swaddled it, Jim Bigelow now damaging the old bandage. Vanderpoel was speaking of the pressures to provide, to be a steadfast progenitor, but his weak eyes had precluded certain fields and experiences, his voracious curiosity returning as punishment. I told him reading did not damage eyes. It strained them temporarily, but some underlying condition likely caused his lifelong deficiency.

He asked my source for this, and I replied that researchers in Edinburgh had tested the proposition and published their results in *The Lancet*.

"You read *The Lancet*?"

"Among other journals." I asked him, "Whom do you love in the world above all others? Don't answer according to plan, answer truthfully. If you can't say it aloud, think it."

He said, "My daughter Portia."

I nodded.

"I love the others too, but she's special to me. She's the eldest." The dark ring around his heart flickered.

"Are you close?"

He crumpled. "When she was younger. She's fifteen now and turning her attention to music and languages."

"And you don't care for music and languages?"

"She's surpassed my ability to teach her. They've all gone to the continent for the right exposures." There was some bitterness in that distance.

"And you let them go."

He flashed anger. "I had no leg to stand on, having been absent for most of five years working for Union and building up the *Standard*." His self-reproach was defiant, but confused, interrogative. How to prove oneself when born to immense wealth?

"I see."

With self-loathing he said, "I was busy."

I knew the words to loosen his storms. It was simple and I paused to fix this image of his composure, regarding the fault lines of his life as if from a height.

He returned to the subject of his father, the high expectations, the admiration, the dismay at how quickly he seemed to forget his mother.

I asked, "What did he seek the second time?"

That angered him, as if his mother had not provided all a man could want. "That's a brutal question."

"No one speaks of your mother."

So off we went in this direction. She was indeed fragile. I might have asked about Elliott's mother a second time but was bone and soul weary. Had he noticed the one-way nature of our conversation? It was my own fault; I had come to help him, and my single stipulation had been to remain invisible.

I said, "Mr. Vanderpoel, I have only one real question for you. The losses of your parents and Mr. Bigelow weigh heavily on you now, but you are built to carry such burdens. So here's my question. Are you a feeling person?"

He looked at me as if I'd slapped him and then retreated so far into himself it felt he'd left the room entirely. He shook his head no, and returned his gaze to me. He would lash out or cave in and I expected caving. I let compassion flood me, a sense of reassurance that all was well, his life full to brimming, and grieving well within his capacity. I sent him mother love.

He received it and fell to weeping, great heaving sobs that swept up and passed through like the stormfront it was. I got up and moved to sit beside him, rubbed his back and shoulder, keeping my thoughts on comfort. His warmth beneath my hand, the fine wool jacket and silk weskit, the linen shirt and beneath it his skin and sinew, required some exertion on my part. My desire thrummed and I did what I could to keep it from him.

He fell toward me and lay in my lap, his arms wrapping his head as he let himself feel. This startled me so much I yanked my hands away. He let me hold his weight for one more moment before sitting up and apologizing.

"Strong emotion makes us into little children needing comfort," I said. "There's no shame in that."

He wanted to speak and exert some control over the situation but found nothing.

I moved just out of reach, but turned toward him. "You're a man of great feeling but have been taught to hide it, as men are taught to do. You must allow yourself to feel, to get in the habit of indulging grief or love or anger when they rise in you. It's all rather normal but you must give it room or it will twist on itself and plague you."

He breathed heavily and was halfway to hyperventilation. I guided him to put his head on his knees, which did not get far as his back was very stiff. No wonder. "It's a lot to feel all at once. You've been holding these deaths at bay for a long time and will feel flooded for a bit."

When he sat up, his face was transformed, as it had been that first night.

"I need to feel the war, finally," he said.

I waited for more.

"What you say about my parents is true, but the real burden that Jim's death brought back to me was the war. All that death and waste. All that starvation. He was so strong and it got the better of him."

I could only close my eyes and nod my head.

He said, "You know about that." A statement.

"On a different scale, I do."

He felt it all, and closed his eyes, exhausted now, seeming years older. Without looking at me he said, "You're very good at this."

"Thank you."

We sat a moment in silence, and when he tried to stand, he wavered, dizzy. I steadied him, and offered to walk him safely up the stairs. My hand in his left me flushed and askew.

I last remembered drowsing in a chair by his bed and woke to morning, my head on Asa's chest, his arms around me. I glanced down and found I was fully clothed and above the blanket. My near view of his collar bones brought a sharp intake of shared air. He smelled of tobacco, that distinctive lemon, and velvety cognac. The rank note, his hell night, had burnt out. At least I had not failed there.

This was a fool's indiscretion but here I was, in my exhaustion having climbed on, my character vanishing. Was I invited? Perhaps it was not farcical romance or physical attraction but a friend I clung to, a comfort and an admiration. Except I'd sworn to hide my occupation. I could not be here.

I lifted my eyes to his face, and found him awake and stunned as I was to see where I lay.

I whispered, "Good morning," backing away. He held tighter for a second, pulling me in, but let go and sat up, staring. I crept backwards toward the door.

He said, "I feel I've been asleep for years." He touched his abdomen with both hands and looked down for two breaths, assessing, then his astonished gaze swung back up to me. "Thank you."

I stopped and stood straighter. "You're welcome. I apologize for falling asleep here."

"Don't."

"I'll leave you to yourself, then."

"Must you go?"

Easing, I said, "Be careful today. You're feeling very free, and I hope you enjoy it. But I beg you to make no decisions, take no new courses of action, until you're under better regulation."

He stood, using his height. "Please tell me your name."

I put my hand on the doorknob and knew I should leave without delay.

He said, "For heaven's sake, you know me better than any soul alive, may I not know who you are?"

His tone was half insistence and half grief. I felt my face darken and a spike of rage. "I should have been a professor of medicine, but was born to immigrants, a woman, and orphaned young." I did not say, unprotected and forthright, I was preyed upon, and maimed. "I made myself useful. My real name means nothing to anyone." As I said it I remembered that wasn't true.

I might as well have run him through with a blade. He whispered, "Forgive me."

I said, "I'm sorry, I meant no commentary on you, sir. I am fit and you are . . . sorted."

"Please call me Asa."

"No, for your own good."

"That cannot be true."

"I may be the greatest hypocrite you've ever met, if by necessity." I shut the door behind me.

The staff posed a far greater threat than the patients. One orderly always found a way to rub up against the nurses. I carried scissors.

But for physical menace, the worst was Dr. Schaeffer. He and his friend Dr. Lund were the staff obstetricians, mysteriously, since they knew little of it. The field was a backwater where incompetents could be marooned. They were graduates of the Medical School of Maine in Brunswick, but only deep-pocketed fathers could explain that fiasco. At that time, the degree consisted of two sixteen-week terms.

The best way to avoid Schaeffer's hands was to stay out of reach, which wasn't always possible when we worked together. He touched my bottom, my neck, and often pulled my hair out of my cap. Protests made him laugh. I dreamt of kicking his manhood but knew the harm would come mostly to me. All the nurses had tricks for managing him, Annalee a devotee of feminine guile.

One day I saw him looming over a girl from the laundry. She was part Negro, with toffee skin, and tiny, no more than twelve, trembling as he cornered her at a bend in the hallway. I stopped myself from charging in, and tried to be both proper and pleasing, always a tippy equation, just sweet enough to correct his behavior without provoking him.

I skated up, sunny and brisk. "Is there some problem with the laundry, Dr. Schaeffer?"

"There's no problem, Nurse, we're old friends."

"Well, you seem to be frightening her. Come," I said to the girl, and held out my hand.

She took it and we sped toward the busier central hallway.

"You all right?"

"Yes ma'am, thank you."

I opened the door to the main supply closet, and let her in, closing it behind us. "What's your name?"

"Wren Harrison, ma'am."

"Does he often bother you?"

She swallowed. "It's not the first time, ma'am."

"You don't have to ma'am me in here. Let me know if he does it again. You shouldn't have to suffer that, and don't ever let him get you alone."

"Thank you." When she looked up, her pretty brown eyes were shy and warm.

EIGHT

I had just fallen asleep when Jodie knocked, shouting, "Doc! Please come right away." Queasy from the timing, I opened the door. Martin Mitchell had brought a girl who was gravely wounded.

"If she's breathing, check her for bleeding. I'll be right there." I did not relish greeting Martin in my shift. As Jodie tore back down the stairs, I heard the girl cry out in pain. It was an animal sound suggesting she was beyond remedy. Martin had never brought a patient before.

The girl lay on her side, ashen and quiet now. It was Catherine Farnsworth.

"Officer," I said, as I felt her pulse and opened her eyes one at a time. "Have you already explained?"

"Awfully sorry, Doc, but I thought you'd want to see her."

"What happened?"

"I guess she made a run for it, and they chased her. She fought back and was run over by a big cart."

"Mother of God!" I said. "When?"

Nina was cutting away her torn and filthy skirt.

Martin said, "Couple of days ago."

I gave him a horrified look and shook my head. "Wait outside."

Nina and Jodie sliced through good homespun. I drew a chair up to the girl's face and began to wash her. "Catherine," I said a bit loudly, "It's Doc. We're going to take care of you and treat these injuries, all right?"

Her eyelids trembled but she did not appear to see. I wiped her face and said, "I'm so sorry this happened to you. We'll do all we can."

Tears began to drip sideways over her nose and into her ear, and I dabbed them. She was thinner than I'd last seen her. One of her hands was limp and broken, and I sickened seeing the pale patches of vitiligo around her wrist and thumb that had kept her from our employ. I took her other hand, and she clamped my fingers as a spasm of pain went through her, an arch of the back and a roll away from me, as if to put pressure into her right side, but the movement made it worse and she whimpered. A crushed kidney and a cracked lumbar vertebra? Nina reported massive contusions to the left leg, and a deep gash above the knee. When they cut the dress from her back I saw a clear track from the wheel, suggesting several broken ribs. I stood to follow it around and saw where it rolled over that kidney. A smell drew me lower. Her thighs were smeared with semen that was newer than a couple of days old. I pointed to be sure Jodie and Nina saw. "Bathe her, bandage that hand and any wounds, and try to get some water into her. No laudanum yet." I might have stitched the thigh but it wasn't bleeding much and she didn't need any more pain. I would give her morphine, but not yet.

I came back to her face. "Catherine, sweetheart, can you tell me where you're from? Where is your family?"

She whispered, "Bethel," but cried from the pressure of the exhale.

"Bethel," I said, but there were many towns of that name. "I'm going to name a few states and when I say the right one, squeeze my hand." I squeezed hers and said, "New York, Connecticut, Vermont, New Jersey, Pennsylvania." Here she squeezed. "Your family is in Bethel, Pennsylvania?" She squeezed again. "Thank you. You're a brave girl, Catherine. Quite the heroine. You did well to fight back and I'm so sorry they hurt you."

Her breathing was calmer now but I heard a rasp in her lung, perhaps punctured by a broken rib. Her tears kept flowing. I remembered another girl, a street harlot who'd been beaten by a gang during the Draft Riots, who died in my lap while we hunkered in the clinic basement.

Betsy, who had apparently been at the Double, brought in cups of tea. "Vivie came back with me."

I was annoyed until I remembered that Catherine fought her abductors. Vivie should see what it cost her. "All right," I said, and she came into the doorway, standing straight, hands clasped in front of her.

I stood. "This is Catherine Farnsworth."

Vivie sat where I had been and took Catherine's hand from mine. "Oh but you're cold," she said, and pulled the blanket closer around her. Nina, who had finished drying her feet, put a second blanket over her.

"If you'll sit with her a minute, I'll speak to Officer Mitchell."

He was outside smoking. I said, "Jesus, Martin." He threw his smoke into the street and kicked the sidewalk, ready to punch something.

He told the story as coldly as he could. She was running east on Fourteenth Street when two men caught up and took her arms from either side. One was tall, dark, and bearded, the other young and fairer. She screamed for help with dozens of people in sight but no one intervened. They tried to stuff her into their cart but she fought them, and it started moving before she was in. She fell under the back wheel as they drove but her skirt got caught and she was dragged a ways before they could stop the horses. A street cop arrived and asked what happened, and the slavers told him she was a crazy whore who dove under the wheel, and took off. The cop arrested her.

Some bystanders shook themselves and said they saw it differently, which made him mad. He manhandled her, and when she collapsed on the sidewalk he roughed her up more. They brought a wagon to take her to the station and stuck her in with the drunks. They dithered for days about medical attention until Martin came on duty and said he would bring her to the clinic.

I said, "What's the name of that street cop?"

He had reasons for not telling me.

"He raped her."

"What?" Martin looked well and truly shocked.

"In the wagon, I assume. Unless it happened at the station. Do me a favor."

"What?"

"Slit his throat."

He bit his lips.

"She's from Bethel, Pennsylvania. Tell him if he doesn't pay for the transport of her body, I'll go to the papers."

"She's dead?"

"Not yet."

"If I still have a job and no one slits my throat, we'll figure something out. Let's live to fight another day."

"And the girls they take in the meantime?"

"I don't know what to tell you."

"You want to sit with Catherine while she dies?"

"Sorry I did this to you."

I rounded on him. "It's sickening, but don't you be sorry for me. Tell your captain."

"He knows. I gotta go."

"Find the damned crib!" I shouted after him, and the plaintive look he threw back at me as he charged away said he knew where it was, had long known. Of course he had. But he couldn't march in there alone to break it up and hope to live. He was waiting for them to make a mistake. Well, he had brought me a tragedy and maybe the long-awaited weapon.

I hoped Catherine might be able to tell me where it was, but she was never again lucid. I sent Vivie back to the Double. "You're sweet but I don't want you to see what comes next."

"Doc," she said, but then words failed her. I walked her into the hall and put my arms around her.

I said, "She's a brave girl, as are you. They shackled you for a reason." I took the hand whose wrist was ringed with shiny scars. "This is your badge of honor, the evidence of your resistance and your courage."

She rubbed that wrist and nodded, tears falling. Betsy walked her back to the Double.

We stroked Catherine's head and shoulders, listened to her cries and whimpers, hummed and sang to her and always sat close by. Her heart was strong. I guessed her family would recognize the way she bore her shock and pain, a kind of sweet strain and disgruntled bother. A valiant girl, moving inward. When her organs began to fail, I gave her an injection. She died around 9 a.m.

When a wagon came to collect her, the precinct captain came along. He had been to the house before, and meant to placate me.

Thinking of Martin, I stayed calm. "I don't know that cop's name, but we both know that he raped a dying girl."

"That could have been anyone."

"It happened at your precinct."

He glanced at me, trying to show he had some heart.

I said, my voice low and shaking. "She was kidnapped months ago, and had the courage to free herself. Instead of helping her, this miscreant arrested her and raped her. What the everloving hell, Captain."

He sighed. "He's connected."

"No kidding," I said. In a desperate ploy, I said, "It's a nice arrangement, his post near the crib." What did I think I could do if I learned the address, send a squad of porters over?

He didn't respond in any way, but stood beside me as her body was carried out.

I made sure Ellen, Jodie, and Betsy were all right in the clinic, then dragged myself up the stairs spilling quiet tears and then heaving great sobs for Catherine and all the girls who'd done nothing to deserve such reckless violation. I put a cold cloth to my face to prepare for the dozens of other girls needing care that day, and tried to be glad Catherine landed with us, that in the end she met loving hands and mercy, but she deserved so much more. I trudged to the Double kitchen for coffee and faced down a slice of sweetbread with chestnuts, chewed without taste or appetite, and felt a quiet dissolution. People will say they snap or break, but I felt an old scaffold built to make the best of the hand I'd been dealt crumble to dust under my feet. Weak voices pled, "these things happen," or "man is born to trouble as the sparks fly upward," but I couldn't swallow Catherine Farnsworth's death. I had sewn and medicated and held countless girls through a war against their dignity, their personhood and autonomy, and it was never enough. The war was always escalating.

Vivie came in and pulled a chair close to hold me while I wept, and Bert put his arms around both of us, and then Perlie came in and said, "Lord above, what's happened?"

Vivie said, "Doc is sad."

I pulled myself partway together, and they all sat close around the table. Perlie watched me, waiting. I said, "A girl died at the clinic this morning."

"Lord help us all. Anyone we know?"

"Catherine Farnsworth, the girl we turned down, who was kidnapped."

"Oh no, Doc," Perlie said. "Bad?"

"Beyond imagining." I looked at her, my tears streaming.

"That's it," she said, slapping the table. "You need to get out of here. The further, the better."

I was in no shape to treat anyone, it was true, but where would this not weigh on me? Vivie said, "Is there anyplace in this city to go ice skating?"

The days had been unusually clear and cold for November, and all New York waited for the ponds to freeze. The porters never tired of debating the East River, which had frozen in the brutal winter of 1866–67, and if it was possible to skate before December. Ponds froze faster, the shallower the better. Corabelle loved the club at Mulvihill's Pond, but everyone agreed that for real New York skating, you had to go to Union Pond in Williamsburg, Brooklyn. We took a chance. For some minutes there was a search of the house for skates and the packing of a picnic basket, and soon I found myself bundled into a carriage with Vivie, Corabelle, and Perlie, with Willy Schor and another porter called Bud Bean riding on the back. We made our way to the ferry dock on the East River at Twenty-Third Street.

I had not seen an expanse of water in many months. Breathing sea air was a bit dizzying, my childhood lurking in the margins between land and water, and water and sky. Beside the odd square ferryboat, a white skiff tugged at its painter. For a moment I felt ten years old, keyed up and buoyed, my own little dinghy loaded with lunch and a net and bucket for the tide pools. I studied the river's brown and gray reflections, the endless tug and chase of light even on this filthy dockside entrancing. Water did this to me, both calmed and agitated.

On the Brooklyn side we took an omnibus from the dock to the aqueduct along the pond where dozens of skaters made their rounds. Without speaking we split into twos and threes. I stood on shaky legs while Vivie and Cora glided off like fish tossed back to the sea, Willy and Bud's eyes watchful. I had learned to skate as a child and had pretty good balance but never trusted the speed. My one fancy was to pivot front to back, and once warm I could skate backwards nearly as well as forwards. The exertion, the satisfying slice of blade across ice, wind and sun on my face, were all balms and I gave myself over. The skill came back to me. The rhythm of my shifting weight, the lengthening of each side again and again, lulled me and revealed how much I needed sleep, a scratchy void where strength should be. Catherine Farnsworth and how many others were forever lost to skating. When I tipped toward that precipice, Vivie took my hand and spun me or just squeezed.

She was a natural, sailing here and there between all of us. I'd never seen her so happy. She took jumps and spins, and stole Willy's hat, taking off for a chase. I wished she wouldn't as it drew attention as flirting, but inside myself I relented. She was newly healed and should enjoy it. So many griefs picked at me.

A childhood memory floated up of a nameless little beaver pond off the Parker River in Newbury one Christmas Eve when a mob of kids with shovels cleared it of snow. Mothers poured hot cider and fathers stoked pondside fires. After church we played the world's messiest hockey game, everyone sailing into the banks for fun. My distance from my parents by that pond had never been greater. Any life they imagined for me was sunk deep. I still preferred my current life to servitude at Portland Hospital, but not perhaps to midwifery in partnership with my mother. Perlie and I made several circles arm in arm, and I told her I was thinking of them.

"Me too," she said. "My mama was afraid of falling in."

We kept to silence, such a rare treat for each of us to say nothing, listen to nothing, answer to nothing. I was grateful she pried me free of my ruts that day.

Both caregivers, Perlie and I never figured out how to be ourselves around each other. We had a lot of affection but it was careful. We deferred at the wrong times. She wanted to mother me and I wanted to spoil her. I tried talking to her about it once, asked if we could arrange anything differently to suit her better.

"I like the back of the house," she said, meaning the work clients never saw.

"Yes, but is there anything about the house you'd change?"

She eyed me like I was drunk. "I'd say if I thought so, you don't have to ask special." She loved bringing girls off the street and into jobs where they were treated with respect. I gave her extravagant gifts—kid gloves and embroidered bed linen and a leather satchel to take when she visited a niece in Syracuse.

I once asked her if she knew why they'd been unable to conceive, and offered to examine her.

"Where's the need for that?" she said.

"Could be Israel's trouble but there are simple matters to treat in a woman."

"I'm near forty years old, what's the point? And there's naught wrong with Israel. I've never been right that way, my courses were never right." She'd been hungry as a child. "You have some tricks but I don't need anyone that far up my business."

Laughter dispelled that unease. Not too many people made me feel I was letting myself down, but Perlie was one. I loved her but often felt wrong-footed. On that day though, circling Union

Pond, we lined up and made our way in symmetry. I held her arm right next to me.

When she wanted to rest, I said I'd take one more turn, but first I hugged her good and hard. Naturally, on that last lap I hit a runnel in the ice at the wrong angle and was falling, thinking how predictable. One knee took the worst, and I slid to full prostration, tugging at my splaying skirts and imagined Asa Vanderpoel observing my buffoonery.

Next I knew, Bud and Willy had hauled me to my feet. I played no part in that repositioning and laughed with relief.

"Very graceful," I said.

Willy deposited me on the bench next to Perlie and I rubbed my knee.

She said, "You all right?"

"I feel a bit unhinged."

"Thank God," she said. "Those hinges been needing oil for some time now."

What could I do but laugh? A lightness came over me then, half love for her and the day out, half exhaustion. We ate ham sandwiches and watched the youngsters make their rounds as I edged my way to the question of Vanderpoel. I liked how he kept up with me. That he could joke when threatened. That his face was so stunning and alive and imperfect and brimming with intelligence. The first thing I offered him was a lie and he sliced right through it. The death of his friend brought the whole weight of the war back to him, and he had no one to talk to. I pictured that enthralling mouth and felt a melting and a choking, a dizzying hopeless madness of longing unlike anything I'd borne before. So many disjunctions and constraints stood between us, or rather, they encircled me.

"Perlie," I said, "Forgive the impertinence, but is it harder being a woman or being a Negro?"

She stared in shock and started laughing. What began as a series of chuckles grew into shoulder-shaking hoots that she kept quiet with her hand over her mouth, and tittering hiccoughs where she dried her eyes and shook her head. I laughed along with her, my directness the only humor I could see.

"What on earth made you ask me that?"

I took some breaths. "I'm sitting here thinking how women are punished and blamed for our gifts, for the most valuable parts of ourselves. It's all beaten out of us. It's the world's most grievous failure: the worst squandering, and the worst betrayal. But it's not worse than slavery. It's not worse than race prejudice."

She frowned, closed her eyes and rocked like she was reading scripture. "It's not a contest, my girl. Plenty of injustice to go around."

"Amen. But I wondered, for you, if one cut deeper."

"Some days one or the other," she said. "I feel one kinship with black men and another with white women. Young black girls are special to me, as you well know."

"And you're a gift to them."

Perlie said, "When I was younger, I might have said I felt safer with women. But now I'm older and not so much in danger that way, I will say I feel more myself among Negroes."

I held her hand. "That makes sense. Thank you. I'm sorry for being so blunt."

The look she gave me began as indulgence, and then sank deeper. She saw something new perhaps, and nodded. Before either of us could speak, the youngsters circled up, and we agreed it was time to leave. The array of pink clouds to the west was a joy and a reprieve.

Asa Vanderpoel followed me then. He watched me walk up the boulevard and take the omnibus. He saw me reckon with water on the ferry and feel ungodly weary, and watched me fall asleep in the carriage in the cross-town traffic and dream of girls bleeding clear to the horizon.

After twelve hours of sleep, I found the need to preserve my own anonymity mattered less than making a furious noise about Catherine's death. Ciara gave me a newspaper row address for Junius Henri Browne, the journalist I'd last seen at the Ball. Perhaps his incarceration with the Confederates had made him sensitive to abduction. We arranged an appointment for one morning when I would be downtown banking.

Junius awaited me in the lobby. "Welcome, Doc. I thought I'd meet you, as not all the natives are domesticated." Office doors advertised importers, investigators, attorneys.

I asked what he was working on.

"A big fat compendium about New York." He wrote books now, and an occasional article. "Cornelius Vanderbilt to the Five Points Brewery, and everything in between."

As if one volume could encompass it. "Good luck with that. What will you call it?"

"*The Great Metropolis.*" I was glad he was thinking at such scale but doubted I would approve its portrayal of vice or women.

When we settled in his two rooms piled neatly with books and papers, he asked if I had come with a story. He was disgusted by Catherine Farnsworth's death.

"Tragic," he said, "in the particulars, and revolting in the implications. I can't say it surprises me, given Tammany's power grab. Let me ask you though, what's your intention in getting it out?"

"A big stick in the spokes of this new ring."

"Tripping up the competition?"

"They're not my competition," I said.

"Aren't they? If Tammany wants to take over prostitution, they'll squeeze you out."

He was right, in the end. It would all go to the pimps and the procurers. My choice would be to cooperate or close, unless I could undermine their plans, which Junius saw as my self-interest. And here I thought I was protecting girls, and women's chance to profit from their own exploitation. "Will you get into it?"

"It's poking a hornet's nest, and to mix all the metaphors, it's not my ox being gored."

I frowned. Of course not. I said, "I hoped you'd have sympathy for the abducted girls. No one works on their behalf."

"I do have sympathy, but I'm on deadline for this book."

How long could it take? "It's the story of one girl, on one morning. I'd be so grateful, Junius." This I said with some import, meaning consideration at the Double. Despite my businesslike tone, I saw a flicker of shock on his face that I would offer myself before he realized his mistake. He was weighing it now, so I said, "There's no one in the city who can stop Tammany's worst excesses except the press."

He said, "I have no desire to live dangerously."

That was fair. Nor did I. "So publish anonymously, and I'll pay you. What's the usual rate for a story along these lines from a freelance?"

"Not enough," he said, "A dollar an inch."

I saw why he wrote books. "I'll pay you fifty dollars if you get it into a paper with a big circulation. And a free night at the house to celebrate."

He was painfully tempted.

"It's a big story, Junius. Be a player in the great metropolis."

"Bah," he said. "Looks like I'll be going to Bethel, Pennsylvania. Lucky for you it's on the Pittsburgh line because I don't go overland for anybody."

I thanked him sincerely. "Talk to Martin Mitchell before you go. I'll tell him to come see you because walking into that station is not advised. I'd love for you to name the copper."

He asked if I cared what paper carried it. "The reputable dailies won't touch it, not until someone else breaks the scandal. A flash paper might be strategic." These were scandal rags catering to sporting men, glorifying the libertine, full of eroticism but hostile to women, Negroes, and Jews.

"Would that be enough to get it into a daily?"

"Maybe." He mentioned the *National Police Gazette*, which was only halfway obscene. They ran a feature called "Lives of the Felons," maybe they could start one on lives of the victims.

Willow thought better of an outing to Hart Island, the potter's field where her mother lay. She preferred to remember her at the Double, where the food and flowers would have made her mother cry with joy.

We made a chapel in the ballroom, rows of chairs and two massive vases of white gladioli. Erroll played hymns. I stood and said, "We gather to remember Margaret Emma Lynch Reilly, to celebrate her life and speed her on her way to paradise. For Maggie and for her daughter Emma whom we call Willow, we mark sad endings and celebrate new beginnings."

Willow wore a simple frock with one underskirt and no cage crinoline. She'd taken well to trousers but thought her mother would not approve for this occasion.

She stood and walked to the front, trembling but not dissembling. "So my mother killed my father and then died quick in prison, but that's not what I want to talk about today. She was a good person with no other options."

The girls cried out a round of "Amen!" and "Tell it!"

"When I was little she was always working. She was funny and had a good word for everyone most days. She'd bring back trash from the street and transform it into useful things, a two-legged table she propped on the wall, a giant cable spool she rolled home and took apart for benches and stools she sold to neighbors. And her sweet tooth. She loved candy, especially candied nuts like pralines, and once ate butterscotch ice cream that she said tasted like everything good in your life happening all at once. Years of being poor and afraid had worn her down, but she always protected me."

Old South Church in Newburyport flickered into my mind's eye, the sharp-edged pews and overhanging balconies, my own mother gone too soon and the rituals cold and paltry. I had cried more for Gwin, who taught me grieving.

In five minutes, Willow had covered all the topics she'd prepared. She grew teary standing there in silence.

Vivie said, "Willow, could she read?"

They'd discussed this before. "She wanted to but never learned, so she asked a woman in the building if she would teach us. Cara and her baby Rufus. We learned the alphabet all together and would read out signs from storefronts and vans, would scrounge handbills and newspapers when we could. When he was two, Rufus could say all the letters."

"Amazing," said Ciara, and we all agreed. "How old were you?"

"Seven or eight. She could sew anything. She could do men's shirts all day and all night if she had a candle."

And her husband drank it all up.

"Where was she from?" asked Meg.

"A place called Carndonagh. They were poor and left in the Great Famine."

Erroll began a sweet melody, and Willow sat down looking settled.

Bert had laid out trays of cakes and cookies in the dining room, and a massive bowl of pralines. The girls told stories of grandmas and aunties who gave them treats when their overworked mothers were spent, took them for walks in the park or down the lane, the friends' parents' kitchens, their dogs and cats, their gentle questions about little girls' likes and dislikes. I spoke of the Horn family kitchen, the home of my childhood friend Charlotte whose parents let me stay when I couldn't face a long night with my father. The raising of children not done by parents, from the viewpoint of the children. I watched Vivie, who was fully on her feet now and radiant. It was past time to send her away, but my feet were dragging.

More than a week had passed since Elliott left me at Asa's. He arrived around seven one evening and found me in the kitchen eating a toasted cheese sandwich.

"Hello sunshine," I said, still angry, though he too had a bone to pick.

He sat down. "Aren't you the dark horse."

I said we needed privacy to talk about what had happened that night at Gramercy Park with Asa, but added, "I do remember you promising most faithfully to stay in the room, and yet you left the moment we arrived."

He looked shocked. "I'd forgotten that."

"Of course you did," I said, with some heat. I brought my plate to the sink and poured myself a glass of cider, offering him nothing. Go to the library, the caucus? I didn't want to be in the house for this.

He followed me through the garden and up the stairs to my flat. When the door closed, he huffed, "You spent the night with him?"

"You bloody hypocrite," I said, "I spent the night with him *fully clothed*. Nursing is a twenty-four hour occupation, idiot. You were supposed to do the physical part."

"Well, he's obsessed with you, and not the nurse."

I was swamped by regret. Asa's regard was dangerous to us both.

"He hounds me daily to bring you back or tell him who you are."

In anger, I mimicked Elliott. "'Please come, I'm begging you. You're the only one who can help him!'"

"All right, all right! Did you have to be so good at it?"

I loathed him at that moment: his childishness, his jealousy, his long use of me for his own needs. "I did exactly what you wanted and if you can keep a secret, it's a great success."

He fiddled with his gloves, unhappy with himself, and stood up. "You were the one person who didn't think Asa was the better man." He drew a letter from his pocket and handed it to me. "This is my last act as go-between. Contact him or not, but leave me out of it."

I set the letter next to me.

"You won't read it?"

"Later."

He eased a bit. "He's desperate."

I said, "He confided in me and is now worried that his secrets are abroad with a stranger."

"No. He's like an addict, pacing around begging."

That picture pained me. Well, I could end his suffering. "If I do see him, it'll be to tell him the truth."

Elliott looked sad now. "Yes. They think you're one thing and blame you when they find you're another."

I'd never made such a confession, but smelled some chance Elliott kept my secret in order to lord it over his brother.

"Tell me something," he said, still standing like he was about to leave. "Did you ever think we could be happy together?"

After ten years he brought himself to speak of our attraction only because he was jealous of his own brother. I thought it Shakespearean and told him so. "A brief affair was never worth the friendship."

He said, "Do you love him?"

I said, "I love you, so get out before you ruin it."

He finally spoke in an unguarded way. "It's okay if you do. I love him too."

I stopped breathing. "Forbidden amours are not for me."

This shocked him. "Forbidden how? Not his wife."

"Yes his wife, and his children, and his good name."

"My God, Doc, you don't think Asa Vanderpoel could take a mistress and keep his good name? Half the clergy in New York have mistresses."

It was so simple. A man takes a mistress, with no thought to whom is taken even if your best friend sits before you or what it might mean to her. Never mind the overwhelming weight of shame and stigma, no matter how unjust or unearned. I didn't want that for Asa, even if he would risk it for himself. I knew how it would end, and whom he would blame.

He said, "Caro left him."

"Doesn't matter." Did it?

"Sometimes," he said, like he was leveling a weapon, "I think you consider all men instrumental. It's like we're not fully human to you."

Laughter blasted out of me, and then I stared at him in gleeful astonishment. "Oh, you feel insufficiently appreciated, do you?" I continued laughing. "As you range everywhere in the world with every privilege and opportunity open to you." I was choking on hilarity. "So sadly misunderstood."

He rolled his eyes and offered a small smile of concession, but still felt aggrieved.

Whatever else he said, I didn't hear it. When he left I sat breathing, holding Asa's attachment as consolation and attainment. How could I break it? I opened the letter. His hand was brisk and efficient.

Dear Miss Warren,

May I offer the most profound thanks to you for twice coming to my home and helping me to fathom my own mind and heart. I feel restored, and more. I am filled with gratitude and compassion for others in their own struggles with death. While I mourn my friend, I can consider his choices as they were without the fog of my own guilt.

Aware that I ask too much, I must beg to see you again. If Elliott felt free to share your address I would come to you. You must understand how difficult it is not to know the identity of my savior, though I feel secure in your character and discretion. The healer in you would not leave this so unfinished, would she? Please, please, may I see you?

Yours,

Asa Vanderpoel

The second please went straight through me.

Meg reported that a new client wanted a word with me.

"Who is he?"

"The name is Singer."

I sighed and gestured for her to take the lead. Mr. Singer appeared to be a cultivated man in his thirties.

When Meg had introduced us and departed, Singer said, "There's a question I've long pondered, and I believe you may hold the answer, Miss Hastings."

"Please." I gestured to a pair of chairs set in an alcove in the salon, in case it was a delicate matter.

Seated, he said, "My brother is a physician at Women's Hospital."

No surprise he wouldn't call me Doc. The medical staff of Women's Hospital was all male. The founder, James Marion Sims, was a surgeon famous for inventing the silver suture technique that revolutionized vaginal repair, that I used myself. "He must be very accomplished."

"Yes. He met a woman who was visiting a patient at the hospital. This visitor claimed to have had a particular surgery performed by a brothel nurse. My brother discounted it, and Dr. Sims was quite offended, actually, that this woman would compare what could be done in a brothel to what they do at the hospital. Have you ever heard of surgeries being performed by your colleagues?"

The temptation to tell him he was an idiot was strong. "Do you refer to a fistula repair, Mr. Singer?" Sims had made his breakthrough while working on slave women in Alabama, without anesthesia. He was celebrated far and wide.

"Yes. The woman said she birthed a large infant."

"What else did the distinguished doctors say to this woman, apart from calling her a liar?"

"They could hardly demand to perform an examination." Singer, I saw now, was a bit bleary with drink. "There was no way to verify her claim."

"And why does this story interest you?"

"It amuses me. They set such store upon their expertise, and were outraged that a brothel nurse might be their equal."

He was seeking to humiliate his brother with the likes of me. "I see." My gut was tight.

"Forgive me, do I offend?"

I folded my hands over my abdomen and spoke quietly. "I would guess the woman in question was a patient of my own, Mr. Singer. Although many brothel nurses do surgeries, chiefly abortions, I believe I am the only one in New York doing fistula repair. I've done upwards of two-hundred procedures since 1855, and have failed about twenty times. But the patients who come to me are not society ladies who have endured protracted childbirth. They are victims of rape, violent gang rape generally, and prostitutes who have suffered objects—bottles, broom handles, knives—thrust into their bodies with the intent to shred and kill. My procedures are on average more complex and difficult than those done on the respectable ladies at Women's, where they would be turned away as unworthy of care, and never make it into the literature. I would take it as a favor, Mr. Singer, if you would keep this information to yourself. I would not welcome scrutiny of my practice, least of all from Dr. Sims."

His slack-jawed astonishment did not justify my recklessness, but it was gratifying. Some days resentment over my invisibility just erupted. I supposed I would pay for it.

"Oh," he said, flummoxed.

"Does that answer your question?"

"Well, I suppose I must consider it."

"If you will excuse me, Mr. Singer, it's a busy evening."

I'd been working too many hours and nearly fell asleep while treating a young mother in pain from a plugged milk duct. I was applying hot compresses and delicate massage to dislodge the original blockage. The baby was fussing so I held him in one arm and kneaded the kink in his food supply with the other. Gradually I became aware of a hubbub outside. Sometimes a line formed outside the clinic that in winter we wound down the alley beside the building out of the wind, lighting braziers when it was truly frigid. I could hear laughing and shouting, and I rushed a bit giving this mother a tincture and instructions.

The clinic was strangely empty. I poked my head outside and saw a fantastical St. Nicholas figure in a fuzzy red coat, a white cotton beard, and slippers that curled up at the toes. My first thought was Elliott but I saw another character, an elf with tiny boots and beaded hat pushing a cart full of cakes who had the shape of Lisa Webber of the Belles. Saint Lydia! Each woman in line got a coin from Santa and an elf cake.

When all the gifts had been delivered, Lydia launched into "Jolly Old St. Nicholas." Everyone went still and breathless with the magnitude of her voice, and then cheered and stomped their feet. I watched the line of patients brighten and thought it was the best medicine they would get that day. Lydia and Lisa waved happy goodbyes to all, and I beckoned them inside. Nina promised the women in the line we'd get to them as soon as we could.

Upstairs I offered tea. "You're too kind," I told them as they removed hats and beards and loosened jackets.

"This is lovely," said Lydia, surveying my parlor, particularly the pillows on the floor by the fire. "Very Turkish."

She spun the Santa hat in her hands. "We found these in our rehearsal space, and one thing led to another. Thought we'd spread a little cheer. John hates it when I give away money." They laughed.

They were rehearsing a show to debut in the new year called *Ernani, or the Horn of a Dilemma*. It was the tale of a Spanish outlaw by Victor Hugo, later made into an opera by Verdi.

When that topic ran out, Lisa said, "We have another reason for coming, Doc. My voice has been tricky, and we hoped you could have a look."

"Certainly." All singers feared nodes or lesions on their vocal cords and she would not want the theater world to know. A quick exam revealed that she had swollen adenoids, the uppermost tonsils. I praised her pain tolerance, performing in that state. She was relieved to hear it was not ruinous. I gave her treatment options from gargling and rest to extraction.

"Will it get worse?" Lydia asked.

"A few days off will tell the difference."

Lisa asked if I could do the surgery.

"You can afford better," I said. "Someone who does it constantly."

Downstairs I made her a gargling solution and Lydia said they'd let me get back to fixing up the lovelies in the queue. "We'll try to come back before Christmas. You're a peach, Doc," she said and kissed my cheeks.

Lifted and grateful, I said, "You're the whole bowl of cherries!"

My bedroom faced Twenty-Fifth Street and my parlor faced the garden, a reversal of the usual arrangement, so the Double staff could see if my parlor light was on. I stood in a shadow beside the bedroom window watching the street, the occasional cart or carriage, men coming and going from neighborhood bagnios. I closed the drapes and sat to contemplate Asa's letter and the question of shame.

I carried the word "unashamed" like a mental talisman, whispered it to myself as I entered certain rooms. An unashamed woman is, however, a scant hair's breadth from shameless, a wanton harridan.

Shame actually has many opposites. Unashamed and shameless with their pitching, wobbling moral weight, of course. But also satisfaction—knowing that you've done well enough—and pride—knowing that you've done well indeed. That was my medicine, but all women swim in shame, respectable or not, proud or not. We drown in the guilt of desire and procreation. An unashamed or satisfied or proud woman invites censure and a smart shove back into that body of water.

In his ignorance, Asa's letter addressed me as if I had no more shame than he did. I tried to tell him as I left that morning with a remark about my own hypocrisy. Presented with my identity, he might lash out or shove me, or he might deny the water existed. My attraction to him, this heat, this rush of blood, was the original shame, and I so rarely felt it. I sat prim as ever, head on my hand, a primordial ache for him up and down my body, and a proud mind trying to ignore, quash, and skirt it. For his sake. For mine.

He had yet to meet me. For his desire, in his ignorance, I felt pride and resentment equally, which was a pretty good description of shamelessness. Any way forward for us wound through a maze of shame. Our intimacy would reek of it, painted so plainly on me. And he knew only half the city he lived in.

I sat in my room and felt myself not telling him, not speaking. I told myself I was not silenced, I was choosing to be quiet. I lived in that difference. People believe that storytelling has the power to dissolve shame and sorrow, and for some that's true. I've preached it myself to those like Asa choking on their own feelings.

But not all histories must become stories. You stop telling some if you ever did. Redemption is not universal; people break beyond repair all the time and it does no good to repeat the injury like an incantation. This is not a failure of nerve, no matter what some may think or say.

This quiet of mine was not shame or neglect or forgetting,

familiar as they were. Quiet is not always silence. Some memories lay dormant for a long time, or remain unspoken. Sometimes they stir.

It was cruel to let him wonder, and also harsh to tell him who I was. I decided I owed him enough truth to let me go. It would be my magnum opus in standing unashamed.

I went to bed sad to ruin the dream of our lovemaking, and dreamt it anyway.

We were catching up in the third floor sitting room when Vivie said, "I don't mean to pry, Doc. You're a very private person." She'd been talking to Meg or Ciara.

"It's all right," I said and swallowed. "Ask your question."

She wore a pretty mauve color, and reeked of health. "Well, I've been trying to decide what kind of future I want. And it seems like it all hinges on one basic choice."

How I loved this girl.

"You know the one I mean."

"Do you want to live respectably, or freely?"

She nodded and said, "You could be respectable if you wanted. Maybe not where you grew up or anywhere. But somewhere."

I had a vision of us taking off with her as my daughter or niece or ward. But that was not her question. She wanted to know why I hadn't done it long since.

I said, "A brothel nurse saved my life."

"Like you and me!"

I twisted my head back and forth between yes and no. "A little. I was near death for a long time, and I was already a nurse. My parents were gone. Afterward, I had no energy for the pretense."

Her face fell.

"You don't have to pretend, Vivie. You can be yourself but omit your history. You're intelligent, kind, and well spoken. That's more than enough to live respectably."

"But it's a lie. How can you be free if no one knows what you've been through?"

I blinked. "You could confide in someone, certainly any husband worth having. But there's shame either way. That's what we're always fighting. We fight it secretly, or we fight it openly. The whole fiction of purity in a woman makes me furious. We're blamed for our fertility, and reduced to it too. It's repulsive, actually, so you have to remind yourself ten times a day that it's all a swindle, and that you're worthy. Especially if there's no one else to tell you."

"That's why you work so hard, isn't it?" she asked. "To show you're worthy."

That was a gut punch, and I gasped for air.

"Sorry!" she said. "I'm so sorry, Doc. I didn't mean—"

I put a hand up, breathing now. "It's all right."

She came closer, slowly, and when I didn't push her away, embraced me. "You do so much good for everyone, I wouldn't criticize you for one second. I'm trying to understand."

I held her close. I hadn't cried so much since I was nineteen.

"Is that what you need," she said, "someone to tell you that you're worthy? Because you're so much more than that, Doc."

"Thank you, sweetheart," I said, wiping my face on my sleeve. "It's kind of you to say. I guess I want to hear it more than I do."

She looked around my parlor, squeezing my hand. "Do you know, I've never known a woman who lives independently before. It's glorious, and frightening."

I saw the shore in Portland where I would walk alone deep in the night imagining where on earth I might live when I left Gwin.

I asked, "Do you know which way you'll go?"

"Not yet," she said. "I keep hoping a solution will present itself."

I should have just picked a city and sent her.

I asked Israel to send a cab to the clinic at the appointed hour. His concern that I wouldn't take my own carriage registered as a question, "Anything I can do for you?"

I almost confessed my feelings for Asa on the spot, wishing to hear what he would tell me about me flirting with a giant of the nation. But I knew what he would say, took heart, and set off.

There was Asa at the door inviting me in. I loved to see him occupy his body and to feel him breathing. He'd vacated the servants again.

He took his cues for our mode of address from me, and I was all business. My letter said I could spare a few moments only. We sat in the same parlor, in different and safely distant places. He thanked me for skillful services rendered, for the precision and niceties of my knife. "It has not been the smoothest sailing, but I do feel better able to manage. I haven't drunk myself into a stupor, in any case."

I was glad to hear it, but had not come to counsel him.

He then broached the subject of my identity. "It's curious that you protect yourself this way. Or is it me?"

"It's you." I told myself to be unashamed and asked, "Have you ever been to a brothel?"

He coughed. "Pardon?" I saw him weigh and dismiss the possibility that I was a harlot.

"Are you acquainted with the inside of a sporting house?"

He took it as another one of my instructive stories. He measured his answer, discretion pulling one way and candor another, urgency in the strong eye. He said, "Since I married, I have entered houses but never gone upstairs, if you understand me. Before that, before marriage and when traveling, mainly, I, um," he paused before revealing yet more of himself, "indulged in the odd evening of sport."

We called such men dabblers or amateurs. "The houses you attended recently, you went to conduct business?"

"Sorting certain matters in private over a good meal can be useful," he shrugged. "There are some very elegant houses in New York."

"And in your travels, what were your impressions of the ladies you found?"

"May I ask to what this line of questioning pertains?" He thought me digging for a sordid history.

"Indulge me."

He smiled to say he gladly would in this or almost anything. Perhaps he thought I was considering an adultery of my own. "Houses vary by class and quality. A cheap floozy may well be diseased, as you are well aware. But a well-appointed house may have many accomplished and beautiful ladies, and the atmosphere is relaxed and entertaining. I've been to the Hotel de Wood, where there was much laughter, excellent wine, a delightful abandon. Secrets tend to spill. I had some memorable nights out west. New Orleans before the war left an impression. London, Paris."

"Did you spill secrets?"

"In those days I had few enough, only my own grandiose ambitions. Why are we speaking of this?"

"I'm telling you who I am."

He came to confusion, and a sliver of panic. "You're not a harlot, surely?"

"Why 'surely'?"

"There's not one ounce of the coquette about you. No one is that good an actress."

I laughed at that. "You're right, I'm not a harlot. I've never taken money for sex myself."

His face went slack to hear those words come from the mouth of a woman he still thought a spinster nurse. I would have laughed but was trying not to shame him for the ignorance I had created. "Have you heard of the Double Standard?"

"Of course, from Elliott and others. He has good friends there."

I took a deep breath.

He said, "What is your connection?"

"I own it."

He drew upon his vast experience, his strength, his knowledge; the rooms and tents he'd shared with more than one President, the sweeps of men and laws and advocacy, and came up empty. He said, "You own the Double Standard Sporting House?"

"I do, and several other businesses and properties."

"You own the house but do not entertain guests yourself?"

"That's correct."

He blinked three times and stayed calm, "You said you were a nurse." Just a little hurt.

"I am," I assured him. "I provide medical care to my girls and many others. I did formal training as a nurse nearly twenty years ago and see many patients daily. I have studied medicine with some intensity my entire life, and have trained many others in nursing. And I own a brass foundry! We make medical devices, though I'm more of a silent partner now. I personally employ—me alone I'm saying—nearly eighty people, seventy of whom are not harlots, and am most proud of a free clinic I run for girls and women."

His mouth fell open and he said, "That's almost the number I employ at the *Standard*."

I looked back at him, feeling myself to be a mirror or a window he'd never imagined.

His intellect rushed forward. "A nurse and philanthropist in the sporting world. A woman of your capability is less constrained in those precincts than in a regular institution."

"Yes, by far. I have greater latitude in every way except respectability."

He sat back, gasping. "Why did you see me?"

"My dear friend Elliott was desperately worried about his brother and convinced me to do him this favor despite my considerable reservations, and the indignity of hiding my identity." I thought back and raised one shoulder. "I was glad to get out of the house for a few hours."

"Why?"

"Ward politics are ugly."

He started to chuckle, and had a rueful laugh. "We have that in common."

"Who's angry at you?"

"I sent a reporter to the quarry where they're cutting stone for the new courthouse." A direct challenge to Tweed.

I raised my eyebrows. "Good luck." We looked at one another perhaps for the first time. "Are you shocked?" I said.

"Not shocked, exactly."

More like disappointed. "I'm a madam. I've never been to medical school but perform surgeries, including abortions. *The Gentleman's Guide to New York After Hours* called me a 'mysterious and bright jewel of the elite underworld.' My name itself invites controversy."

His face was open and empty, and I interlaced my hands so I wouldn't reach for his cheek. He said, "My previous beliefs do not prepare me for the present moment, and I begin to appreciate your reticence. You implied that first night that you had some notoriety, but I assumed it was domestic, like your husband left you. Well, I'm a fool. What is your name, then?"

"I go by Nell Hastings, but most people call me Doc."

"You're Doc Hastings!"

My heart ached.

"I've heard of you. I thought you were a man."

That was funny. "Naturally."

"Nell Hastings is not your real name either."

"It's not the name I was born with, no."

"And what was that?"

I said nothing.

He said, "May I call you Nell? Though I can't say it suits you. You're more of an Eleanor."

"If you prefer it to Annalee. As I say, my friends call me Doc." I stood, and he followed.

"Doc, Nell, Annalee, where are you all going?"

I looked right at him. "Prudence would dictate my earliest departure."

"Yes," he said, standing between me and the door. "But who would not want to know how a trained nurse came to own the most elegant brothel in New York?"

He wanted me to justify myself. I folded my hands in front of me. "I don't tell that story. I'm sure you understand."

"You insisted I tell mine."

"I'm not on a bender."

He flinched and saw his romance run aground, his new fantasy of saving me as I had saved him flagging, and came back on a disappointing tack. "You own the house but do not engage in its business."

"The main business of the house is liquor, followed by food."

He blinked. "How does a woman of your wisdom and capability end up in the demimonde?"

Painfully disappointing. Tartly, I said, "That's the wrong question. How many women do you employ at the *Standard*?"

He was taken aback. "A few. Cleaners, mainly."

Only, more like. "Are they harassed, fondled, made the objects of jokes? Assaulted? Are they paid more than a pittance? Can they feed their families?"

Now his face was slack and pale. "What's the right question?"

"Why do so many men do so much harm to women?"

His mouth dropped open, and he put his hand on the door to steady himself.

I said, "But that's rather philosophical. Let's begin on a more practical level. How many women run hospitals, or hotels, which is the closest business to a brothel? How many women earn their own fortunes or lift up hundreds of people from the street?"

He stared and I drove on.

"Why did you visit brothels before you married?"

He thought I'd changed the subject. "I wanted educating, to have the experiences a man should have."

"And you could not get those in your usual social circle."

"Not without being a cad."

"So in one setting sex makes you a cad, and in another an educated man of the world. Did that ever strike you as hypocritical that you would exert yourself to protect some women from an experience you would gladly purchase from others?"

"Well, the world presented me with two kinds of women."

I smirked about Matrons and Vixens. "Do you imagine a house with the name 'The Double Standard' celebrates that split?"

"Do you mean to say you operate the house as a way to thwart it?"

I laughed. "If such a miracle ever occurred, that would be a bonus."

He was shaking his head in confusion.

"Heaven's sake Asa, do you think hypocrisy only, or even mainly, affects men?"

He was speechless and it was time for me to go. I needed to offer him a place to rest and close the case, so I said, "All I ever wanted was to take care of women. When I was a student nurse, I was not allowed to take care of patients beyond cleaning them, though I was more skilled than many of the doctors. That really is the answer to every single one of your questions. Good night, Mr. Vanderpoel. Thank you for your hospitality."

"Please don't go."

"I must."

"If you're trying to protect me, don't."

I glared at him. "Your career and your children mean so little to you?"

"There's no one here but us."

That hurt, that he thought we could settle it with a quick tumble. "No thank you."

He looked so sad. "I had thought you—but no, now I see how little you think of me."

Sweet Jesus. Softly I said, "On the contrary. I refuse to be the means of your humiliation and dishonor." Or to come into public view for an affair. I steadied my voice. "It's been a great pleasure to meet you sir, but I think we must say good-bye." The word 'unashamed' was no match for my pain and regret as I walked away.

It wasn't that I feared sex, exactly. I had an abundance of shame about my body, but a few men had snuck past it. At the Silk Pillow, an Italian count (so he said) fell ill while bedding a harlot.

He tended to faint when he'd gone too long without food, so I gave him a sandwich and he found in me a puzzle, ventured informed guesses of my history. He offered to rectify my aversion. "A virgin cannot work in a brothel," he said, "it's against God and nature."

"I'm not a virgin," I said.

"Whatever that was doesn't count."

More than twenty years my senior, he had a seen-it-all drollery and a twinkle. He enjoyed eroding my restraint, and brought me to greater and greater intensities of pleasure until I could lose myself in release. It was all highly educational and good natured but a lark with little emotional connection. He was no count.

A few years later in the early days after Fort Sumter, I ran into a client on Broadway. He had a friend with him, a veteran of the Mexican War who was deciding whether to take up his old commission despite an injury that left him with a limp. They came to the Double and over dinner this Colonel Robert Hess spoke of sorting his fear and his duty. At Buena Vista, he'd been burned on the leg by a comrade's accidental weapon discharge, but he believed in Union and abolition. I admired him.

After dinner when we stood, he whispered in my ear, "May I see you?" For two days we melded and slid and slammed ourselves together. He chose to fight.

Asa Vanderpoel unsettled me body and soul, but that was nothing compared to the threat I posed to him.

There was little call for midwifery at Portland Hospital. Only a few laboring women ever came in. General practitioners had begun attending home births, but traveling midwives still saw to most of them. Annalee and I began discussing training like they had in Boston. Portland Hospital always needed more money. Why not create a lying-in ward, and bring a skilled midwife to teach us? Dr. Lund and Dr. Schaeffer presented unpleasant obstacles, but we began to formulate a proposal to take to Nurse Pell and Dr. Jordan, the medical director.

Most of the nurses and students said Dr. Jordan was full of himself, and perhaps that was true, but I thought the greater share of his hauteur was from being in charge so young. He was no more than twenty-eight when he became medical director of the wards. He looked older: grave and slightly stooped, with light brown curls and dark, wise eyes. He never raised his voice, and remembered people's names and backgrounds. When he learned I'd been raised in a surgery, he took me on rounds and said I did my parents proud. Once when an unruly patient was thrashing in bed while orderlies tried to restrain him, I saw it was a seizure and took a pen from Dr. Jordan's coat pocket and put it in the man's mouth.

"Quick thinking, Nurse," he said later. "Why the pen and not some other object?"

"It appeared to be ebony, which would not crack."

Nothing very special passed between us until one winter night when I was sitting up reading to an old woman on the verge of death. It was a cancer of the breast, and she was in terrible pain, and frightened. I read to her from Waverley, *which I found in her possessions. Dr. Jordan came by, took a chair on the other side of the bed, and fell asleep himself. Soon after the woman began gasping her last, he woke and held her other hand as I sang to her. It was quick. Before he left, he took my hand in his two and held it near his heart, saying nothing but with his eyes saying thank you for being kind, and perhaps something else.*

I should have asked him about the training program then but didn't, entranced by the something else.

NINE

I received an unsigned cable, presumably from Junius. "*Weekly Rake* on Saturday." Ciara brought the paper to me at breakfast. The cover article carried no byline but had a lurid illustration of a girl manhandled on the street, skirts flying and bodice gaping, the headline, "Sex Slavers at Work in New York, Latest Victim Suggests Police Complicit."

"Gracious," I said.

Junius told the story of Catherine Farnsworth's last days in graphic detail, then circled back and gave particulars of the family farm in Bethel where they raised pigs and chickens. She was the eldest of seven, and when her father died a year past, her four brothers and grieving mother resolved to keep the farm in the family. At seventeen Catherine secured a referral for work in the city, planning to go into service and go ahead as best she could.

But then Junius bowled me over by naming two men who had wronged her unforgivably. She arrived at the home of a family called Wilson on Washington Square, whose son raped her, something Junius must have learned from talking to her friends among the street girls, bless him. She made a fuss and was dismissed without a reference, ended up on the street for a few months before being kidnapped. Then he named the copper with the Fourteenth Street beat, one Dale Donovan, who had since resigned his position and left town. Donovan's connections were not apparently good enough to prevent him taking the fall for Catherine's death, to protect the larger operation. Perhaps the precinct captain had drawn a line.

Ciara said, "Our Benno's in some shite now." I wondered what form the slap from Tammany would take, if any. Meanwhile, it'd be the end of the house or worse if Benno learned I'd loosed the journalist.

The name Dale Donovan meant something to me, but I couldn't remember what until Vivie flew into the kitchen, eyes blazing and jaw hewing forward. "Donnie!" she said, seating herself at the table and spreading her hands. "That's what they called Dale Donovan. What a total bastard."

Ciara said, "The villain who cut you is a copper?"

"Maybe so, but either way that man is a devil, always smacking you one for nothing, or choking you while he—you know. A monster. I remember once after he beat me, Mrs. Wrigley shaking her head and saying he did it all for free."

I sat numb, feeling no satisfaction from this revelation. "He's on the run now. I hope Catherine rests a little easier."

Vivie said, "I hope he burns alive."

Ciara said, "Amen, sister," as I noted that Vivie had reached the furious stage of recovery.

Late that night, Martin Mitchell sat at the kitchen table with a cup of coffee, the twins on either side of him. He brought the news that Benno had sent a bully called Goliath to the *Weekly Rake* to threaten the staff and extract the author's name. The gentlemen of the paper, among whom were several former police officers acquainted with Goliath, welcomed and flattered him until he sat down for an interview about his line of work while two sketch artists took his likeness for a feature.

We considered if the *Rake* was now in the clear. Their stance was so unpredictable, celebrating wild girls one week and condemning them the next; excitement and titillation all mixed up with affront and blame. Likewise with sports and gangsters, they spewed print from all directions, lascivious to churchy, so it'd be easy enough for them to butter up Tammany in their next issue.

Ciara asked Martin, "You taking guff at the station?"

"No more than usual."

Junius kept Benno and Hank's names out of the paper in part to protect me, but also to protect Martin.

I reminded Martin, "Keep your distance from Junius?"

He said, "Oh we agreed never to have met or to meet again. And too bad, I liked that cranky little wizard."

We'd avoided exposure, but I reckoned we'd trip into the light pretty soon.

I had a note from my reformer friend Viola Hill asking if we had read a recent article in the *Weekly Rake*. She proposed to introduce an activist newly emigrated from England who turned out to be a minister from Liverpool. The Reverend Albin Birchdale had a copious head of gray hair untamed by oil and a voice booming with the joy of the gospel. I doubted he could counsel anyone on death while exuding so much rapture.

Taking Viola's arm, I led them to the salon and invited the twins to join us. Shaking Meg's hand, Viola stared in awe. "You're so lovely," she said, meaning, I believe, that she'd never been so close to such a frankly sexual creature.

"Thank you," said Meg, admiring Viola's hat.

"Forgive me," said Viola, now shaking Ciara's hand. "It's like coming upon a pair of DaVincis." Her interest in prostitution was adorably eager.

We persevered. When settled in with tea, I asked Mr. Birchdale what kind of work he'd done in England.

"Are you familiar with the mission of Mrs. Josephine Butler?"

I was not.

He said, "I had the privilege of ministering to girls at her Industrial Home," and offered to give a brief account.

He was loud but likable; still couldn't see him at a bedside though. He knew nothing about bodies, tried his best to ignore them. He described his Mrs. Butler as a prophetess or an angel, that rarest of all things, a true Christian. Meg found this implausible. She was a society belle and wife to a university don, mother to little children, called to serve the most downtrodden of girls, bringing them off the street and right into her own home. Two years prior she had prevailed upon Liverpool's merchants to fund a place where girls could learn an honest trade without the shame and strictures of a reformatory.

Ciara said, "And you say this Industrial Home is successful? Girls leave and don't end up back on the street?"

"Oh Mrs. Butler does not mean to stop there, she agitates for more access to education and employment for women, but meanwhile, yes. The home places many girls."

"How inspiring," I said, imagining this Mrs. Butler's faith was both sword and shield, protecting her from taint as she carved out new opportunities, but in service of a serious practicality. These were the kind of reformers I could do business with. "What brings you to New York, Reverend?"

"I seek to spread the word. Also, my bride is a native of this city. I have come to the pulpit of St. Michael's."

I looked to Viola. "That *Rake* article alarmed you?"

"Indeed." she said, "The syndicates appear to be moving toward industrial scale procurement!"

They knew even less than we did. "Yes, it's concerning." I hoped it was clear that my worry was not for my profit margin.

Viola stepped past such questions and said they wanted to propose joining forces. "You have ways to infiltrate and gather information; we have the credibility and connections to make the case to the authorities and the public."

The twins and I sat silent.

"Have I overstepped?" Viola asked.

"To what authorities do you refer?" said Ciara.

"Oh," she said, "I suppose I mean those with the power to stop them. Police and courts?"

Birchdale saw the point. "Who may themselves be part of the scheme, however."

I explained that not all police, district attorneys, and judges were corrupt, but that precious few would risk outright warfare on Tammany's interests. The only remedy, we had concluded, was through the press.

Viola made a face. "I don't like that *Weekly Rake*, and would rather place it in a respectable paper."

Meg said, "They're respectable because they won't touch scandalous subjects."

"Well," Viola said, looking at Birchdale, "I don't want to get ahead of myself but we have a connection at the *Standard*." My belly lurched. "Their city editor is married to one of our members, and they do take principled stands on public issues."

I said, "They've never shown any interest in women's issues. They have no female reporters." In no scenario could this involve Asa Vanderpoel.

Birchdale said, "That may be so, but it's to our advantage."

Ciara said, "In the *Standard*, the issue is machine expansion and ambition."

Meg said, "Abducted girls are incidental?"

Birchdale said, "To us they are central, of course, but we're speaking now of putting this procurement ring on the front page for general discussion."

We faced both fear of Tammany and a disinclination to speak of fallen women, let alone slaving, so the *Rake* was the better option and I said so. "The flash papers exist for provocation. Whatever they publish of import sifts into general awareness and the other papers eventually."

But this was not a tangible question until we had more information. We agreed to meet a week hence.

Mr. Birchdale asked if he might tour any parts of the house. I offered the parlor floor, and the twins led him while I lingered with Viola, anxious to hear reports she might have received on the failed infiltrators of the Merry Hypocrites' Ball.

She said, "Mr. Beltron said he was turned away at the door."

"Ah." I tried to stifle my smile and failed, given his thorough ravishing.

"He's been scarce. We thought him abashed."

Poor man, I thought and nodded. "I'm sure he's very hard on himself." I was sorely tempted to tell her but did not.

When they left I wondered what more I could need to thwart a cabal of vicious slavers than a bookish journalist and some highborn churchmen and women.

A week after I said goodbye to Asa Vanderpoel, a letter arrived at the Double.

Dear Miss Hastings,

You made clear your wish to sever our acquaintance, but as the days go by I'm less amenable to that ending. Please forgive my impertinence. You have taken up residence within me. You have infiltrated my way of thinking, from the deepest well of my own interior to the way I approach my role at work. I often imagine what you would say to this or that but do not know you well enough to answer. I throw myself upon your mercy for further education. May I call on you?

Yours,

A.

He gave no details lest the letter be intercepted, which was evidence enough that we should go no further. I had no desire for more of his opinions but his gaze was still on me and I spoke to him, yearned for his skin, his scent, his expressions. His face was faraway in daytime and at night too close. He stole my sleep.

A year past I might have given in, but with Benno and the slavers it was all too risky. Each day I half expected to find myself a headline in the *Rake* or its ilk, but how much worse to be the subject of an investigation in his paper, or the lurid detail in a story about him in the *Times* or the *Herald*. I let him go, but saved the letter.

Junius arrived by prearrangement on the same night that George brought an unexpected Peter Sweeny for a drink. A meal was quickly arranged upstairs in the caucus dining room with Meg and Tatiana as entertainment. I gave Junius brief instruction on Sweeny's temperament.

George had never met Junius and wanted to hear about his stay with the Confederates. "Did they provide you with any women?"

"Nothing very worthy." He winked at Tati, who looked ready to spank him.

George wanted more, so Junius said, "It was bad enough watching friends die of typhus and dysentery. No one wanted the pox."

The smallest and least imposing of the men, Junius was the only one who'd been to war, though he wielded a pen. Sweeny said, "What'd you do your first night out?"

"I made it to a Union encampment about fifteen miles east of Knoxville, a huge one, like a city. I'd been walking for a month, four-hundred miles through snow-covered mountains held by the enemy, including the previous twenty-four hours straight. I ate and slept. But that week I stopped in Knoxville, Nashville, and Louisville before I got home to Cleveland, and I will tell you that I don't remember much about Knoxville, Nashville, or Louisville except clean glasses and perfumed sheets."

There was much sly laughter at what pleasures Junius indulged after twenty months in captivity.

When conversation lulled, Meg asked, "So which is tougher, Junius, the enemy's mountains or the docks of New York? It's open warfare over there, from panel-houses to shanghais—some guy waking up on a ship a day out to sea, girls abducted off the street. It's worse than ever, and I grew up in Five Points." Oh, she was good.

Sweeny turned to her. "I grew up in a tavern in Jersey City. It's no worse now than it ever was."

She winked at him. "You know because you ride your carriage from City Hall to Delmonico's?"

Defensive, he said, "I'm well informed."

Junius said, "I'll take the city, thank you, with a bed and ample food to eat. But you're right," he raised a glass to Meg, "it grows faster than any ability to police or govern it. Tammany keeps a certain order but someday we'll need legitimate power to keep crime in check."

Meg cried, "Junius Henri Browne, do you have a death wish?"

Junius smiled, expansive. "Oh Maggie dear, you don't get to be George Barnard or Peter Sweeny by being too delicate to hear the truth. These men should be proud of what they've accomplished."

George said, "Tammany indeed does what no one else can do, and the Boss above all brings will and unity where there was none."

I said, "The average man admires him for brass and for dining with millionaires."

Sweeny said, "We never lose sight of the street."

Junius said to him, "Do you still frequent the taverns?"

He grew stiff. "Not as often as I did."

Junius hit the table with both fists. "The night is young, Mr. Sweeny! Let's seize it and commune with the common man."

It was too bad I couldn't accompany them, but I did suggest they begin at the Reveille.

Another letter from Asa arrived at the Double. I squirrelled it into my pocket to read alone, which I did before bed.

Dear Miss Hastings,

I revisit our encounters like a miner with a pan. You found me at my worst, and turned me around, sent me back toward myself. The second time you peeled me like an orange, and I often wish for your counsel and reassurance in my ebbs and flows. When I woke with you in my arms, I was filled with joy.

I abhor my memories of our last meeting. Forgive my ignorance, my confusion, my petulance. My only consolation is that you took the trouble to disabuse me. You do not fade, and so I write. Please forgive. Please take a meal with me.

Asa

He was not used to refusal, which was good reason to refuse. I thought back to that morning when I woke in his room, our smells in the bedclothes and his eyes open. And the night before returned too. I had placed a chair by the bed to wait until he slept. Soon I dozed and laid my arms and head down to rest a bit before I set off home. Sometime later, the room fully dark and both of us all but asleep, Asa shifted over and drew me up, the most natural movement in the world, and we fell back to dreaming together. I remembered the warmth and weight of his hands on me, and wept.

Two days after Junius took Peter Sweeny to the Reveille, Hanky Pank turned up in mid-afternoon at the Double. Ciara sent a note to the clinic, where I was treating a girl in the midst of a bloody late-stage miscarriage. Nina could keep watch for a couple of minutes.

But a torn placenta was messy and my sleeves were bloody. I wrapped my wrists in the ends of a shawl and sped over, finding Hank alone in the salon with a bourbon.

Having gathered his inconvenience, he said, “You’re busy.”

“I have patients. What can I do for you?”

“I’ll be quick. Peter Sweeny stopped in at the Reveille, for a better view of the ward, he said.”

I nodded. "I saw there was something sticky between him and Benno and thought it might help."

"Help who?"

"Benno, you, the ward. It's better if he feels connected, no?"

"Well, he felt so goddamned connected, he suggested we make better use of you."

My first reactions to that were incoherent, but then I understood. There was no more pretending, so I said it aloud. "In whatever you're planning for girls."

"He said we'd be fools not to."

I took a breath, and swallowed a laugh. My ill-conceived matchmaking between Sweeny and Benno had ended with Sweeny making a much worse match between Benno and me. "But he's worried I won't answer to him."

"It has crossed his mind."

They would have ignored a casual suggestion, so Sweeny had more or less ordered this, for no reason I could see beyond my actual utility with girls. Benno and I were on the road to confrontation now. My first instinct was to slow things down.

I dropped the stupid shawl, poured a bourbon and threw half of it back. Hank saw the blood on my sleeves and flinched. Benno might just want a steady supply of chloroform. I loathed that prospect, but talking to him was the best way to learn about his plans.

I said, "I don't have time to work for Benno, Hank, more than I already do. But I can find him the right people to build up his operation. You need someone who understands how girls work and can recruit without making a fucking mess."

He said, "Do me a favor."

I raised my eyebrows.

"Stay away from my bars."

"Never set foot in one," I said, opening my hands. He didn't appreciate Sweeny inspecting his place, and having seen Junius, doubtless suspected he wrote the *Rake* piece. I wondered if he'd say anything to Benno.

I asked him, "How do you work it for girls at your places?"

"It's all on them," he said. "As long as they sell drinks. If they want to take a guy upstairs, they pay the floor manager for the room for half an hour."

That was sensible. I said, "It's nice you let them decide."

He said, "What's your interest in this?"

"Same as ever. I'm an open book, Hank. No slaving. Treat girls well, not like punching bags, or pin cushions, or target practice. Like you do at your saloons." I put down the glass, ready for this to be done.

He said, "You're swimming upstream."

He didn't know what I had on Sweeny. Or what Vivie did. "Aren't I quixotic."

Hank said, "They want to set a meeting here next week."

"They're welcome, as ever." I did hope "they" included Vernon Trent, ostensibly Benno's slaver-in-chief.

So did Vivie. She asked for the chance to confront him if he showed up, and I agreed as long as she understood she would have to leave New York directly afterward.

I sat alone in the caucus, waiting to offer Junius the chance to listen to my meeting with Benno from a hidden vantage. My list for the meeting was not long: the crib's location, as by now the one Martin knew might be out of date; the condition of the girls and if they were being abused or worked to death; anything about Vernon Trent and his connection to Tammany; anything that could help us stop their operation without going to war. This last was terribly unlikely. When I refused to participate in slaving, Benno would refuse to deal with me, and I'd have to close the house. I couldn't imagine anything that would save us, and held scant hope for something unimaginable to come along.

Junius agreed to listen in and to write it up if publicity was indicated, tripling his previous fee. I asked Israel to instruct him on using the back entrance.

When Junius had gone, Israel returned to the caucus with something to say. "Doc, what's gotten into you?"

Trying to be honest, I said, "I think it started with Vivie."

"What hold does this girl have on you?"

"The sum total of sorrow handed down through all of womankind?"

He scoffed.

Ciara and I had kept the revelation about Sweeny to ourselves and Vivie, but now I figured it was time to tell Israel and Meg, if Ciara had not already told her.

He wiped his mouth with the back of one hand. "And what? You're going to risk the house to prove something to this child?"

"The house is already at risk. It can't last, Is. You know it."

He huffed. "Benjamin O'Connor cannot kill the Double Standard."

"He can raise his percentage until we lose our margin. I won't run a house for him."

"So you're going to let a child torch it."

I smiled. "More likely it'll be a newspaperman."

"Now I know you're done, Doc. It's against everything you've said since I met you."

I was quiet, and wished I had some filthy and dissolute habit like young boys or absinthe because I'd go on a spectacular bender.

"There's more to this than you're saying."

To myself I could admit that was true. First came Catherine Farnsworth, and then there was Asa. Giving up the house could not bring us together, but the way he looked at me mattered. Some fuel in me had run dry.

"You're not sick?"

"Just tired."

He said, "If you were anyone else, I'd send you to Doc to figure out what was wrong with you. Haven't you spent every waking moment trying to build and preserve something? You've made a thousand careful choices for the long run, things you hated doing because it would hold up the house and the clinic. The idiots you suffered, my God, to protect all of us."

The sight of his kind face moved me to tears. "I've had enough of girls' pain."

He blinked twice, and exhaled. "You won't stop healing."

"No," I agreed, though I wanted a break. And I'd had enough of hiding. I wanted colleagues, I wanted all of medicine, unlikely as I was to get it. Then I said, "If I thought you and Perlie and the twins wanted the house, I'd give it to you, but you don't want it under these conditions."

"And if us taking it from you would stop this craziness, we would."

I nodded.

"I don't see how this ends."

"Maybe that's it," I said. "I want to find out." I'd begun wondering what might come next.

Christmas preparations usually cheered me. We held a decorating party each year with porters on ladders around the tree in the salon and girls laughing as they unboxed glass ornaments and paper garlands. Georgia wanted to add candles and Ciara asked her pleasantly not to burn the house down.

Each year I gave girls variations on the same gift, crystal

beads in different colors or a classic book. This year I'd splurged and gotten nine pendants with their birthstones. Perlie would have a jade bracelet and Israel a matching watch fob, and the twins would each have mother of pearl opera glasses. I had not intended to give Elliott a gift but when I bought the glasses I saw a pocket spyglass perfect for the little busybody. Vivie would have a pair of new hats, one for day and one for evening.

Christmas Eve was a big night for business, but on the day we gathered in the salon after breakfast to exchange gifts. Erroll played carols, "O Come All Ye Faithful" and "Joy to the World." "God Rest Ye Merry Gentlemen" gave way to "Silent Night." That one hit me, the echo of the unsung lyric less evocative than the lilting melody and its lullaby qualities. I had no childhood memories of it but grew wistful. Marianne sat by me and when it was done, she said, "That one has the proper spirit."

We applauded Erroll and he bowed his head.

"It's restful," I said. "Christmas should be restful, don't you think?"

"Not too likely," she said, taking in the spirit of the room. "Any special plans, Doc?"

"Me? No. You?"

"A couple of us are going for a quick skate in the park. Would you join us?"

"That sounds fun," I said, planning to read or sleep. No one ever knew what to get me. I had years of books I'd never read, jewels I'd never worn, bottles I'd never drink. A pair of tickets to the opening night of *Ernani* on December 26 had arrived in the post, which I passed to the twins.

Would Elliott make sure Asa didn't sit alone all day at Gramercy Park? They had no family except on Caroline's side, but he had friends and colleagues to welcome a distinguished guest to their tables with his wit and elegance, far from Benno and that inevitable fiasco.

The next morning early I found Vivie waiting in the clinic, arms folded across her belly, rocking.

"What's wrong?"

"I'm bleeding." Her voice was knotted with fear, yet full-throated. Her color was fine.

I sat down next to her, crooked a hand through her arms, and interlaced our fingers. "Take a breath." When she inhaled a teaspoon of air, I said, "Bigger than that. What do you feel in your abdomen?"

"It hurts. I'm so scared, Doc. What if the cuts to my bladder can't be fixed? You said an open fistula is very dangerous."

"What did you do yesterday? Go dancing, carriage riding, falling down the stairs? Did Georgia tickle you again?" Vivie, it turned out, was very sensitive in her underarms.

Not the smallest glimmer of amusement. "No, nothing."

"Did you eat anything unusual?"

She grimaced. "Aunty Laure made shortbread and I ate five pieces." Her lower lip trembled. "Six. I took one when she wasn't looking."

Oh dear. We had a grim conversation ahead of us different from the one she expected. "My darling, I think you're menstruating. It's actually wonderful news about your recovery."

She burst into tears and sobbed with something like relief as she fell into my embrace. "It feels wretched!"

I rubbed her back. "Oh yes. I can do an examination if we're at all unsure, but let me ask you some questions. Is the feeling in your abdomen crampy and heavy, or sharp?"

"Crampy."

"Does it hurt more when you move?"

She shook her head no.

"And your mood is bleak, you're sure something is very wrong."

She cried some more, and I drew her closer.

"Hmm, let's see. And you're tired and want to crawl into a hole, but want dessert at every hour."

Finally she laughed. "I feel like such a simpleton. But I panicked when I saw blood. I can't stand the thought of bed rest again."

We sat back, breathing freely now. "Of course you worry about your healing, and bleeding will bring back all those terrible memories. They will come, maybe every month for a while, and you'll get better at recognizing the signs of your cycle."

We found some cloths and belts for her in the clinic closet, and set her up in an exam room while I explained how the Double maids managed the menstrual laundry. "Once you've arranged the paraphernalia, come upstairs. There's something else we need to talk about."

The stairs felt steep and long as I climbed back up. I set water to boil and filled a strainer with mint for a mild anti-spasmodic, and wondered how to conduct this conversation and keep my own composure.

We sat at my dining table. "Vivie, do you understand what it means that you're menstruating?"

She made little birdlike movements of her head, and then her eyes widened. "My mother said it meant I was a woman."

I said too abruptly, "It means you're fertile. That in all likelihood you can conceive a child. In the middle of your cycle, between bleeding, for a few days."

She nodded over and over. Then she said, "Well I don't plan on doing anything that would lead to that, so."

I closed my eyes for a moment. "I know you have no interest in men now. That may last for the rest of your life, or you may meet someone, perhaps years in the future, and decide to marry. You could take a man as a lover for pleasure."

"Not likely!"

"All right. But there's something very important about this that you have to know, and it's upsetting. It's sad, and I'm sorry to tell you."

"Doc, what is it?" She could see that this was costing me.

I took her hands. "Sweetheart. The repair to your vaginal wall would not likely sustain childbirth. Birthing a child for you would be a terrible risk, and you must take extreme pains never to conceive. I'll teach you many things you can do to prevent it. And if you do anyway, which sometimes happens, you should end the pregnancy."

Her face had gone slack and full white, but she held my gaze. I tried to offer consolation or resolve or steadiness with my expression, but probably failed. She tried to swallow. I saw her waver, but then she made a wry face, and shrugged. "That'll keep suitors off."

Her skill at deflection had grown an edge.

She said, "So I get to suffer menstruation for no purpose. Isn't that just the icing on the cake."

My jaw dropped open.

She said, "If I'm ever tempted to marry, I'm going to remember this conversation."

"Indeed."

"And this anger. I hate the way it has nowhere to go. It's so helpless."

"Yes," I said, hoping she would say more.

"Meg found me crying yesterday and took me into the garden to throw stones at the wall and stomp my feet. She said there's a crossroads between anger and despair, and that I should always choose anger, but not to swallow it. 'Better out than in.'"

Ah, bless her. Meg and I often threw rocks in our early years together when the burdens of shame and stigma grew heavy. I learned that trick on northern beaches. "Vivie," I said, "it's all right to grieve this. You'll never be a mother, not that way. There are other ways, of course. But if you ever had the dream of motherhood, you may need to mourn it. Now and maybe again later."

She looked at me, some of that fire coming in my direction. "Are you sure? I mean, if I had a great healer, might I be all right after all?"

I looked right at her. "It will always be a grave risk. Terribly grave. Down the road you could have someone examine you and reassess, but for your own well-being you should consider that road closed."

"Can we close the menstruation road too, then? Because this is miserable. It goes off a cliff."

I gave her the mint infusion. "This will help with the cramping. If they're not too bad, you can let the cramps come, it'll end sooner. Your uterus is doing its job. But if it's painful, lots of mint."

She looked at me in puzzlement, but this was not the day to discuss the biology of conception. "I'll explain menstrual blood and cramps some other time."

Now she looked irritated. "I suppose it's better than dying of infection."

I snorted, which made her laugh, which made me laugh, and I thought we might end puddled and philosophical.

But then she said, "You can't, either, can you?"

She saw me as well as anyone ever had. My eyes crinkled with a faint smile, and I said, "No."

We could hear the clinic day starting below, someone calling out, "Have you seen Doc?"

"Okay," she said, stood, and kissed my cheek. "Let's put that on the list of things to talk about later."

The pile of girls' journal pages needing attention was deeper than ever. Two days after Christmas I sat in the clinic office trying to catch up when Meg arrived.

"Hey." I said, "You all right?"

Smiling, she said, "Fine. There's someone at the house asking for you."

Yet she hadn't sent a porter. I moved some papers off the only other chair in the room. "Do you want to sit? Who is it?"

She was bemused, holding a piece of information she thought would surprise me. I half expected her to say Bill Tweed.

She sat. "It's Asa Vanderpoel." I must have flushed crimson as my heart lodged itself in my throat. "Just as I suspected!"

I tried to swallow but could not. "What did he say?"

"That he needs to see you urgently, but to be sure to tell you it concerns Junius."

Anger swept over whatever else I was feeling. "Fuck all!"

Meg waited, and I realized she was hurt that I hadn't confided in her. "What's going on?"

I closed my eyes, furious.

"Are you seeing him?"

"I treated him, and he's been writing to me."

"Do you love him?"

"I can't," I said, well aware of the admission and the stupidity.

"Well," she said, "that makes sense, because he choked when he tried to say your name."

I covered my head with my arms.

"Doc," Meg said gently, "why not have a quiet affair with this man? He's splendid. The girls are tripping over themselves to get to him."

I sent a pleading look at her, miserable that despite all my efforts, Viola's friend had dragged him into this.

"Where's the harm? Don't you deserve a little happiness?"

There was too much at stake. "I couldn't bear to see him disgraced."

She stood up in a rush, angry with me now. "Bloody hell Doc, you're no disgrace. We're going to have words about that later, you and me. What should I tell him?"

I stood too, and took a breath. "Give him his coat and send him into the garden."

"Do us all a favor," she said as she walked away. "Take the handsome and distinguished man who loves you to bed."

For the length of time it would take him to get outside I tried to slow my breathing. Our progress toward one another across the dark garden was both too long, as I had nothing to do but watch him move and feel joy in my limbs that Asa was alive in the world and had come to see me, and too short, because I had no idea what to say. He came closer than expected, took my hand, and kissed it. I trembled despite my heavy shawl, tried to breathe, tried to form words that would slow the thrashing in my body. He looked concerned and put his other hand on my arm, and there we were, halfway to an embrace, my senses clattering like a child's when he took me into his arms. I expected wild danger, a kind of planetary cave-in, but all tumult ceased. Then he kissed me. My mind fell silent as the world floated upward, a noiseless rising and lightening. All mass and heaviness eased. Asa's mouth searched in this ether and found me, sweet and earthy, warm and liquid, that trace of citrus, the way he stood on his feet and pulled me in, one hand on my sacrum and one behind my heart like epic poetry. Another moment and this airborne connection would have landed and demanded another kind of action altogether with far more friction, so I put my hand to his face and stopped us. That left me so dizzy I dropped my head to his chest and he kissed my hair. "Doc," he whispered, his arms tender and strong around me, "how I've longed to see you."

I balanced on the edge of that peace, that thrumming silence. "Please don't," I said. "We have to stop."

He said, "I came to say that you mustn't put yourself in danger."

That helped. I took my first full breath in several minutes as I pulled back. Separating pained us both. "Let's sit."

On a bench in shadow by the clinic, he tried to take my hand but I evaded touch. He turned sideways and stretched his arm along the seat behind me. "Is it true that Junius Browne is the author of that piece in the *Rake* and you a source?" The publisher had arrived. "Because exposing a procurement ring in a flash paper is about the most foolhardy thing I've ever heard."

I sat in stillness.

"Why would you?" he pleaded.

Tears came to my eyes for how little he knew me and how little it mattered. "You're not really asking me why slavers must be stopped."

He blinked, the strong eye fierce. "I'm asking why you would take the risk."

It was a fair question. I stood and led him to the clinic. The gas light in the east treatment room dissolved all romance. He circled the examination table the better to see it, stared at the chest covered with bandages and instruments. I put fingertips on the table and said, "Catherine Farnsworth lay here bleeding. Her kidney was crushed and she had so many broken ribs she couldn't breathe without ungodly pain. In that state, she'd been raped by a policeman." He was truly shocked. "She died right here, in my arms. Over at the house, there's a girl who was kidnapped from a family party and chained to a bedstead while she was deflowered. Fifteen years old. I paid $650 to free her, a bright and beautiful child." My voice held sobs as I said it.

His horror was partly at me.

I saw the error in how I said it, and a far worse one in how he took it. "Jesus, she's not working, Asa! She stays at the house because everyone understands what she's been through and she feels safe with us. She's a guest, she's family."

"I'm sorry," he said, confounded both ways. "I misunderstood."

That was despair for me, the very bottom. I felt hollow and ill but now I knew what to do. Didn't men try to shield women from the cruel realities of life on the street? Shaking my head, tears falling, I said, "It's not foolhardy. It's all I can do. You're so far from the lives of Catherine Farnsworth or"—I almost said Vivie's name but caught it in time—"that it's almost sweet. My only purpose is to help them. I know running a brothel seems an improbable way to do it, and I don't expect you to understand. But we're so far apart that you imagine me doing the very last thing I would ever do."

His face had fallen to misery. I was drawing the line for both of us, again.

"Asa. You're brilliant and soulful and funny and handsome and I . . ." I closed my eyes and sought grounding in my feet. "This is a gap we cannot bridge." My head shook no as I spoke. "I'm so very sorry, but please, I beg you, leave me alone." I kissed his cheek, pointed toward the street door, and sent him out.

Those last months of my training as a nurse at Portland Hospital are as dim in memory as they were to live. Annalee and I made our proposal to Nurse Pell but she refused to discuss it. We began sneaking out of the dormitory to walk by the wharf and talk about what to do.

I wrote to every woman's hospital I'd ever heard of, but I'd never get a place without a letter from old Pell. The Newbury house and practice had not sold so I had no money. I considered returning there to set up an herb dispensary, and begged Annalee to come with me. We'd teach ourselves.

One evening Dr. Jordan found me for a quiet conversation. Nurse Pell had told him I was agitating. I began to apologize, but he put a hand on my arm. "You mistake me. This place is ill-equipped. If I can help you move on, I will. Your talents are wasted here." I promised to bring him names and addresses.

He was trying to protect and warn me. I hope he got out of there.

TEN

All along Vivie had expressed the wish of confronting Vernon Trent, if he showed up. If Benno saw her, he might finally grasp that she could testify against Trent and Peter Sweeny.

We ate dinner in my rooms the night before the meeting. Watching me sort mail and clear the table, Vivie said, "Were you always so patient, or does that come with age?"

Why did every compliment have to hurt? Chuckling, I said, "I don't find demanding, impatient people endearing, do you?"

She made a silly, self-mocking face. "I suppose not."

"Anger and insistence can be childish, but not always. I try to take the long view, which often translates into small, slow, moves, showing up every day, doing the work, keeping my head down. I usually get what I want without all the drama and bother."

"Small sounds like a good place to start," she said.

I agreed. "I love the clinic's dailiness, one girl and another and another. Being consistent and reliable is a part of the job."

She crinkled up her face. "Actually, that sounds terrible."

We laughed. "You're young for that pace yet."

She looked pained, but then worked herself up to say, "I think I want to travel. Do you suppose I could be a companion to someone or a nanny to a family going abroad?"

That was an interesting prospect, and I flattered myself that the pain was from putting so much distance between us. "We can look into it. Are you thinking it'd be easier to conceal your past in another country?"

"More that I wouldn't be so often reminded of it."

I doubted that was true but kept it to myself, and would consider destinations far afield where prosperous Vermont farmers were unlikely to go.

"Not England," she said, dreamy. "I think maybe Italy or Switzerland."

To fall was to be lost, but it was only the end of the first act for the woman herself. In act two, she adjusts to her new condition of body and mind. My own rather elaborate second act, with its long views and small moves, had lasted fifteen years now. Vivie's would be far quicker for having landed at the Double. If we're lucky, fallen women get a third act beyond crippling shame and desperation.

I said, "Disappearing from your life is hard enough; losing everything familiar is harder still, but it's an act of great creativity. Do you have languages?"

She spoke a couple of sentences in French. That presented possibilities.

"Let me tell her." I could hear Junius from the open caucus door as I approached from the hallway. The meeting with Benno would begin shortly and something unexpected was brewing.

Meg and Ciara were in the room with him. "Tell who what?"

Junius looked abashed. "Hello Doc. Why don't we sit?"

I closed the door behind me and stood.

He said, "It turns out that the Female Moral Reform Society has a contact at the *Standard*."

"Yes," I said, a warning.

"So, as you have heard, one of their members is the wife of a city editor. At his wife's prompting, that editor took it upon himself to speak to Asa Vanderpoel about abductions, and about the efforts of a certain brothel owner."

Not two days past I'd sent him away.

"And he spotted my work in the *Rake*. Knew it right away, he said, and came to me this morning."

I should have known that keeping secrets from Asa was foolish.

"The truth is, Doc," Junius continued, "He's the right person for this. He owns the paper, he's unassailable, and he's interested. I worked with him for years and we understand one another. We talked it over. We can get it right."

I knew what Asa's interest was. "Do we have to decide this now?" I asked, unhappy that they'd already spoken. "We're just gathering information today."

Ciara said, "He's downstairs."

I stared at her and then at Junius.

Meg said, "Can you two leave us alone for a moment, please?"

Ciara's eyebrows hit her hairline.

As they left, I suggested Ciara introduce Vivie to Junius.

As she closed the door, Meg said, "I take it you didn't sleep with the handsome man who loves you so much he's trying to help you stop some slavers."

I put my face in my hands. "This is him not taking no for an answer."

"That's a new one." I wanted to laugh but couldn't. She said, "You need to focus today, so the real question is how much of a distraction he is."

She laughed in sympathy at my pitiful look.

I said, "Let me think a minute. If Junius says he's the right person we have to consider it." Asa would get an education, which could only help the working girls of New York now and later. Any hint of an affair would be calamitous in this context, so that bolstered my resolve. "We'd need some assurances about sentiments to be kept out of a paper like the *Standard*. I won't have sanctimonious editorializing about prostitution. Slaving is our only target."

"I'm sure Junius can handle that."

It was ridiculous. Idiotic.

I went to see Asa in the salon. It was the first time we'd met in daylight, and I kept myself far back on my side of a line despite the gentleness in his face and voice as he assured me that all decisions about publication could be made later if publicity was needed, and not before.

"Forgive me for turning up," he said, "but first Alfred came to me, and then I spotted Junius. He may have an idea that I . . ."

"He has a taste for gossip," I said, tight. But at least Junius would have some context for my work and position.

"He promised to keep it quiet. Doc, look, I begin to appreciate what you're trying to do, and want to help. You're risking a great deal for these girls, and it's very brave."

"Thank you." He gave no instructions and asked for nothing. His presence actually settled me, like having Elliott at my back. "You can observe with Junius."

We arranged the listening post on the floor above the caucus in a gown closet that nicely dulled noises. They could lie on the floor and look through slits hidden below by plaster leaves in the ceiling medallion, or sit up to listen. We gave them blankets to lie on and to baffle the sound of notebooks, and insisted they remove shoes and buttoned coats and cufflinks. A certain amount of noise was expected but no conversation to betray direct connection to another room, and they settled in amidst acres of perfumed silk and satin.

Israel brought Benno, Hank, and Vernon Trent to the caucus where Meg and I waited. Israel paused in the doorway but closed it behind him and sat next to me. Benno stared at him like he'd lost his mind.

I said, "Benno, I believe you've met Israel Bixby. He's run security here for many years and knows more about brothel traffic and operations than the rest of us put together."

Benno sneered at all the women and Negroes, enjoying his supremacy.

Israel nodded without a hint of deference and said, "Mr. O'Connor," in that formidable baritone.

Benno sat down and said, "What's up with you and Sweeny?"

I very much wanted to ask him the same thing, but said, "As you know, he's a client of the house. He's very particular, and our girls are special."

"Yeah, but why'd he make me come here?"

I reminded myself to take my time and try to show him the way I saw girls and his possible future in the ward. "That surprised me too," I said. "I suppose he thought if you're getting into prostitution, I might be able to advise you and save you some trouble, having done it successfully for many years." Benno showed no interest in learning anything, so I shrugged and added, "He likes the way we do things here."

He showed no intention either of introducing the man beside him, so I turned to Vernon Trent, the source of so much havoc. "I'm Doc Hastings." I loathed him for Vivie's sake, and he just sat there. Where I thought to find a strategic juggernaut sat a lump of impulsive beef. After a long moment, I said, "And you are?"

He glanced at Benno, who had probably told him to keep quiet. I said, "He has to tell you your name?"

Benno said, "That's Bobby the Snatch."

Meg said, "Your mother must be so proud."

I said, "Who's Vernon Trent?"

Trent stirred himself. I knew he could speak because he'd wheedled his way into that party in Vermont. "Nice place you have here, Doc. I bet a man could enjoy himself." His voice was slow and sleepy.

I realized that we could have done this over drinks and dinner, using and also demonstrating all our arts and guile, with the promise of girls at the end. I had designed it instead for Junius to listen, and now Asa, and had to hope it was the right move. I would play the successful entrepreneur.

"Thank you. I've been hearing reports of your enterprise for months now." He preened at this, a vacuous half-lidded smile. "In this business, that's a problem. If you want to last more than a few months, you've got to be discreet. That means quiet."

Trent shrugged, but I'd gotten Benno and Hank's attention.

I ticked off on my fingers, calm and matter of fact, "Reenie Byrne, Catherine Farnsworth, whom I held as she died, and was all over the papers. That's just sloppy, and totally unnecessary. Killing girls is not popular, nor is it particularly sporting."

Trent smirked and said, "Never got in my way before."

I looked to Benno and sighed. "This is your plan? Seems like a pile of liabilities, including whatever's out of joint with Peter Sweeny."

"All right, all right," said Hank.

I took a big breath and said, "Here's my best advice, Benno. If you want to succeed in the flesh trade, you need people who can groom and manage girls. Kidnapping and smacking them around might be where some people get their jollies, but it's not a smart or viable way to run a business."

Trent laughed, an embarrassing sound.

Meg said, "Benno, why don't you give us an idea of what you're trying to do, and we can tell you how we can help."

"And what exactly do you do here?"

Meg metamorphosed before us, becoming a temptress, her voice a river of juices. "I'm the one who keeps New York's most gorgeous and alluring women sober, cheerful, on time, and still working for us a year from now."

Trent laughed again, and she looked him over like he was yesterday's news.

Her voice was still silky. "I'm the one who can tell at a glance if a man gets off on tits or ass, being whipped or tickled or fed with a baby bottle, if he keeps his clothes on, his shoes on, his hat on."

I thought she'd gone too far but she knew what she was doing. Benno was aroused enough to ignore the insult, and was likely expecting to throw her up against some wall when we concluded our business. He didn't seem to register her skill in reading men, let alone manipulating them, that men were even legible, and some obvious, or that people could be good or bad at reading one another. He said, "Sweeny fucked you?"

Before she could deflect, we heard a girl shriek directly above our heads. It sounded like Susannah had gone into the gown closet and found Junius and Asa on the floor. It was too loud and my heart pounded, my face flushing. "What are you doing?" she cried. There was no audible response, but presumably a lot of gesturing for quiet. I pictured Asa rolling from belly to back and lost the first seconds.

Israel got calmly to his feet and was out the door. I recovered and said, "The girls' rooms are directly above. Sorry about that. Someone probably found another girl wearing some of her underthings." Benno was listening for more, and next we heard two girls giggling. "They're jealous of one another's finest silks and lace." Trent's gaze went long and Hank rolled his eyes.

Soon Israel's voice rumbled but too softly to make out words, followed by footsteps moving away.

"Boys," I said turning back to the business at hand and offering praise, "you have so many strengths. A smooth graft operation," here I threw Hank a small smile, "all those patronage jobs to dispense, friends at the station house, pretty much free reign in the ward. You're perfectly positioned to do great business if you keep your operation tidy. What you're lacking is a clear plan and experienced hands to execute it."

"And that's you?" said Trent, cluing in.

"No thank you," I said, "I already have two jobs. But I can suggest qualified women to run it for you. You need women to run girls." Though he showed no pleasure, Benno clocked that I did not want in.

"Okay," said Trent, "let's talk percentages."

I grew more affable. "Now keep your pants on, big boy." I turned to Benno. "Can you give me a sense of what's already in place?"

Israel returned, cool and steady as ever. Benno nodded at Trent, who puffed up to brag. "We got a lotta pretty girls, maybe not so pretty as yours," he said, winking at Meg.

"How many?" I asked, lightly.

His face went slack and he blinked a few times, started to count on his thumb and fingers. Benno wasn't watching but Hank was horrified. Trent said, "A dozen. I can get more."

"And how do you do that?"

"I used to work upstate, whatever, Pennsylvania, but now I stay in town."

"Kidnapping, you mean."

"Well, usually they just come. I offer a job or a place to stay or something."

"And a drink with something in it?"

"Well sure, if you want to move them."

I explained that I thought that was the wrong way to go about it, that so many girls were actually looking for work that it was a waste of energy and an unnecessary risk to hold them against their will. If they were planning to scale up, it wouldn't work.

"Yeah," said Trent, "but if you offer them a job, you have to pay them, see. This way we pay a few guys to watch the place and it's much cheaper."

I nodded. I swallowed. Everyone around the table had their private reactions to this. Benno and Hank at least understood that we wouldn't like his answer, and waited for my response. I said, "So you work them until what, they die?"

"Nah," Trent said, "til they're used up."

I said, "Obviously I have a very different approach. I treat girls well and keep them healthy, which clients appreciate. The girls look great, they're not mean or strung out on laudanum, and they don't spread the clap. It keeps clients coming back." Then I made my case that Jane and Lizzie had to move their establishments every few months, and that even they trapped their girls with debt, not force.

"Nah, it's fine," said Trent.

"So far," said Meg.

Benno's eyes went to slits. "Is that a threat?" He spoke one language only.

She smiled, indulgent. "An operation bigger than one little crib will attract attention. You need happy girls. The key to your whole expansion plan is happy girls! Girls who work for you because you pay them and treat them decently, so all your advantages in the ward can protect you."

Benno glanced at Trent and then at Israel, who wore a rather grave expression.

Benno said, "What are you looking at?"

Israel said, "Slavers."

"What?" Benno wasn't sure if it was an insult. I did a double-take when Israel used that word.

Israel said, "You're slavers. Lotta people don't like that much. Doc's trying to tell you you can get all you want and more without slaving and save yourself a lot of trouble. Pretty simple, be a slaver, or don't."

Benno probably wanted to say he had no problem slaving but Israel was big and had the home advantage. I'd have liked to see what happened next, but Trent piped up.

"Oh now, we're just having a bit of fun. Who don't like a pretty girl? We have all kinds of people come through. You know boss, we could have a crib for colored folks too."

He really was dim, and I guessed childhood hunger or head injury. The aw-shucks talk was probably an imitation of someone he once worked for.

I changed my tack, thinking that my advice might land better if it appeared masculine, if it smacked of Tammany. To Benno I said, "The patronage system works so well because it's a trade. You offer benefits. Jobs, belonging, clubs, a hand when it's needed. If Tammany gave out nothing, do you think it'd command so much loyalty or be so powerful?"

Perhaps he'd understood this in regard to votes and jobs, but had trouble connecting it to girls, who got neither. Maybe he expected everything to come easily now because of his connection to Tweed. Or maybe he had a diagnosis. I examined his face for signs of mercury poisoning. I said, "How long do you expect to stick around? Because if you're talking a year or two, sure, go for it. I've been here almost a decade."

That got his attention.

I said, "Can I at least see your girls to make sure they're healthy? Syphilis will kill the whole plan."

Hanky Pank spoke. "Not a good idea. Boss, let's wrap this up. Doc is offering a different way to get and manage girls than

Bobby the Snatch here. There's a lot to consider." That confirmed the girls were on his property.

Benno looked at Hank like he was a wad of phlegm that had landed on his shoe. "What's got into you now? Why not have both? Bobby has a knack for one kind of girl and Doc another. Then we got something for everybody." He looked at me like he'd discovered electricity.

"Sorry Benno," I said. "If you want my help, it's one or the other. Abducting girls is totally unnecessary, and will ruin everything. I want no part of it."

"Is that so?"

"It is."

"What about your friend Sweeny?"

"I'll tell him just what I told you. I have reason to believe he agrees with me." This tipped Vivie's hand somewhat, but he missed it. "Maybe that's why he set this up, so I could persuade you to do things differently."

"Jesus Christ," he said, raising his voice, "You pretend to be such a high and mighty goody-goody but you're just a fucking baby killer. I've had just about enough of you thinking you're better than me. You can be replaced like that." He snapped his fingers. Moral outrage fit him like a Sunday bonnet with buttercups.

"Sure," I said. "But keep in mind Benno, we've hosted thousands of men here over the years."

"So what?"

"So I have a good memory."

Finally, finally, it dawned on him, the men whose tastes and histories I knew, and the secrets spilled at the Double, plus the girls I'd put back together, and what I might have on Oakey and George and Sweeny. Trustworthiness was outside his experience.

He'd never considered the thousands of times I'd kept my mouth shut, and what trouble I could make for him if I began to speak. He knew he was out of his depth, and despised me anew.

I tried to make it easy. "Here's the key to me, Benno. I protect people. Girls in particular. That's the whole story. If you treat girls well, I'll help all I can."

He was pretty much deciding he'd have to kill me when I said, "And by the way, we do keep records. Some are stored here, some there, some with an influential gentleman, who would be very distressed if anything should happen to me." It was the first and only time I'd threatened him, and his last chance to do this the easy way. My ace waited in the hall.

He stood up, knocking his chair over. "We're done."

Israel and I stood as well, though Hank, Trent, and Meg kept their seats as a way to cool the temperature.

I said, "As you wish." He waited before moving toward the door so Israel could open it for him. Israel's movement was so menacing even as it took the form of service, that Benno slid sideways through the doorframe. It had always been a long shot, that Benno would absorb what I could tell him. His power was built on violence and he'd stick with it, and the threat of exposure was too abstract. I guessed his next move would be to take out his anger on someone who worked for me.

In the hallway, Vivie stood between Willy and Ciara. The look she gave Vernon Trent would have flattened most mortals, but after registering her face, he lit up and greeted her like an old friend. "There you are, little princess! Landed on your feet, didja? This is some nice place."

"No thanks to you," she said, offended. "You're a cursed brute and I hope you rot in hell for all eternity!" Benno didn't know Vivie. He might never have seen her, and as usual showed no interest in a girl he wasn't fucking or stealing.

"Oh now," Trent said, laughing. Whatever came out of her mouth had no effect on him. The only information related to Vivie that penetrated his skull was her diminutive size and sweet appearance. She made him happy, and he had no idea what sexual slavery meant to her. He felt jubilant having escaped the meeting, and greeted with her presence, thought to express his pleasure by collecting her. "Come on kiddo, let's have some fun!"

He bent low and I thought he might kneel and play at begging forgiveness, but he plowed right into her belly, grabbed her wrist, and slung her up and over his shoulder. He no more respected her person than he would a poppet. Her appearance and size were enough for him to do with her as he pleased, his for the taking. I would have tackled him myself, as would Willy, but Trent stood between us and the stairs. I begged him to put her down. Israel was charging down the hall and I put out a hand.

Vivie was not his. She screamed and thrashed and he laughed. "Oh now," he said and only once did I see doubt flicker in his posture as he bounced down the stairs. He began to sing some filthy drinking ditty. I don't know if he expected to carry her for the procession to the door with Hank and Benno or to take her home and ravish her, but while he was busy navigating the two turns in the staircase, she had stopped screaming and kicked out a foot and reached around his body, fumbling with her skirts. Israel had raced ahead and put himself between them and the door, but by that time I'd registered a sound, a sliding, ripping, thrusting sound, a third, a fourth, a fifth repetition, a movement of her arm. Israel recoiled.

On the bottom step Trent paused and beneath the fall of Vivie's hair I saw her fist around the handle of a blade. Trent registered some pain.

There was a pause when he began to groan and fall. His grip slipped off her as he grabbed for his back but never reached it.

Vivie landed on her hands and knees. I moved toward her but she leapt to her feet and scrambled to the door, shoving Bud Bean and running out into the cold.

"Vivie, wait!" I said to Willy, "Go with her!" and yelled for someone to bring my bag. Willy and Ciara took off. Trent's wheezing told me she'd hit a lung. He had landed face down and I tried to lift his coat but it was pinned under him. "Who has a knife? Quick!"

Hank handed me a switchblade that sliced through many layers of fabric. There were five distinct punctures. One had glanced off a rib and got a little messy but the others penetrated. If that blade reached deep he was a goner. I felt for a heartbeat and sited a wound that pierced the pericardium. He began to convulse: once, twice as time slowed in death, and it was done. I kept my hand on his back until I was sure there was no pulse. Ciara dropped my bag beside me as I fell from my knees to my bottom. I looked at the blood on my hand. It wasn't much. All the damage was internal.

Benno was pale and blank, and Hank said, "Jesus, she killed him." I stood and handed him back his switchblade.

"The fuck she did," said Benno and kicked at Trent's shoe.

"Bloody moron," said Meg, "picking her up like he owned her after kidnapping her before? Scared her out of her wits!"

Ciara said, "Adiós, slaver." Benno finally registered Vivie's identity and glared at me. I saw him realize that I knew what was between him and Sweeny, and that Vivie had been at the Double for some time. The rage that turned his face purple seemed very distant to me. All I could think was, where would she go?

Hanky Pank had the most presence of mind. He said to Benno, "We had nothing to do with it, boss. Let's get out of here." With Trent dead, did Vivie even pose a threat to them? She'd never seen either one of them before.

Benno tried to menace me but he barely reached my nose. Israel stepped right between us, forcing Benno to fall back. "You'll pay for this," he said, turning to go.

That struck me funny. "I pay for everything else." Hank kept him moving out the door.

Bud Bean, Israel, the twins, and I looked at one another. Putting my hand on his arm, I said to Israel, "Get Asa and Junius out of here." He moved toward the stairs. To Meg and Ciara I said, "Where would she go?"

We had no idea. She had no friends in New York outside the house. "To Bud I said, "If Willy found her, where would he take her?"

Bud said, "He lives somewhere nearby, further west on Twenty-First maybe."

I told Ciara, "Get him cash, all we have on hand." She ran. To Bud I said, "You can scarper with it, or you can search them out and give it to her. To *her*, not him. If you bring me a note from her with the number you delivered, I'll give you the same amount. Israel may have the address."

Israel had brought Junius and Asa back down the stairs. I went to them, sending Israel to Bud. They stared at the body lying on the floor as I said, "You've got to go. Stay away from here, no letters unless you use a third party."

Asa said, "Are you all right?"

"I'm not stabbed." To Junius I said, "Did you get what you need?"

He began to speak but Asa said, "Watch tomorrow's *Standard*."

Now Junius and I both stared at him.

He said, "We'll go write it now, the two of us, including the death and why it happened. Can you send someone who witnessed it to my office before 8?"

I looked to Junius and he said, "Better to get ahead of it."

I said to Asa, "Meg will walk you out." Stepping closer and looking him fully in the face, I pleaded with him. "After every sentence ask yourself if you're doing any harm to women including—no, especially—abducted girls and girls trying to survive. No moralizing about prostitution."

He said, "I'll do my best," and I believed him.

To Meg I said, "Walk them out on the far side of the clinic."

My worry for Vivie pulsed and twisted all that evening as the police and morticians came through and the twins sorted the mess of canceling, for now, two days' worth of clients.

Bud Bean returned with a note from Vivie that said, "Thank you for everything, $760, we disappear and begin again, all my love always. Someday I'll find you." I gasped for breath.

Brushing off any award, Bud promised to say nothing of Willy. He told me nothing of their plans if they had any, and I insisted on giving him $200.

"Hush money?" he said.

"A reward for keeping faith with them while they flee for their lives. Use it well. Use it so it helps you or someone else."

He shook my hand, and said he would.

I wrote and posted the delayed letter to her parents, hoping it would reach them before the newspapers did, and never said a word to them or anyone about her wanting to see Italy or Switzerland.

Bert sent home roasts with maids and porters. Some girls rushed off for the rare night on the town, some stayed in to speak of Vivie. A crowd of reporters tipped off by police waited outside, tried to get in.

Corabelle was spooked, afraid Vernon Trent would haunt us.

"Do you feel a presence?" I asked her. She wasn't sure. "He

didn't strike me as vengeful," I said, and referred her to Aunty Laure for further inquiry.

Martin arrived and said no one had seen Hank or Benno. I wondered if they'd get word to Peter Sweeny, at home in his townhouse with his mother, that the women of the Double Standard Sporting House might know he raped Lavinia Curtis, or if he'd find out from the morning paper.

Late that night I fell out the back door into the garden, lingering a moment where Asa kissed me. Thank heaven it had gone no further, because at that moment he was composing an article that would put my business on the city's front page. Wishing he had met Vivie, my composure frayed. Of all the people to tell our story. Abuse is such a strange prism: a clear light like hers pours in and exits in a ray of murder. My own culpability weighed heavily. In teaching her shamelessness and self-defense, I'd given her potent weapons. How far would it take her that she acted on her own behalf for all of Trent's victims past and future, for Catherine?

I slept well enough, considering. Meg came to the clinic office early, and handed me the *Standard*. The headline read, "Kidnapper of Innocent Girl Meets Surprising End."

> *A note to our readers: The subject of this article is far outside the bounds of propriety, and we publish it knowing some readers will take offense. We apologize for the affront to delicacy, but believe it imperative to bring public awareness and ultimately prosecution to recent shocking developments in criminal vice. It is not pleasant reading, but it is an authentic record of verifiable facts, and we publish it from the deepest regard for the public interest and safety. The power of the press is one of the few countervailing powers to the rampant crime and corruption in our city.*

A man whose real name is not yet revealed, known upstate as Vernon Trent and in the Sixteenth ward as Bobby the Snatch, died at an uptown brothel yesterday, stabbed by a sixteen-year-old girl he kidnapped, ruined, and sold earlier this year. She defended herself when he put her over his shoulder in an apparent attempt to kidnap her a second time.

Trent met Miss Lavinia Curtis at a family party in her hometown of Bennington, Vermont, in the spring. He posed as a traveling salesman to gain entry to the home of a local merchant hosting an open house on a Sunday afternoon. The sweet and educated daughter of a dairy farmer and Vermont State Legislator John Curtis, Miss Curtis was drugged and abducted for the purpose of selling her purity. When that was done, Trent sold her again to a downtown bagnio. All the while her captors claimed she was accruing debt and kept her under lock and key while forcing her into the most degrading and unrelenting employment. They also addicted her to laudanum.

After Miss Curtis was gravely injured by a patron wielding a knife, her life was saved by Miss Nell Hastings, a nurse who runs a free clinic for girls and women. She was moved by the girl's plight and purchased the debt allegedly accrued to her, freeing her from servitude. Miss Hastings also owns the Double Standard Sporting House, an elite brothel serving a wealthy and important clientele. Miss Curtis resided at the Double Standard during her convalescence, as a guest and not an employee. Ruined for Bennington but unwilling to suffer prostitution, Miss Curtis was invited by Miss Hastings to heal and to recover from her ordeal, and to consider her future life.

Miss Hastings became aware that Vernon Trent was conducting more widespread slaving operations in Manhattan. Recent accounts in the Weekly Rake of the kidnapping, escape, and assault of Catherine Farnsworth of Bethel, Pennsylvania, that resulted in Miss Farnsworth's death have shocked the city.

Hoping to learn the whereabouts of other missing girls, Miss Hastings agreed to meet with the presumed members of the slaving ring. Under pretext of bestowing her expertise in more high-class forms of prostitution, she met with Vernon Trent, Tammany's Sixteenth ward chief Benjamin O'Connor, and Henry Philip Wotley, owner of several concert saloons. Members of the press were concealed nearby in service of disrupting and exposing the procurement ring.

Little concrete information was disclosed by Trent, O'Connor, and Wotley, beyond the gangsters' desire to create a vast prostitution operation and to populate it with kidnapped girls in order to save the trouble of paying them.

As the meeting ended, Miss Curtis revealed her presence to Mr. Trent, the man responsible for her enslavement and ruination. An imposing man, he was delighted to see her and in a most misguided show of power, threw the diminutive Miss Curtis over his shoulder and proceeded down a staircase and toward the street door.

Terrified to be enslaved a second time, Miss Curtis withdrew the blade she had understandably begun keeping in her boot against such incursions against her person, and thrust it into Mr. Trent's back several times, including one blow that pierced his heart, killing him. She bolted out the door while Miss Hasting tried to save the brute's life. Miss Curtis has not been seen since.

Infrequently do we have occasion to report satisfaction in any crime, but this brave young girl acted in self-defense. Surely she served justice and the women of New York, avenging herself and forestalling large-scale abduction. We can only hope justice catches up with the other masterminds of graft and corruption,

> **rackets and schemes that prevail in our city. We do not sanction vigilantism, but hope our justice system will recognize the true heroines of this day, and hold more gangsters to account.**

I was flooded by noise, by the specter of tens of thousands of people reading my name and Vivie's over breakfast. My face and scalp, my chest, my hands, all flamed in different ways and directions. I put my head down, and Meg threw an arm over me. "Well," she said, "this will be an interesting day. Shall we sell tickets?"

So this was exposure, as if I'd been placed downstage center with all the lights up and a full house staring at me. Meg said there was a cacophony of reporters, police, and outraged citizens congregating on Twenty-Fifth Street. Either Benno or I was finished, perhaps both. We opened the clinic in a limited way but I stayed out, useless.

The morning was a blur. The twins thought house breakfast would put all the girls on the same page, and allow me to feel their solidarity. What they knew about Vivie and Trent was so far hearsay.

When the girls and the Bixbys and Aunty Laure convened around the table in the dining room, Meg stood up and said right to me, "Let's talk about revenge."

The room fell silent for three seconds and then everyone began speaking at once. Meg rapped on the table. "One at a time, please. Vivie had good reason to hate Vernon Trent, but she never would have killed him if he hadn't been such an idiot as to pick her up. He put her over his shoulder like a sack of potatoes, and she was done with being treated like that. And brava to her for it."

Girls cheered and clapped and pounded the table, Tatiana most loudly.

Meg said, "Who here has taken revenge on a man who wronged you?"

The girls looked at one another, and Susannah said, "A friend did."

I stood. "I did."

This was not premeditated. I had a good answer to the question and could not remember why I'd never told the story. What was the point of keeping these old secrets? No one moved or made a sound as I paced behind one row of girls and went back the other way. "It will come as no surprise to you that I made a mortal enemy of a doctor in a hospital where I worked when I was nineteen."

Everyone laughed and resumed breathing as I kept pacing, circling the table one way and then the other. Most girls averted their eyes, but not the twins. Meg and Ciara sat at the opposite ends of that long table and their attention held me as if I were about to fall all over again but this time they would save me. Each one stood and closed a door as I gathered the breath to say it. I spoke quickly.

"While I'm sure I was insufferable about it, I did have quite a bit of experience."

I stopped pacing and stood taller.

"Alfred Lund was his name. A lazy drunk, actually. Obstetrics and gynecology are the lowest prestige fields in medicine but that hasn't stopped them from trying to take birth away from nurses and midwives. He was this close to incompetent. Closer." I held my thumb and finger together. My voice evaporated and I stopped pacing to leverage what I could. I tried to remember the girl I was. Tears fell, but my voice returned. "There was a mother in labor, her name was Lily McBride. She came already a whole day in travail, already bleeding. The babe was breech, but Dr. Lund had no experience. He examined her, his clumsiness causing her to scream, hemorrhage, and fall unconscious. This offended him, and he left with no further instruction to me or anyone. The girl was bleeding to death. I sent an orderly for another doctor or anyone, and after a moment, I acted. I had attended breech births with both my parents and I thought I might save the babe if not the mother. I turned the child with external manipulation, and in two contractions he was born. My friend Annalee Warren and another nurse, Dara Bauer, helped me. Dara took the babe and I did all I could for Lily. We could have said she delivered the boy on her own. There was no accidental way to surgically repair a perineum, but it turned out the main tear was deep in her uterus, something yet beyond me.

"The nursing supervisor came in when I was finishing. Lund had not returned. You would think his dereliction was the main scandal. His abandonment of Lily, his incompetence in the face of an ordinary complication. No, the scandal was a nurse trainee delivering a child and performing surgery. I was upbraided and nearly assaulted by this horrid woman called Christine Pell. I apologized and asked, sincerely, what I should have done instead. Her only response was that there would be hell to pay. Poor Lily died anyway a few hours later, but the child lived. She called him Samuel.

"Where was this, Doc?" asked Ruby, and Ciara looked daggers at her. You didn't interrupt a woman in the middle of a soul confession.

"Portland, Maine," I said, undeterred.

Ruby nodded, flushing.

"Of course I explained Lund's failure and flight, which was grievous for him, but also made my position more difficult." I swallowed, and found my throat clear. "A week later, Lund and his friend Schaeffer threw a sheet over my head and drugged me, and I never knew what they did to me until it was all over. That, I will tell you, is a mixed blessing." I heaved a sigh. Had they intended rape or murder? Rape could have been hushed up or as usual blamed on the victim, but no one would have to guess who mutilated me. It was perhaps their way of working up their nerve for murder.

"Two women saved me, a girl who worked in the hospital laundry called Wren who found me, and a brothel nurse in the neighborhood she brought to see me." I patted my bodice and began unbuttoning. My voice had become childlike.

Faces went slack and disbelieving. Meg was crying, Israel kept his head down. I loosened the ribbon on my chemise and worked it open, revealing a network of shiny scars from hectic shallow slices to my skin, and puckered voids where my nipples used to be. I turned so everyone could get a good look. The girls were shocked and sad but a few were angry. "I woke bleeding everywhere, including inside. They raped and cut me. I should have died. I was meant to. It's strange that I lived, but Wren was quick to get help and Gwin was very, very good. She sewed me up and kept all this clean." I passed a hand over my chest. "Later we experimented on the wounds to my bladder, using a technique originated just in time. It took a full year to heal me and on many days I gave up. Gwin saved me again and again." Sims published his paper on silver sutures in 1852, and this was 1853.

Ciara stood up as if to come to me but I shook my head and she sat. I retied my chemise and said, "The question was revenge."

The room began to buzz with energy. Ruby said, "Please tell us you got some."

I nodded, buttoning. "Once for fun and once for real. I'd gone to work as a nurse at the house where I landed, helping Gwin. It was called Rosetta's, but Rosetta herself was long gone. Gwin ran it for an absentee landlord, a sailing captain. Lund came in one night. We put all sorts of emetics and laxatives into his drinks to make him puke and shit himself. That was entertaining. I hoped he'd die but he didn't.

"We treated men as well as girls. One night this bruiser came in after a fight. He'd been scarred and broken many times. I took care of him and when he was fit, he offered his services. Nobody but Wren knew where I was. I had disappeared from the hospital, they never knew what became of me or if I lived. They all knew who was responsible, especially after bloody instruments and towels were found in the basement. They resigned in haste before they could be arrested. Later Wren heard they'd landed at a maternity hospital in Hartford."

Shock and outrage around the table.

"Well, I couldn't have that," I said, which the girls loved. I supposed Lund and Schaeffer might have repented, might have tried to learn or improve, but the odds were slim. That was my only regret, that I wasn't sure they hadn't tried to be better. But this was a tale of revenge. My emissary's name was Gary. I'd forgotten the rest if I ever knew. "So the bruiser, I asked him to break all the bones of both their hands."

After a beat, Ruby said, "Fucking hell Doc. Did he?"

I received in the mail a newspaper article, and was surprised that Gary had that degree of literacy. "He did." I never told Gwin. The girls clapped and shook their heads. I didn't know if Lund lived. "Doctors Attacked Outside Tavern," was the headline. I wondered if they tried to set the bones or amputated. The pain would have been ungodly, suicide by drugs or drink likely. I wasn't proud, I wasn't ashamed, but I ended their ability to do a certain kind of damage. I wouldn't call it justice, maybe good hygiene.

"A woman may not know more than a man in a position of authority, no matter how unworthy. The worst part is that I never spoke up when I saw mistakes, and there were plenty. I only tried to save Lily and her baby because we were left alone. I never corrected him as he jammed his hand into her womb and flailed around like he was digging potatoes."

I sat down and said, "I wish I'd done it myself, like Vivie did."

The girls mobbed me, took my hands and kissed me, wrapped me up and petted me. I let them. It was a half measure, that telling. I dreaded someone from Newbury or Portland reading the *Standard* and making connections. I never wanted that circle to close and tighten. Oh Vivie, I thought, I wish we could have ridden out this storm together.

The Standard of December 30 created a tsunami. Newsboys were mugged for copies and they reprinted three times. Bets were taken for how long Vivie would remain hidden and Benno would remain ward chief. He and Hank were in hiding. The flash papers dug up all sorts of dirt on Vernon Trent, and I waited for the news that their crib had been found and the girls liberated.

The one surprise came in the *Herald*. They ignored Trent's death and the slaving ring but chose December 31 to publish an exposé on an investigation underway by Dr. Peter Singer of Women's Hospital on the number of surgeries being performed in the city's brothels. He reported that one shameless but unnamed Satan's Circus brothel nurse claimed to have more skill even than J. Marion Sims, father of gynecological surgery. Indeed I would have happily put my rates against his but I was fairly certain he had never consulted on the repair of his own vaginal wall. My clinic practice was not illegal yet, but that was coming.

We did open for New Year's Eve, regulars and friends only, but notably, Peter Sweeny, George Barnard, and Oakey Hall stayed away. The city paused on the brink of 1869, and New

Years' Day brought a bit of snow and quiet. Meg dared venture the possibility that Vivie, in her refusal to submit to abuse, had saved the Double Standard.

And then this limbo ended. Early on the second as Nina, Betsy, and I resupplied the exam carts in the clinic for a full day, a loud knock sounded at the door. Betsy opened it to four puffed-up men, two in uniform, asking for me.

"Nell Hastings, you're under arrest."

I asked, "What's the charge?" aware that Tammany didn't need a pretext to punish me.

He said, "Kidnapping and procurement of Lavinia Curtis."

Part 3

THE FALLEN WOMAN PLOT

ELEVEN

Thirty years past, the city of New York built a jail atop the old Collect Pond that straightaway began to sink. The stench inside the hulking Egyptian revival mausoleum known as the Tombs was a fair effigy of hell. Did ancient Egyptians believe in hell? I retched upon entry and remained sleepy and nauseous as long as I was there. It's a miracle anyone functions in that miasma, and it explains why it took me days to question why they'd bypassed the local precinct and brought me straight there.

At the entrance a hulking pharaoh bedecked in diamonds enthroned himself on a prehistoric easy chair. His duty to wear jewels fulfilled, he asked no questions and showed no interest. A holding cell was next. A gray matron opened an iron gate and one of the arresting party pushed me through and vanished. The room was fifteen feet by forty with a slab along one wall where sat several young harlots. None looked up, so I sat apart.

Sooner or later someone at Tammany would realize the gravity of their error. The longer my stay, the more they would owe or fear me. Meanwhile I was a girl on the bench: slattern, dollymop, whore. Or rather, profiteer, procurer, slaver.

Had I not paid Emily Wrigley $650 for Lavinia Curtis and kept her within the Double's walls for months? In Vivie's absence any defense might as well be stated in German. I bought her to free her, absolutely.

I slid toward sleep and dreamt of rooms and roof lines and earthquakes and mudslides and woke to a girl rummaging in my skirts. I grabbed her wrist and bent her to her knees, the offending arm twisted behind her. "Oy!" she yelled.

"Keep your hands off me."

"Okay, okay, I didn't think you could fight."

I jacked the arm just to the point of shoulder dislocation and she howled before I released.

"Looks can be deceiving," I said and she scurried back down the bench.

Fatigue, nausea, and shortness of breath registered. No wonder I slept but this was no time to be unguarded. Israel would have fits.

"Hold up," said another girl. "Hold up, I know you."

I shook my head no. "You don't."

She understood. I remembered her, but not her ailment. Termination? Syphilis? No recollection, but I'd seen that daffy sneer before. She said to her companion, "Leave her be. She's all right."

"Fuck I will, Daisy! Twat almost broke my arm." Right, Daisy.

"You were rolling her! It's only fair. Leave her be, I'm telling you."

"Bloody hell, it was you who said that's a prize and no mistake."

"Sorry Doc," said Daisy. "I'll keep these ruffians off you."

I blinked my thanks and wondered how long before I was hearing their stories and inspecting their vulvas. All I wanted was to close my eyes.

Soon a skinny goon was calling out, "Nell Hastings!" The three girls were gone. I had slept for some time, my joints stiff. My jailer gripped my biceps and steered me down the hall to a room marked, "Court of General Sessions."

It was a busy place, full of defendants and their warders. I was the only visible woman. The judge was predictable in his type and manner, peremptory and flashing his authority. Any kind of resource detectable in the defendant and bail was set; you could buy your way out. That was easy. I imagined the twins securing lawyers and bail bondsmen and whatnot. Most cases were of drunkenness and vagrancy, disturbing the peace and disrespecting officers.

Memories of Newbury pushed up through the trance of charges and dispositions. I had glimpses of my parents in a rare relaxed mood in high summer sun, striped patterns on the swaths of sea at Plum Island, light shining green through mounting swells and breakers. I was held tight in vast cold water against the weight of wet fabric. Later I learned to swim, to submerge my face between inhales, slicing circles and kicks with my limbs. I shared precious little with my parents now beyond medicine, certainly not the small-town rectitude that dignified our poverty. I retained their arrogance, anyway, despite unpromising circumstances.

That was a waking memory. Drifting into sleep in the long hours of lengthening light, I dreamt I was sent to the hospital laundry for clean sheets. I set my lamp on the floor and was grabbed from behind. I yelled and kicked but was quickly insensible. I woke to Wren taking the cover from my face and cutting the bonds from my hands. "Oh gosh, you're alive. What do I do?" she whispered, panicked. "You're bleeding everywhere."

I dropped my chin to see fields of blood across my breasts and belly, feeling the penetration and seepage of my vulva. I tried to speak but my jaw wouldn't move, and felt my eyes roll up as I passed out.

When they called me to face the Court of General Sessions, daylight was gone and the place nearly empty. My warder steered me to a platform before the judge. I felt myself waver and pressed my feet into the floor. "Miss Hastings, are you drunk?"

"No sir, I'm a bit ill from the air in here."

He didn't hear my answer, as he was reading a set of papers. "What the living hell?" he said, looking up at me. "This is most irregular."

"I would have to agree, sir."

"This is a warrant from Commissioner Goodson."

"Commissioner of . . . ?"

"Police, Madam."

"Thank you."

"He alleges you procured a young girl."

"I did not, sir."

He peered down his nose at me. "I wouldn't think so. He's a lame duck."

"Pardon me?"

"It's January the second. Well, I can't sort this, I'm sorry. I'm remanding you to the Court of Special Sessions. You'll have to wait until they can schedule you."

"Pardon sir, but what does that mean?"

"It means they'll give you over to the matron and set a date for another hearing where evidence will be required. It's not in my power to let you go on bail." He banged a gavel that startled me and waved his hand. "Next!"

Turning to my warder to ask the meaning of January second I realized: the new Governor was sworn in on the first. The office had swung from Republican to Democrat, and the Governor appointed the three Metropolitan Police Commissioners. But that meant it wasn't Tammany who charged me. Why would some outgoing Republican be bothered?

The women's block was much smaller than the men's, three tiers of about fifteen cells, each with a narrow bed and a tiny window, the cell doors standing open. Clumps of girls sat chatting and sewing along the galleries and on the main floor, with Sisters of Charity moving here and there. At suppertime a silent functionary distributed a hunk of bread and a ladle of tea. Breakfast would be the same with rye coffee; at midday the meal was a thicker stew, just enough to keep one alive. More than half the girls had friends bringing food from outside.

I asked for nothing. I was tired of talking, reacting, adjusting. None of my choices mattered and for the moment I found that freeing. A swarm of opportunists tried to sell me their services. Called steerers or drummers, they would make sure a prisoner's case made its way through the proper channels or died a proper death. Some worked for lawyers, some operated singly. Some were charming or funny; I sent them all away. On the men's side a squad of keepers reigned and all they understood was money.

On the women's side everyone answered to the matron, who was out when I first arrived. I heard her long before I ever saw her. Girls called out, "Oh Miss Foster, oh Miss Foster, I'm back!"

"So you are, poor dear," came a strong voice. "Maybe this time we'll get you to the Home for Fallen Women, and let the good shepherd fill your soul."

"Oh now," said the girl. "Not sure I'm ready for that."

Later the matron stopped by my cell and watched me try to wake and sit. A bright presence with a prow of a bust and shrewd expression, she turned her head back and forth as she assessed my situation.

"Never mind, Miss Hastings, we'll speak tomorrow." Her expression said she'd heard about me. "I hope you get some rest. The first night can be confusing."

"Thank you, Matron."

Soon we were locked in darkness, light not worth the risk of fire. I shook all night with cold.

I woke to Gwin praying, which she did in silence. It was two weeks before I could stay conscious, and two months before my broken jaw healed enough for speech. They gave me soups and juices through a straw, made me drink even when not fully awake, even when it dribbled out of my shredded bladder. I knew when Gwin was there, her eyes closed, her breathing regular. More than regular: controlled, intent. Fully present. I woke enough to tell her not to bother, to leave me in that basement. My body was evidence. I was looking for a way around my shock and pain, which she well knew. I choked on sobs that compounded my wounds. Gwin prayed at my bedside several times a day, and breath by breath I sank into her resolve that I should live.

My first visitor in the morning was Meg. She brought clothes and blankets, food and money, a hair brush and soap and towels and candy.

"Thank you," I said, leaving it piled on the bed, except the cash which I put in my stocking. "Next time, water and tea. It's foul in here."

Meg looked horrified. "What happened?"

I shook my head.

"Oh Doc, don't be discouraged! The charge is groundless and you'll be out soon." She withdrew a *Standard* from the pile and brought me up to date on all the fallout from the first article. Benno and Hank, found hiding in an attic at the Eureka, had been arrested. Asa or someone had gotten to the new District Attorney, and Tammany had sacrificed Benno faster than you could say "liability." So much for his lifetime of loyalty. Even so, he had a lot of friends, and plenty of money, and probably wouldn't do real time. New York would never be quite safe for me.

Martin Mitchell had finally taken a squad to break up Trent's crib, which was all the way west on Fifteenth by the river. The two goons keeping watch had been arrested. There were eight girls but they said there'd been many others. I was glad for that. Eight was plenty. Martin brought the freed girls to the clinic, and Nina sent for Minnie.

Meg reported, "They all stayed, it's like a party. Phila's giving them clothes, Bert is feeding them beefsteak and soup and cake. Laure's moved in too as mama bear."

I smiled at that and teared up. "Did you open the house?"

"Sure! Why not?"

I admired her brass but said, "I'm not sure I would. We're still exposed."

She said, "Benno's in jail and Vivie's hailed as an avenging angel! This is our against-all-odds best-case-scenario victory, no?"

I cocked my head and looked at her, given that Vivie was on the run and I was imprisoned.

She sighed. "Fair."

I said, "Benno might be back. And if he's not, who's the successor? It could get even worse."

Meg put her hands to her face, which had no makeup. "Tweed's no fool, Doc. I bet he leaves the Sixteenth alone, for months at least. He'll let the dust settle and see who bubbles up as a likely boss. We've got a little breathing room, I'd bet my life on it. Or Tweed's, anyway. And George and Oakey can be useful now as well, they'll put in a good word where it's needed."

I shook my head over those two. Spending years in prison would certainly set back my plans for a third act. Her confidence that the house was safe gladdened me, but I was pretty sure I would not be going back.

She put her arms around me and I rested my head on her shoulder. "Oh Doc, it's everything, isn't it? Vivie, and being in the paper, and telling your story to the girls—you shook up even Tati with that one. And Asa Vanderpoel showing up, twice. In here at least you can rest!"

I laughed and cried at that. "I'm sorry."

"For what?"

"For all of it. For not protecting Vivie and everyone better."

"None of it is your fault and I sure hope you're not sitting here blaming yourself. I wish we knew why they arrested you."

I told her about the Republican police commission and the Court of Special Sessions having to sort it. "Did you get a lawyer?"

"We sent word to George and Oakey but haven't heard back yet."

"Find out if they've appointed new commissioners."

She asked if she should go to Peter Sweeny, and I said no. "He may realize on his own, but don't ask him for a favor."

"Why not? The slavers are done."

I was in the Tombs because of Vivie. Sweeny might read a request for help as a threat, as extortion. I said with a warning, "Leave him alone. Let him come to me."

She said, "Okay. The courts will figure out you saved Vivie, eventually, I suppose." I wasn't counting on that. We shared a pained look. She said, "Remind me the locations of those affidavits."

They were in my safe, with my attorney and man of business, and Junius, plus one I didn't tell her, Bim Farley at the Wayward Academy. "Please don't mention it to anyone, though. Let someone in Tammany remember the secrets I keep."

I once asked Wren what she said about me that Gwin would treat me in the basement of a hospital full of doctors, and once they'd moved me, give up her own bed, an ancient woman sleeping on a pallet on the dispensary floor. Wren said I was kind and that was all. She must have mentioned my attempt to save Lily McBride.

When I could stay conscious for more than a minute and insisted on trading beds, Gwin said only, "What do you do to prevent apoplexy?"

I wrote with chalk on a slate she had given me, "A vegetable diet and a light sedative, Madeira or small doses of laudanum."

"Never laudanum," she said. "Puts the bowel to sleep and it's hard to shake. Madeira or brandy if they can afford it. If the person is impoverished?"

I wrote, "Patent medicines." High in alcohol but cheaper than wine.

Gwin narrowed her eyes. "Your father is European."

"Was. German. Both parents."

"A doctor?"

"And a midwife."

"She died first."

"By seven years."

She said, "Cannibis, betel nut, coca, even tobacco, can all be grown and in some cases are more salutary than alcohol. You can have the pallet."

I heard what I took to be a Sister of Charity interrogating a young Negro woman. The Sisters worked for the matron. "Are you a Christian?"

"No Ma'am."

"Have you heard of Christ?"

"Yes ma'am."

"And you don't love him?"

"He's very lovable, I'm sure."

"So why not be a Christian if you love him?"

"I've seen many things, Sister. I've been a servant to them who called themselves Christian and I can't be one."

My heart sank for that girl, not least because the idiot nun lectured her on forgiving sin and not holding herself above others. When that had gone on for more minutes than I could stomach, and more loudly than would allow me to sleep, I stood up. In the next cell I found them, a vagrant and this parasite. They both looked at me. I nodded to the girl.

Turning to the nun, I said, "Do you ever try listening instead of prattling on about a God who has clearly forsaken them? I mean, do you have any curiosity at all about what those so-called Christian employers did to her, or are you that intent on making it worse?"

I winked at the girl while the nun said, "It's up to us to seek God. He doesn't forsake us."

"Go away," I said. "You're unequipped for this work."

She was so shocked she forgot to be angry. "You could do better?"

"A toddler could do better. She wouldn't shame this girl for what she's done to survive. That's against God, and no mistake."

"Are you an apostate?"

"Are you a moron?"

The woman was literally cloaked in charity but wouldn't have known it had it smacked her.

"How dare you speak to me that way?"

"How dare you speak to her that way, without empathy while blathering on about love and faith. How many have you saved? Can you count to one?"

Her jaw flapped up and down a few times before she fled. "Bye," I called. Girls in the nearby cells applauded.

"You all right?" I said to the girl on the bed. "I'm Nell."

"I'm Josephine."

"Talking to me right now might not be a good idea, but later I'd be keen to hear what you have to say about those employers of yours."

She said, "I got nowhere to be."

The matron's summons came quickly. Her office on the ground floor was ringed by flower pots. In the depth of January she had blooming geraniums.

"I see you're awake Doc Hastings, and eviscerating a young Sister."

"She has no aptitude for this work whatsoever."

The matron pursed her lips but did not disagree. "And who are you to tell her so?"

I told her I'd helped hundreds of girls find employment to suit them.

"As harlots?"

"So they can cease being harlots."

"Praise the Lord."

"No thank you."

She laughed and said, "Well, that's a first. Have a seat. What would you do with her, then?"

I said a girl who clings to doctrine might learn kindness and compassion with the right teacher, but meanwhile I'd give her solitary, detail-oriented work such as copying or gardening or cooking.

"She claims a vocation for this."

"She craves adulation as a savior. She'll fail and grow cruel and do harm to girls."

The matron sighed and conceded defeat. "My name is Flora Foster, by the way."

I bowed my head to her.

"Trafficking?"

"I don't traffic. I saved that girl from enslavement. I was trying to expose a band of slavers and it worked. Someone is angry and retaliating."

"You exposed a band of men enslaving girls?"

"With help."

A quizzical smile warmed her face and I realized she was older than I had thought, even elderly. There was a statuary quality to her features, a beauty and a purity after all. "Heroic, then," she said, unconvinced, and I shrugged.

She'd had an unusual request, she told me, to make me more comfortable than inmates on the women's side usually enjoyed. There were six cells on the men's side where furniture and women could be brought in for a price. Benno was doubtless setting up there.

"Who made the request?"

"I believe it was a judge of the State Supreme Court. Friend of yours?"

"Something like that," I said, given that George was arranging for my comfort in the Tombs rather than getting me out. "It's not necessary, thank you."

"Well then," she said, peering, trying to find me a pigeonhole.

I stood. "Thank you, Matron."

I lay on the pallet weeping, my home gone, my parents gone, my frail sinecure gone, respectability gone, my health and ability to bear or nurse children gone. There was nowhere in the world for me, nowhere to stand within myself and gain some footing, let alone move forward.

Gwin stood in the doorway watching me, and I cried harder for my failures, including to heal. My body cried for movement but I couldn't leave the house. I wanted to swim, to let my shredded skin and organs soak in the salt of the sea, to float untethered. A plan had begun to crystallize.

"Not that," Gwin said, seeing it as clearly on my face as words on a page. "That's despair and you'd change your mind anyway. Life will have life."

Half a mile into the open Atlantic, I thought. But floating away called to me.

"Where's your anger?" she asked, peremptory.

I flashed it at her. What would anger get me besides a confrontation with my own weakness, the injustice in my particulars and all our generalities?

"Yes," she said, "Despair and anger are two sides to the same feeling. The difference is resolve. Your anger will be grand when you own it. It will propel you a long way, but you need a destination, a goal to move toward with all that fire."

I got a glimpse of what she was saying and whispered, "Can't."

"Why not?"

I wrote on the slate, "Would tear me apart."

"Ha!" she said. "You've been feeling it and swallowing it all your life. The trick for you now, Rafaela, is to choose work into which you can pour it."

On Monday Ciara and Elliott visited. He would dine out for years on the women's block of the Tombs. My stock with the inmates jumped.

Josephine next door had done my hair that morning. We'd been talking about those Christian employers of hers, two women who treated servants abominably, abusing with words, switches, and withholding pay and food. She'd come to New York searching for her sister but ran out of money and broke into a basement apartment to get warm.

I told her she could stay with me and I'd help find her sister, last seen working in a dockside tavern.

She said, "You have people coming today?"

I nodded.

"Best do something with that hair."

I touched my head and found it standing up and tangled. A brush was in reach and I began taming it.

"That hair do something to you?"

"Pardon?"

"You going at it with a grudge."

I rolled my eyes at myself and she reached for the brush. She did a kinder job and French-braided it, tied it with a ribbon from her pocket.

"That's special to you, isn't it? I'll make sure to get it back to you."

"If you put me up and find my sister, you can have that and a lot more too."

"Okay," I agreed, happy.

"Why you so nice?"

"It's free."

She barked one bitter laugh.

I said, "Josephine, what would you do if you could do anything? Do you have dreams, a way you'd like to live if you could?

"If we're talking ways to earn a living, I like to cook. If we're talking dreams, I like music. Singing and dancing. I'd listen all day if I could."

"Can you sing?"

She sang a few wordless syllables in a pretty alto. "How about you, Nell? Something you always wanted to do?"

"I always wanted to be a doctor. To teach other doctors, really."

She tipped her head. "They let ladies be doctors?"

"Some few so far. But that's not my biggest hurdle, unfortunately."

"No?"

"I work in a brothel. Not as a harlot, but still."

"That hair so pretty you could swing it."

We laughed, and memories that had been floating up since she began brushing reached the surface. Dr. Schaeffer behind me finding the side of my waist. "Oh pardon me," he'd say. Another day from behind he put one leg between mine and sniffed my hair. I threw an elbow and he pulled a clump out of my cap, which would give Nurse Pell fits.

I had suffered a hundred such humiliations in that hospital and I shivered for the girl I was, desperate for the smallest acknowledgement from Isaac Jordan.

Elliott inspected my coiffure and said, "A little demure for you."

I ignored him. He handed me the morning's *Standard* in apology as Ciara pushed past him and embraced me. She said hello to Josephine, who left to make room for them in the cell.

A Medical Prodigy and Philanthropist Hidden in the Sporting World

Note from the Editor and Publisher: Since our publication of the account of the fate of Miss Lavinia Curtis and the role of Miss Nell Hastings in her rescue from a downtown brothel, we have been flooded with every kind of reaction. Some praise and some blame Miss Curtis for defending herself against the slaver Vernon Trent, some praise and some blame us for putting the story in the public eye. But one element of the story has prompted a most unexpected outpouring. We've been inundated by letters and visits from dozens of people who have been helped by Miss Hastings, known affectionately as Doc. Her healing skill is uniformly and highly praised, but less so than her kindness. Here follows a fraction of the stories that have come to us.

Gerta, 26, credits Doc Hastings with saving her life and giving her a place to stay after she was brutally beaten by her drunken husband.

Jennifer, 19, was treated for an ailment given to her by her husband, and aided in her attempt to reform the young man.

Lenora, 30, was employed as a maid at the Double Standard Sporting House, where she was well paid and well treated, and Doc helped her establish her own bakery.

Patricia, 37, says Doc gave her a tonic that eased a painful condition she'd suffered for years.

Tilly, 31, says Doc took her into the Double Standard during the Draft Riots of 1863, sewed her wounds and fed her for days along with dozens of other people, until the streets were safer.

Christopher, 42, reports having worked for Doc for years and finding her a fair and generous employer.

Sophie, 20, maintains that Doc has conducted landmark studies of women's health for decades and has made many important discoveries, but no publication will print them because of where the research was conducted.

Abigail, 29, claims that Doc performed surgery on her after a terrible childbirth, and saved her life.

Randy, 25, reports that Doc is the best employer in the city of New York, everyone knows it, and that the real purpose of the Double Standard is to raise people up.

We can also report that Catherine Farnsworth, the girl who escaped the slavers' redoubt and fought her brutal pursuers before being jailed, was brought to the clinic in the middle of the night. Doc Hastings eased her suffering and sat with her until she died the next morning.

Think what you will about prostitution—the poverty that forces women into it and the exploitation of that poverty by men of all stations—but we urge the citizens of New York not to let the learned delicacy of turning away from all such questions deter us from recognizing the contributions and achievements of Doc Hastings in easing the pain of the women forced to it.

Why then was she arrested on Saturday for alleged slaving when she is its pre-eminent opponent? She languishes in the Tombs for no clear reason, though her role throwing a most unflattering light on unscrupulous bosses in the Sixteenth Ward would be a good place to begin speculation.

Sounds escaped me as I read, laughing, crying, shaking, and snorting. Ciara kept an arm around me, patting. This was how it would have felt floating too far offshore, bleeding heat into endless iciness.

I read and re-read that page. "Sophie" was clearly Sophronia. The rest I mostly remembered. The Draft Riots were my high-water mark for philanthropy. As the city burned and raged, we housed two hundred people in various buildings, and stripped our larders and the surrounding shops bare feeding them. I spent half a year's profits that week, and gladly. We put all our white porters on horses fetching family members and delivering messages. They carried a lot of people to safety. Israel and the Negro men for whom the main streets were too dangerous made a cordon around our block. We kept some few weapons in the house before those riots, and afterward more, well hidden but ready for such days if they ever came again.

Elliott snapped me out of my reverie by saying that Asa sent his best regards but the paper was overrun and he thought it best not to come. "I'm to ask if there's anything you want from him."

I must have flushed crimson, because Ciara burst out laughing.

Elliott said, "She's so bad at this."

Ciara said, "Yeah, well, not much practice."

She saved me by saying they had other news not so congenial as Asa making blanket offers of assistance and publishing paeans to my skill and character in his newspaper.

I squared myself to hear that the mystery of my arrest had been solved. Who had exerted pressure on that Republican police commissioner? A Mr. John Curtis, Republican state legislator from Vermont. He had read the first article in the *Standard* as anticipated, and boarded the first train to New York in a vengeful rage. It turned out that one of the outgoing commissioners was the brother of an old Harvard chum of his who had taken pity on the poor father and, in the absence of Vernon Trent, offered me up to satisfy him. We shook our heads a while over that.

I heaved many sighs that day over all the people who'd been moved to write to the *Standard*, and Asa who'd been moved to put them in the paper. Elliott told me it now had the largest circulation of any daily in the city at 100,000 copies. I could barely sit and kept popping up to pace the three steps each way in my cell. The differential between so much praise and amazement at my achievements and my present incarceration was laughably familiar. Praise most often came with punishment. Dr. Jordan frowning in disapproval as he complimented the stitches I'd given Lily McBride. George Barnard pronouncing the Double's perfection as an institution for the purchase of girls. John Curtis punishing me for saving Vivie.

In a dream I lie on my left side near sleep, hands palm to palm tucked beneath my cheek. My right hip feels precipitous and ripe. Asa's knee weighs down the bed as he lays himself behind me, one hand on that hip, and then the hand cradles my belly to draw us closer when he's settled. "Meine Liebe," he whispers. I'm flung awake and cover my mouth. When I'm calm again I murmur to the dark Tombs, "Ich liebe dich," and pray the dream resumes.

I was never called to the Court of Special Sessions. On my eighth morning in the Tombs, the matron told me I'd been summoned to the warden's office and walked me there herself. I saw the famous "Bridge of Sighs," where prisoners passed on their way to hang.

The warden wasn't in, but Peter Sweeny stood beside his enormous desk. It was the first time I'd seen Sweeny feeling his full power, and I hesitated. Before the matron could arbitrate, he said, "I'll speak to her in private."

She looked to me and I nodded. I didn't fear him physically, though I should have. She said, "I'll wait outside."

When she was gone, Sweeny shrank a bit. I said, "Shall we sit?" There was a table with six chairs. He sat at one end and I sat to his left.

He said, "It's not right that you're in here."

"No," I agreed.

"I had nothing to do with it."

"I wouldn't think so," I said.

His voice climbed as he said the next sentence, full of tension and pain. "You tried to stop them from taking girls against their will."

"Yes."

"But you own a brothel."

"I don't force girls, Mr. Sweeny. They work for me because I pay them and treat them extremely well and help them not be harlots anymore."

He shook his head in abject confusion. "Why did you try to help me?"

I smiled. "I'll give you three reasons. First, Judge Barnard and Mayor Hall asked me to. They could see your discomfort in social situations. Second, I had hints that slavers were ramping up and suspected Benno was behind it. I thought he would be cruel to girls. If you and I were friends, and if you agreed with me that slaving is wrong, you might help me stop him. This was a long shot, but it seemed worth trying. I never did ask, as you know."

"And third?" He couldn't bear to leave the list incomplete.

I tried to lighten my tone after the effort of saying the second reason without offending him. "When we met, I found you interesting. I found your wit refreshing."

He looked at me. "My wit?" The man should have been on stage. The guileless menace was comic genius.

I tilted my head. "I know you don't always mean to be funny, or understand why people laugh, and I'm sorry for that. But you often put your finger on the absurdity of a situation in a way that tickles me. You make me laugh in the best way."

He blinked repeatedly. "Why didn't you solicit my help when they put you in here?"

"I don't trade on people's fears or call in favors, if I can help it. I build friendships and alliances."

"George Barnard said that yesterday. He said he trusted you."

So Sweeny finally bestirred himself to speak to George about my imprisonment a week after it began. I said, "I can keep a secret."

"You knew about that girl. You could have snapped your fingers."

"Yes. But to be clear, I didn't know about that until after we met."

"When?"

"The ball. Election Day."

"How?"

"She saw you."

"She was there?"

"In costume."

"And you didn't extort me or make demands."

"No."

"Why not?"

So many reasons. We decided to wait and play that card later. It was Vivie's to play in any case. Because it probably wasn't his idea, and he might not have known she was kidnapped. Because Benno probably convinced him he wanted her, or should, when he didn't. I said, "Because I think you were sorry afterwards. I think you regretted it."

He stood up and took a step toward the door. To be seen that way terrified him.

"It's all right," I said. "We all make mistakes."

He turned back and stood across the table from me, hands on the back of a chair. "How did you know that?"

"Vivie told me. For better and worse, you are built differently from other people. Remember our conversation about kinds of sight and blindness? I can see how you're different and have a lot of sympathy for how difficult that must be."

"You're peculiar too," he said.

I laughed. "Indeed."

"Well Doc Hastings, I don't know anyone who would have kept quiet knowing what you do, even when they put you in this place. I'm indebted to you."

"It does smell terrible in here, doesn't it?"

He shook his head both yes and no. "I want to repay you somehow."

"I'd like to go home."

He looked alarmed. "Yes, yes. And I've told them to leave that house of yours alone. I mean something for you."

Funny that my release and the Double's future were each a given to him, quite incidental. "Thank you," I said, moved and gratified, perhaps even vindicated. "What I'd ask of you has not changed. It's not small and you may not be able to do it, or do it for long. I ask only that you try as long as you're able."

This confused him, so I rushed to clarify. "Stop the slavers. As Tammany expands its vice operations, don't let them abduct or procure girls. Let girls apply as they would for any job, and pay them fairly. Forcing unwilling girls is unnecessary, and cruel, and truly abhorrent to me. I think to you too, so it's simple. To the extent that you can exert your influence, stop them from slaving."

He stared into the distance for a moment, and made a decision. "All right. It speaks to the Catholic in me."

I swallowed the hilarity of Catholics for better prostitution. My guess was that Tweed had another two or three years before a journalist or district attorney got the goods on some aspect of their operation and summoned sufficient courage and backing. For that brief time, some number of girls might make it home unmolested because Peter Sweeny forbid abductions. I was curious how he'd enforce it, whom he would direct or pressure, but didn't ask.

He said, "If I fail?"

He certainly would. I said, "Do your best, and the rest is between you and God."

He said, "You're not selfish."

Strangely grateful that he'd noticed, I said, "Not much. What will happen to Benno?"

"Sing-Sing, I imagine."

I would still be *persona non grata* in the ward, no matter who took over.

Sweeny said, "I don't pretend to understand half of what you say, Doc Hastings, but I like you too."

"Thank you, Mr. Sweeny."

We shook hands before opening the door to the warden's office, his grip clammy and tight.

Matron Foster said, "I sent word to the Double Standard Sporting House to bring your carriage."

On the street Meg and Ciara enveloped me. "Thank you," I said, "for whatever you've done."

"About a million people want to see you. The mayor sent flowers."

I rolled my eyes and heard further updates, though few registered.

As the carriage ground to a halt in late-day traffic, I said to Ciara with her taste for gossip, "Tell me about Caroline Vanderpoel."

They glanced at one another. Ciara described an old family invested in mills, alleged to have bought southern cotton during the war. That would be a brother or cousin of course, as she would have no hand in the business. She had excellent taste in fashion and did the requisite charities: orphans and art museums.

Meg said, "Elliott told me they're separated. He also asked if he could bring Asa over, by the way." Her off-handedness had some message I couldn't figure for the ringing in my ears.

Ciara said, "What kind of separated?"

I said, "She's in Europe with the children. Three girls."

Meg said, "He's a workhorse. You don't start a successful newspaper in three years without being married to it."

"Or act as the president's eyes on the battlefield for two years," I added.

"They haven't spent much time together since 1862."

I pursed my lips and felt my throat tighten. "She's still his wife."

"That's his problem," said Ciara.

Meg said, "I'll tell Elliott to bring him in a couple of days."

Home felt immaculate and grand. I ate favorites that Bert sent specially, toasted cheese sandwiches, a hazelnut almond torte, and a bowl of dried pineapple. I drank about a gallon of clean water and made tea. The rituals of cup and leaves soothed me.

I nearly cried for the hot bath Nina filled. My eyes and ears were rheumy and the steam inviting. I sank in with a rumbling sigh and soaked up the heat, washed my hair and oiled it, my skin as well. Drying my hair by the fire in my favorite shift, I did cry for no particular reason, glad to be alone.

Minnie must have listened for my movements because she knocked at the right moment. I asked her to examine my throat and ears and to check my hair for vermin.

"You look fine," she said.

"The worst was dehydration. I might have died of thirst, the options were so repugnant."

"You smell exquisite."

"Lavender and jasmine oil."

When she asked what I needed next, I thought about a Scotch but could already feel the headache. "What's good for sleep?"

"Chamomile?"

"Makes me itch."

"Hot milk with cinnamon?"

"Now you're talking. Where are the girls from the crib?"

"We moved them to 136 Twenty-Fifth so you could have quiet."

"How are they?"

She laughed. "Rowdy."

"I'm glad they called you. Would you stay? I'm not sure what I'll do now and it'd put my mind at ease if you were at the clinic."

"Sure, Doc. Let's talk about that later, though. You rest."

While she went to get the milk I lay on my bed and sighed the sigh of my life. There was one more sob at the bottom. Asleep by the time Minnie returned, I had some memory of her leaving it and woke hours later with an absurdly full bladder. Nina dozed by the fire.

"Hi sweetheart," I said when she bounced up to attend me. I kissed her and sent her down to bed.

"Meg and Ciara were here, they said they'd see you in the morning."

When I'd been at the Silk Pillow for two years, Wren sent word that Gwin was very ill. Beadie let me have a week and I arrived just in time to witness Gwin's death. Wren said she was waiting for me, though she never regained consciousness. It was sudden, probably a cancer of one of the organs, or just a general failure. I had imagined she was in her early eighties but it turned out she was ninety-four! We found some few papers in her room. I've never before or since met anyone of that age. We buried her in a pretty plot overlooking the sea.

She left Wren and me fifty dollars each, the sum total of her savings. I gave mine to Wren, who used the windfall to move to Boston and try to find work as a nurse. Gwin also left Wren her Bible, and me the turquoise pendant she wore on a leather cord. Wanting her scent to last as long as possible, I rarely wore it. In the dark all those years later, I felt for it in my jewelry box, squeezed it in my hand, pressed it to my cheek and lips.

In the morning a porter came with the news that Mr. and Mrs. John Curtis awaited me at the Double. My letter had arrived in Bennington after Mr. Curtis left for New York, and Mrs. Curtis—Amelia—had followed when she grasped how wrong-headed his demand for my incarceration. Ciara and I met them in the salon, where they were still at cross-purposes. She embraced me but he wouldn't shake my hand. He wasn't offering any apologies. Vivie looked just like her mother, but had her father's posture.

I said what a lovely girl she was and how fond we were of each other.

"Why didn't you bring her back to us?" demanded the father.

I reset my own shoulders. "I urged her repeatedly to write to you, but she didn't feel ready."

"Ready for what? Why would she need to get ready?"

Amelia Curtis said shakily, "Because, John, she didn't know that we'd welcome her home or know what to do after what happened to her."

He looked daggers at his wife, and I sat by her, hoping to calm her but agitated myself. "I also offered to write to you myself, to arrange a meeting at a New York hotel. She didn't feel able to go to Bennington. She worried about your position."

"Position!" erupted John Curtis. "What would that matter if we had her home?"

"She could hardly resume her life with you."

"How dare you."

"That was her sentiment, sir. If you'll allow me, I would venture to say I have rather more experience with what it takes to recover from sexual enslavement and laudanum addiction than you do. Vivie was also gravely wounded and required surgery to her uterus, after which she had to rest immobile for several weeks. We had many occasions to speak of what she planned to do."

Mrs. Curtis cried now, shaking and moaning. I patted her back. She asked, "What did she say?"

"She was trying to decide whether to change her name and live respectably, or as I did, serve fallen women. She thought of being a teacher or a governess, and hoped something would present itself."

"Well it certainly did," muttered John Curtis.

I sighed, nodding. They were right to be angry with me. I said, "Can we agree it's best if she's not found right now?"

Amelia looked to her husband. "John?" He nodded once.

"I kept this from the police. It all happened so quickly. She ran out the door and I sent a young man who worked here after her. He found her and he hasn't returned. We gave them a good amount of cash. He's a capable young man, worthy I would say, fond of her. They'll travel as a convincing couple. In any case, the police are looking for a single girl. He's resourceful and will keep her safer than almost anyone would."

"What's his name?"

I shook my head. "They wouldn't use it anyway."

"What worthy man works in a brothel?"

I said, "A protective one."

He paced. "You kept her here."

"To heal. It's safe, and we have a kind staff who cared for her."

"You're telling me she stayed months in a brothel without—"

"Yes, I'm telling you exactly that. No one touched her except for medical exams and the many hugs she got from the girls and myself. We kept her hidden to protect her from her kidnapper."

"To whom you then presented her."

"Obviously we did not expect what happened and I'm very sorry for that. But confronting Vernon Trent was Vivie's idea. She was intent upon stopping him from doing to others what he'd done to her. She had already told her story to a reporter, and had some rather potent things to say about abduction. She wanted to say them to Trent's face."

Amelia put her hand to her heart. "What on earth did she say to him?"

"She told him she hoped he'd rot in hell for all eternity." A single sob escaped me. I had to wonder if she had that blade in mind all along. "But then he picked her up. It was so unexpected. She was terrified." I turned to Amelia. "Whatever he intended, she saved herself from it. She was incredibly brave."

John Curtis said, "And now she's a murderer and a fugitive on top of being ruined."

The police were not actually searching for her, as they had no idea where to start. The sentiment in the *Standard*, that she was a heroine, was in general acceptance with the feeling of Trent's good riddance. Before I could say that, Ciara spoke for the first time. "Mr. Curtis, may I suggest you try listening instead of trying to throw blame around. Doc saved Vivie from forced prostitution, repaired life-threatening knife wounds to her uterus, freed her from a laudanum addiction, and also from despair. She *saved* Vivie in ways you can't begin to imagine. Did you protect her? Did you teach her to defend herself? And I've been meaning to ask for a while now as you've been spraying your venom all over us: exactly who invited Vernon Trent to that party in Bennington?"

His jaw bobbed up and down.

"Oh," said Ciara, "I thought so. You should stop talking now. And by the way, Doc paid $650 to the owner of that filthy downtown bagnio where she found her, so if you're so jealous of what she did for your daughter, you might pay her back."

"Please don't," I said.

Amelia said, "But why on earth would you do that?" Not an accusation.

"You may well ask," I told her. "She certainly didn't belong there, not that anyone does. I just liked her. I swear there was nothing untoward about it. Her predicament moved me, and I was in a position to help." I glanced at her husband and back at her. "I'm so sorry."

She said, "Someone did the same for you."

I nodded many times before I could speak. "That's exactly right, Mrs. Curtis, and Vivie knew that too." But Gwin left her cloister with deep habits of abstinence, penitence, obedience, and silence. What had Vivie seen me do? Defy Benno and court Sweeny.

I offered to show them where Vivie had been staying. The four of us trooped upstairs, Ciara waiting in the hall. The room was how Vivie had left it, tidied up. Some flowers dried out in vases, her books and medicines, clothes and bits of jewelry the girls had given her. We found her sketch book with drawings of girls and maids, and the façade of their house in Bennington. When John Curtis saw it, he wanted to cry but contorted his face to hold it in. He put his face into one of Vivie's dresses and caught her scent. That was the only moment I saw what she meant to him, a sprinkle of sugar across his bitterness. When I looked with compassion, he spit in my face.

"John!" cried Amelia. "For shame! I don't know you." Ciara whipped inside, ready for battle.

I wiped my face with a handkerchief of Vivie's and said, "I wonder where she ever got the idea you wouldn't be kind or understanding."

"Come, Amelia," he said.

She jutted her chin. "I'll make my own way back to the hotel, thank you."

"You'll do no such thing."

"You've made enough mistakes today, sir. Order me around again and see where that gets you."

He stomped out and I signaled to Ciara to make sure he found the door. I returned to Amelia who was sitting on the bed holding a pillow Susannah had embroidered.

She said, "I'm so sorry. I have no idea what to say about that. He's never done that in the twenty years I've known him."

"He feels powerless."

"Well it certainly doesn't sit well on him, my goodness. I'm grateful she found someone who understood what she needed."

"And I'm so sorry for the way it ended, and that you haven't yet seen her. She wanted her ordeal to have meaning, to help end that slaving ring, and she did. She did. She ended it."

Amelia looked to heaven, and noticed the hatboxes atop the wardrobe. We took them down, and I explained that they had been my Christmas gifts for when Vivie would leave the Double, but she never got to wear them.

Inside one box we found several abandoned drafts of letters beginning, "Dear Mother." I gave Amelia the sketch of her house but kept the notebook.

Gwin insisted on house breakfasts and Rosetta's girls resisted. I asked her about it.

"Do you imagine girls arrive as novitiates in circumstances very different from the way they arrive at this sort of nunnery?"

I had never considered it.

"Family poverty, sexual adventuring, disobedience. A rare girl had a true calling to God."

"You did, I think."

She said, "Yes, but also a father desperate to shed himself of dependents so he could get on with drinking himself to death. The girls are angry, scared, and lonely, and it takes time to inure oneself to a long day of prayer and work. The only sweetness is the sisterhood found between these poor creatures who nestle side by side for warmth as they pray or eat. I saw girls settling in over meals as they shared their stories. It was the most familiar part of the day. Good mothers allowed the young ones to chat if they didn't get boisterous. Those girls fared better than the ones forced to silence."

When Gwin left the mountains, she landed in Portland where the pre-eminent brothel needed a healer. She found it familiar, at least in daytime.

The edges of my mouth kinked up.

"Out with it."

"I wondered about your education at that late juncture."

"I was no virgin."

"Forgive me, but may I ask if that was force or seduction?"

She looked at me with an affront I'd never seen before. I was about to beg her forgiveness when she mumbled, "It was love, and later it was cowardice."

"But not your cowardice."

"Oh yes it was." She squared to face me. "Tell the truth of wrongs done to you if you wish, but own your mistakes."

My heart sank that she thought me easy on myself.

She said, "How else but at meals are you going to get a bunch of selfish, distrustful girls to look out for one another?"

I swallowed and said without much energy, "Make the rules clear. Treat them well and equally. Condemn bad behavior but don't get angry or shame them for it."

She laughed, "Hoooooo! You have been paying attention. You were born to be in charge and you know it."

I closed my eyes and doubted I would ever be allowed to run anything.

She said, "Don't let them improve to please you. You know what I mean."

"It's for them, for everyone."

"That's a challenge but try anyway. Show them how to think for themselves, and to take care of others. That's a woman's work." This was her apology for speaking harshly.

That talk seeded my scheme for a clinic and a house together.

I was minutes from bed in a silk chemise with a shawl around my shoulders, under a blanket in my big chair dipping into *David Copperfield* when I heard heavy footsteps on the stairs, two men. A soft knock and Elliott's stage-whisper followed, "Doc?" My heart coiled and shook like an unbound spring.

The door was unlocked because Minnie and Nina and the twins were still fussing over me. "Come." I stayed where I was, being barely dressed.

"You all right?" Elliott asked.

"Fine," I said. "Just cold."

Asa, soft-spoken and humble, understood the various reasons I was frozen in place. He said, "I'm glad you're well. I wanted to see you, and Elliott thought the late hour prudent."

Elliott said, "Ruby's waiting for me, so I'll leave you to it. Asa, you'll get a cab?" Elliott winked at me, which was awkward.

I offered Asa a seat on the sofa. "Forgive me for not getting up."

"Forgive the intrusion." He put his hat and coat aside before sitting. He looked around and said, "It's what I imagined, cozy and full of books."

"Thank you for the articles," I said.

He brushed it off. "That was little enough, but I wish you had seen the effect on my staff of all those letters and visitors. Two junior editors in particular, intellectuals of a practical bent questioning every use they'd made of their lives, pledging better service to women and humanity. They're interviewing women writers to hire."

"Good luck to them," I said.

The way he looked at me seemed to shift the earth's axis. He knew me so little but his gaze went clear to my foundation. "What makes you sad?" he said.

Everything, but what to tell him? "My time at the house is done."

"Not because of the *Standard*?"

"No, you put it in the best light possible, and I thank you for that. Benno will nurse his grudge wherever he is, and any Tammany boss will find me *persona non grata*. It's time." Asa had some part in that, but not the paper.

He blinked and stopped himself from saying anything about what I might do next, perhaps that he'd be glad for me to leave the trade. Then he sat forward. "Well, I came to tell you two things, and now that I'm here I'm hesitant about both and which to say first."

I licked my dry lips. "No happy endings."

His face fell, full of regret. "I wish I had one to give you. You deserve one." It was a funny question, what would happen if we tried to knit our lives together. A burlesque, actually.

As he looked at me, his face shifted to appreciation. "Your hair is beautiful." It was loose around my shoulders. I'd forgotten, and smiled self-consciously.

He sat further forward and interlaced his fingers, then splayed them wide. "I love you, Doc. You, more than anyone." My heart stopped, then shivered. He paused for the length of a breath while I sat with ears ringing, waiting for the second thing, the certain sting. "And I'm leaving New York for several months at least. I sail for London in five days."

My breath frayed as it restarted. I was glad he would follow his daughters, glad he would protect them from scandal. Two sobs escaped before I could swallow.

Then I couldn't sit still and shot to standing, letting the blanket drop. "Would you like a bourbon?" He stood as I did. If we touched there was no returning and I found that what—inevitable, delightful, tragic? One night or none? I'd be heartbroken either way, with a dash of rectitude or a dash of indulgence. I raised my eyes to his. The longing and the apology were excruciating. It was like trying to tear ourselves out of gravity. I said, "Excuse me for a moment."

I went to the water closet and applied a pessary and sponge I'd kept there for years unused.

He was pacing the parlor when I returned. "Look at us, always so restrained and courteous."

"I hope not," I said, and took his face in my hands, ran a thumb across his lips. I barely contained the kiss that followed, my whole body curving into him. It swamped me, love and passion together, the force pulling us close, and the brief joy we found in full propinquity.

Remembering that night, I summon details but have lost the sweep. I warned him of my scars and their origin. When he drew the silk over my head and saw them, he cried, "By God you've battled monsters," and pulled me in again.

There was his beauty, and our skins. How candor lived in his hands. His thigh's long septum. The dip of each inguinal fold, the spines of his scapulae, my fingers mapping soft swirls of hair. The surprising grace with which we moved and sealed ourselves together, our rhapsodies of sound, taste, and tempo. The steep crescendos of pleasure that tousled an errant hem of heaven.

Our desires differed slightly. He wanted tenderness and I wanted emphasis. We coaxed each from the other. Between acts,

I liked laying on him, he liked roaming me. We tried to laugh. Expressing a lifetime's devotion in a single night is not easy.

Dawn was a plague. We said our goodbyes, though we planned to see one another once more before he left. At the door I said, "That morning you asked me my name. I was born Rebecca."

He closed his eyes and kissed my forehead. "Yes. Thank you. It suits you."

I stood still because any movement felt like shredding.

He said, "Is it possible to take this gift and not be greedy for more?"

"No," I said. "I love you, Asa, though I can't quite grasp it. You, more than anyone."

"Yes." He kissed me again and whispered, "*Adieu.*"

TWELVE

The Double girls were reorganizing the gown closet. The third-floor hallway was lined end to end with fabric; Meg and I escaped downstairs. I was in the process of transferring ownership of the Double Standard to the twins and the Bixbys, holding a silent twenty percent. No one beyond the principals and Lyman, Meg's paramour and my attorney, yet knew. They would keep funding the clinic, with some additional cash from the brass foundry, and Minnie would run it.

I was proud that each enterprise would survive without me, and felt the most immense relief to let go of the daily responsibility. Meanwhile Meg and Ciara grew even shinier, Perlie hummed as she flew up and down the stairs, and Israel developed a tiny kink in the corner of his eye that looked like secret mirth.

Georgia and Marianne followed us to the salon in their underclothes to ask about the possibilities for fur purchases at the same moment that Israel ushered Viola Hill and Albin Birchdale into the hall.

Georgia made her usual cheerful conversation while Marianne put her breasts to use. Albin Birchdale averted his eyes while Viola stared in open lust. I sent the girls upstairs.

Other changes were underway. Corabelle departed to marry Gabe Mayer, and Tatiana set up her own boite in the neighborhood with a couple of regulars. The twins were interviewing girls, but there was some discussion of running the house instead as a mixed hotel. They could keep the whole staff except the harlots, whom we'd help to their next employment, and had already hired Honey away from Bim Farley with his blessing, but to what role was not yet clear. Perlie wanted her for an assistant but that would pay quite a bit less than being a top harlot. I'd bailed Josephine out of the Tombs and put her to work helping both Bert and Erroll. Laure adopted her and half the staff was searching for her sister.

Lyman had informed me that morning of the number the four partners typically would pay me as a landlord for the Double plus the building next door where they all lived and their share of the clinic. I didn't think they could make that figure as a hotel, even with a full dining room, so was inclined to charge them less. The buildings would accrue value, and I had other rental income, so I wasn't worried. I also had an idea involving Elliott, who was due later that afternoon.

Meanwhile our reformers had come to debrief the results of our silent collaboration. Their one role had been recruiting Asa.

Albin Birchdale was penitent over Vivie and Vernon Trent, whose real name we learned from the *Standard*'s investigations was Mark Tyne, born and orphaned in Baltimore in 1839. His unwed mother died in childbirth, and he learned his trade supplying girls to both armies during the war.

Viola asked me if I was all right. "You're less vital than usual."

I assured her that apart from the foul air, the Tombs was a respite. While Vivie's whereabouts and condition troubled me, I couldn't grieve Mark Tyne. "No one deserves a violent death, but the man did no credit to living."

Reverend Birchdale said, "We'll have to disagree on that. That young woman was never meant to be a murderer."

I sighed. "No, nor a fugitive. But Tyne made her that a year ago." Then I asked them both whether they found any healing for Vivie in having saved herself. Rather than spending her life as a victim, she now walked abroad as her own avenger.

"It's God's place to judge and punish," said Albin.

"What are the courts for, then?"

Viola said, "Doc, I appreciate the spirit of your question. Abducted girls are rarely avenged. But we mustn't let that injustice lead us to embrace another. Vivie herself would agree his murder was not the right outcome."

I doubted that. But this was the character of all my life's decisions. "Do we call it murder when one soldier defends himself against another?" Or call it exploitation when you run a brothel to lift girls up?

"This isn't war," said Albin.

"No? Is self-defense murder?" If prostitution is inevitable, why not use it to help the people it exploits? I asked them, "Is prostitution inevitable?"

Meg laughed.

The reformers looked to her.

She said, "It is as long as there's marriage."

They were shocked beyond speech.

Meg took her time. "A woman can't make a good living working respectably, right? She needs a husband, but not everyone finds one. There are plenty of poor, single, widowed, and abandoned women. And most marriages aren't satisfying, apparently. So a girl needs a buck, a man seeks satisfaction. I call that inevitable. But if women could make a good living doing something else, most would. And if men could live without a yoke around their neck, people could come together to suit themselves."

Viola, who had never in her life contemplated paid employment, if one didn't count marriage, heaved a sigh as if Meg had never spoken and said, "Well, we came to say we're glad that hideaway was revealed, and that Mr. O'Connor and Mr. Wotley are in prison."

I informed them that some freed girls were staying with us as we sought them places or positions, and asked if they wanted to meet them. They both leapt.

We set some ground rules. No coercion over faith—we'll give you this if you commit to Christ—no coercion period. "Just listen to their stories and give them time to grieve and sort out their aspirations."

Reverend Birchdale said, "We need some maids at the church."

Viola said, "And I'll need a nursemaid." We all perked up and congratulated her.

I disclosed that two girls would need weeks of treatment, but not what for. One would probably be well, the other was an open question. The newest reporter for the *Standard*, a young Vassar graduate, had been to the clinic to meet the abducted girls and would shortly publish a story about them.

We walked Viola and Albin to the clinic, where the freed girls had resumed residence. Nina pulled me aside and said, "Church folks?" They were a rather drunken and disorderly lot of girls. We were weaning them off the hooch slowly.

"Let's see what happens. They'll make their own choices. Be sure they can decline any opportunities offered."

Meg and I said good-bye to Albin and Viola, and climbed the stairs to my place. She poured us brandies.

"Any idea what you'll do?" she asked me.

"Maybe," I said. "You wanted to go to Paris."

"I might when we get through this next stretch. Care to join me?"

I covered my face with one hand. She waited. I coughed out, "Asa sails tomorrow for London."

Her face fell. "I'm so sorry, Doc."

"Me too, not least because it'd send the wrong message to sail with you."

She giggled. "So don't tell him. We wouldn't chase him and the wife. It's a big continent."

"I did have one outrageous idea."

Her face said, let's have it.

I told her that I had long considered trying to go to medical school in Germany or Switzerland.

She stared at me, floored. Then she cackled. I'd never heard such a sound come out of her. She grabbed my hands and danced me around the room. "That's the best idea I've ever heard!"

Slowing her down I said, "Don't get too excited. I doubt they'll take me. I need a way in, despite or because of my disadvantages."

"Show them the damned newspaper! I saved a dozen copies of all those days, by the way. I'm having the testimonials framed." She said, "Doctor Hastings."

I shook my head. "Sternfeldt. *Herren Doktor* Rebecca Sternfeldt." I walked over and put out my hand. "Nice to meet you. I'm Rebecca."

"Damn glad," she said, shaking my hand with a teary smile. "I'll call you Becca."

"Just not Becky," I said. I hated that. My mother called me BB.

I received a letter at the Double that saw me squawk with laughter and then cry freely, inordinately, joyfully.

Dear Doc Hastings,

I read accounts of recent events in New York and suspect we are acquainted. Forgive me if this is a presumptuous misunderstanding but I risk it with every gram of my intuition. Your past is safe with me; please have no fear of any public revelation. I heard that dreadful doctor is dead. I would be relieved beyond measure after all this time to confirm that you're one and the same with my old friend, thankfully alive after all (I knew it!) and tending girls and giving hell to slavers.

With love and hope,
Mrs. Annalee Warren Sedgwick
Fayerweather Street
Cambridge, Massachusetts

No scars would heal from that bit of news and never would, but a bit of tissue somewhere near my heart long denied blood suffused, puffed up with liquid and began to pulse. I wrote back at once.

Elliott and Asa came to dinner. I asked Bert to serve an informal meal in the caucus for seven—the Bixbys, the twins, the Vanderpoels, and me. Family style meant it could be quick. Bert made one of my favorites, pork cutlets with apple fritters and onion relish, and Israel's favorite, a rum raisin brioche pudding.

The main topic of discussion absorbed me enough that Asa's presence was not a constant disruption, though each time my eyes landed on him my heart and groin ached. Someday I might consider him with equanimity, but for now all I felt was ravenous need. The room observed us.

Israel addressed himself to Elliott. He explained their exploratory plan to run the house as a hotel, but the necessary refits to the upper floors could not be met with innkeepers' income alone. A restaurant was part of the solution, but an opportunity presented itself with the ballroom. "If someone wanted to run it as a club, sort of a high-class concert saloon, we could sell a lot of food and drink and draw the needed foot traffic. For that we need a reliable producer and entertainment manager."

Elliott looked around the table, mostly at me and Asa. He said, "I'd need the right manager. A woman, probably."

I said, "Clemence might suit you. She has the right experience."

"Not Ruby?"

Ruby might come to regret that partnership. "Feel free to ask her. Clemence, Ruby, Willow, and Susannah all have experience on stage. They might make a core troop of performers." I suggested that his next conversation should be with Erroll.

Ciara said, "Georgia and Marianne would make good managers."

Meg said, "That leaves only Sophronia."

I told them what Sophronia had told me that morning, that she had saved every penny of what she'd earned at the Double and intended to start a boarding house for girls. Over time she hoped to build a charity. Elliott registered some regret over the shelving of her other talents but kept it to himself.

He thought out loud for a few minutes about what kind of shows he'd want to produce and how this venue could serve the class of performers hoping to reach Broadway. With Hank's saloons in disarray there was another opportunity. He envisaged buying the Reveille and the Eureka too.

Asa said, "Maybe start with this one venue and see how it suits you."

"Oh it suits me." He looked at the Bixbys and the twins. "As does working with you all. But are you prepared for me? I'm not by the book."

Perlie said, "Let us approve your manager, and the manager's assistant."

They began to discuss particulars. I worried that Israel and Perlie would take on most of the work, and planned to warn them all to make sure everyone's role was clear. Meanwhile Lyman would negotiate for me and I would tell him to be generous. It was restful to hear this talk of a future in which I would be a spectator.

My attention filtered back to Asa, quiet across the table, and found his attention entirely on me. We breathed in synchrony.

As the table adjourned, Elliott to further planning with the Bixbys and twins, I led Asa downstairs to the library. He'd never seen it and was well pleased. He said, "You astound me, always. Thank you for what you've done for Elliott."

"I hope it works out. He'll make a great producer if he bothers."

"Could you lose money?"

"It's no risk for me."

He came near and took my hands. "Rebecca." He kissed my cheek, and I held myself back, desperately.

I said, "I may go to Europe, but not to chase you. I'll stay away. I'm thinking about medical school in Heidelberg or Zurich."

"How exciting. They'd be lucky to have you."

"Probably too old."

"Never." He pulled me closer.

I gasped for air and whispered, "I wish you every happiness, especially the love of your daughters." I kissed him, looked him in the eyes, and fled the room. I ran down the hall, down the stairs, and into the freezing garden where I threw myself on a bench under a grape arbor and heaved breath trying to haul myself together. Head in my hands, I missed the sound of the door but heard his footsteps. I wrapped my arms around myself.

"Forgive me," he said, sitting close but not touching me. "I wasn't finished. I hate to hurt you, but I feel the same pain." He took a jagged breath. "I ask nothing of you, Doc. You're free, of course. Maybe we'll never be close again. We may not be on the same continent. But perhaps we'll find our way back to one another after all, somehow. You know all of this."

I agreed, hiccoughing.

He reached into his pocket and pulled out a little box. I froze in shock and his face said yes, listen. From the box he took a ring. "You may think me mad, but please accept this token of my love for you, which you can wear, or keep in the box, or throw into the sea. No promise is intended. Still, I wanted something tangible to say that no matter how long or how far, for the rest of my life, I will love you. And I hope to return to you in a way that won't hurt you."

He held the ring up for a moment, a slender circle set with small pearls and gems whose color I couldn't tell in the dark. He took my right hand and slid it onto my fourth finger as torrents raged and arguments clashed in my head. I wanted no hope.

"It's beautiful," I said. "Thank you."

He kissed the velvet box and tucked it into my pocket, touched my hair and my face. "Do you like sailing?" he asked me.

"Why?"

"I have a sloop and imagine you on it."

"I grew up on boats," I said, my heart lightening as I ran my hands over his neck and shoulders. "I'm able." That pleased him.

We held one another until I sank into his arms and stopped shaking. He kissed me twice, once long and once short, and drew me to standing. "Let's get you inside, it's freezing."

"I'll go this way," I said, pointing toward the clinic, while he would re-enter the Double to meet Elliott.

He squared us face to face. "The best part of me will always be waiting to see you again," he said.

"Yes," I said.

I have no memory of climbing the stairs or if I wept that night, though I would guess so. I would not have known how to turn our love into less of a loss and more of a gift, but Asa knew. Those pearls and sapphires lit my hand for many years, while I slept.

One morning soon after, a woman came in who was not like our usual patients. She was a few years older than me, well dressed and well educated, German or Polish. She told Nina that she would consult only me and waited, having heard of my diagnostic insight. It was odd but I listened to her complaint. She told a tale of post-menopausal bleeding with no apparent pattern.

"Why did you look for a pattern?"

She pursed her lips. "A physician suggested I count the days to see if it mimicked courses, a kind of vestige." The word physician stood out.

I asked various questions about her reproductive history. She had no children. "And may I ask, do you have a profession yourself?"

She told a story about having been a teacher, but either it was a ruse or she was a very unusual person.

"Well Madame, I suspect that you have uterine cysts that often accompany menopause. They tend to shrink over time and rarely present a problem, unless they are large or painful."

She averred that she could not attest to their size, if they existed, but she did not have pain.

I regarded her for a few moments. It was a ruse. She was testing me. "I believe you're having normal symptoms of menopause, quite common and benign. If you seek further testing to confirm that diagnosis, I could do a brief internal exam, but that would not yield much information and it carries the risk of infection. What is your level of anxiety about this bleeding? Do you have the feeling that your health is amiss? If it would put your mind at ease I could do the exam."

"That does not appeal," she said.

"I don't recommend it, unless, as I say, your intuition tells you differently. Tell me, are you local to New York?"

"No, but I visit."

"Well, you're welcome to return at any time if your symptoms change."

"How often do you perform such examinations, may I ask?"

That was it. I stood and said blandly, "Do you work with Dr. Singer?"

She made a sour face. "Forgive me. I am not acquainted with this Dr. Singer but from what I have read he's a spiteful sort of toad." I yelped out a laugh and she stood and looked me full in the face for the first time, put out her hand. "Dr. Marie Zakrzewska, Miss Hastings. I'm pleased to meet you. You have a most excellent arrangement here."

I gasped, then stopped breathing. She'd gone to Cleveland Medical College and worked with Elizabeth Blackwell before founding her own Women's Hospital in Boston. She was on the faculty of the Boston Female Medical College, my childhood dream. Finally I coughed out, "It's an honor to meet you Doctor, but why the subterfuge?"

"Oh the consultation was real enough and your discussion sensible, I must say. I considered the exam if only to observe your skill. If I did want one, I'd come back."

"But that's not why you came."

"No," she agreed. "Mr. Asa Vanderpoel is an acquaintance of mine and he wrote to me."

I must have gone full white.

"He wrote to sing of your many accomplishments and your unconventional use of resources. He mentioned that you have done several longitudinal studies of fertility and disease."

"Yes, that's true."

"I take it you have a full roster of patients today?"

"I do."

"Would you be amenable to my observation for an hour or two? This is not a population I usually see. The directors of my hospital require that poor patients prove their respectability."

"How do they prove that?"

"Don't ask. Or ask later. May I observe?"

"Of course."

"And perhaps one evening this week we might meet to discuss your research?"

I must have looked puzzled, unsure if this was a swindle or the teacher I'd been missing for years.

"Miss Hastings?"

"Yes, of course. Of course. Please forgive my addled state. I never expected such a visitor and I'm a bit in shock."

"Indeed. Tell me, what are your plans now? I hear that you have sold your sporting house."

"I was considering formal training on the continent." In German I told her I was born in Darmstadt and wondered if I could gain admission to medical school.

In German she said, "You're a skilled surgeon and have practiced for decades, why go to school?"

I blinked. "To fill gaps, to be taken seriously."

In English, she said, "As it happens I have two positions to fill at New England, a nursing supervisor and a surgeon. Would either interest you? Is that serious enough?"

For some reason this terrified me. "I do only gynecological surgery."

"If you can repair a fistula and terminate a pregnancy, I can teach you how to remove an appendix or any number of tumors in an afternoon."

Still, I could not imagine being welcome. "Would you consider dropping the requirement for respectability? How does one prove it?"

She sighed. "They need to provide a letter attesting to their worthiness from some reputable individual. And we treat only the first pregnancy of an unmarried woman."

It wasn't the worst I'd heard but bad enough.

She said, "You ought to make the case for abandoning those rules to my board of directors. We've been open for a decade and they should hear it."

I said, "I've run my own establishment for a long time. I'm not sure I can take small-minded orders from anyone."

She laughed. "Then don't go to medical school."

Dr. Zak, as everyone called her, Marie, stayed through that whole day and over supper in the caucus I walked her through the scope of my research and preliminary findings. She listened eagerly, exclaiming over my intricate cross-referencing and nuanced conclusions. "You have a unique perspective, having escaped the narrowness of most medical institutions, but real stringency nonetheless. It has a practical bent rather than a scientific purity which is refreshing. We should consider a collaboration. I might be able to help you publish."

I feared the appropriation of my work, and said so.

She nodded. "We would have to know one another better, and talk it through. I appreciate your hesitancy, but while I'm a stubborn mule and my students think me antiquarian, I'm not a villain. Your work should not languish in obscurity. This aggravates me."

"Me too." We laughed.

"It's amazing what you've done without teachers or colleagues. Whom do you ask questions?"

"I do have colleagues, though uncredentialed. And I read journals."

"Remarkable. It's a pleasure to meet you, Doc Hastings."

Packing my things was more difficult than I'd imagined, having been so rooted in the ground beneath Twenty-Sixth Street and the walls of those rooms. The goodbyes were awful. But once aboard the moving train looking outward, I felt better. Intending to see Annalee, look for Wren, and inspect Dr. Zak's hospital, I made for Boston. And then I might visit Newbury and even Portland, and a further plan had begun to take shape, a house on the beach for the summer to revisit the pleasures of tidepools and surf rhythms, to reclaim the shoreline and the ocean, to remember the wonders and fascinations of the girl I had been.

EPILOGUE

In 1883 I published the monograph *Bodies of Knowledge: The Medical and Psychological Treatment of Fallen Women.* Despite some lingering resistance to treating sexually active, unmarried women in hospitals and clinics, the book became a standard part of the curriculum in women's colleges of medicine and nursing, and is now in its third edition.

Its greatest controversy came as a surprise. Critics dismissed the use of storytelling in recovery from rape and forced prostitution, saying I proposed to cure sin with fairy tales. I actually reported that survivors fare better when they can shape their experience into an ongoing narrative that turns pointless suffering into meaningful sacrifice. I had long observed this in individual patients, but the inspiration for quantified research came from doctors serving Union veterans. They discovered that injured soldiers who believed in Union or abolition had better outcomes than those with no moral or social connection to the cause. Some blows wound both body and soul, and their united healing can be heroic.

There is no elevated cause to which fallen women can assign their sacrifice, but if they find solidarity and community with other women and help one another, they fare better than if they struggle alone. Meaning grows in connection and service, and in naming the common patterns in their experience. What men demean as chatter can be the most potent medicine.

Students often ask how I developed this field of study, so I began to reflect on how I might convey the answer contained herein despite it lying far beyond the bounds of respectability. It upends conventional portrayals of prostitution by contending that fallen women use what little power they are allowed within a society that enforces their legal and economic dependency on men. The arts of comfort, compassion, and pleasure can provide the rare path to self-sufficiency.

Of course I do not recommend it. It carries serious physical risks in disease and assault. Stigma and shame are flung at fallen women from every direction, even by frequent customers and from within their own psyches. But prostitution is a means to an end, and demand is always robust. For a medical practitioner excluded from traditional avenues of education and practice, brothels present a mutually beneficial opportunity. The family I found in brothel life shared more love and purpose than anything I found before or since.

I have spent the last twenty years practicing and teaching in Geneva, Berlin, Boston, and London. I started a journal for brothel nurses, with some help from friends in publishing, that ran for a decade before folding into the *Women's Medical Review*. The Minerva Hotel and Cabaret lasted seven years until Israel and Perlie retired. Meg spends every other year in Paris, and visits me often. In 1869 Ciara married Martin Mitchell, who became an attorney and then a prosecutor who dogged Tammany. They have two boys. Her past an open secret, Ciara helped to found and run an industrial home for girls modeled on the work of Josephine Butler in Liverpool. They train apprentices to be theatrical costumers, hairdressers, teachers, and nurses. Elliott is a Broadway producer, and Asa still runs the *Standard*, with the highest circulation of any New York paper, and dotes on his daughters and eleven grandchildren. We write on Christmas and our birthdays.

Bill Tweed died in prison, George Barnard was impeached and died of Bright's Disease, and Oakey Hall was widely reviled as mayor. Blaming his dead brother for his crimes, Peter Sweeny repaid $400,000 to the city of New York, married and raised a son in Paris, and recently returned to the Hudson Valley.

Occasionally I receive news from a fine school for girls. Its headmistress is a cultured woman married to a prominent merchant. They have many adopted daughters, some taken in as infants and some as displaced adolescents. On my next journey to the US, I hope to visit.

London, 1889

ACKNOWLEDGMENTS

To Marjan Kamali and the members of the 2021–22 Generator, deepest thanks for lessons in craft and camaraderie, and for the miraculous worldbuilders. To Kelly Buchanan, Rick Finkelstein, Peter Spiers, and PK Simonds, heartfelt gratitude for free-ranging advice, opinions, prescriptions, and hilarity, for fine reading, fine art, access to national historic sites, and the essential friendship that saw this through.

I'm grateful to Brett Gary, Sonya Green, Monika Gupta, Nancy Kopans, Abby Laber, Mindy Lerner, Eliza Margolin, Barbara Schwartz, and Francesca Vitale, who read various drafts. I've waited my whole life to find an editor as gifted as Jane Rosenman.

Love and thanks to Jake and all the Bernhards and Margolins; Blanca Alcaraz, Jaclyn Kryzak, Janelle Browning, and everyone at Be; The Gang, Liz Perlman and John Murphy, Melissa Buffer, Matt Prouty, Reimagym, and all my friends and loved ones, so many of whom are caregivers and community builders.

To Brooke Warner and everyone at She Writes, thank you for a smooth operation, and for the twist in my tale of a thousand nos.

And to David, for endless patience and faith in me.

ABOUT THE AUTHOR

Photo credit: Eliza Margolin

Nancy Bernhard is a journalism historian and yoga teacher, fascinated by how survivors of political and sexual violence heal through storytelling and movement. She was born in Brooklyn, and lives with her family in Somerville, Massachusetts.